The Pelicans Fly High

Christie Peavyhouse

For my mother,
who is always anxiously awaiting
to hear about my next crazy adventure.
Hang in there, Mama. I have many more to come!

CHAPTER 1

"K immy, come pick up your clothes from the bathroom floor!" I can hear my mom yelling from the other side of the house. I lie in my bed and ponder what I will do today. It's the first week of summer break, and I'm already bored out of my mind.

My best friend, Maria, is coming over around noon, and I am supposed to be cleaning up the house, but I need more motivation to get out of bed.

"I will in a minute!" I yell back at Mom. I hear stomping coming toward my bedroom, and the door flies open.

"Kimmy, you get up right now and help me straighten up this house, or you won't have any company all summer long!"

With my eyes closed, I pretend I don't hear her, but she knows I'm faking.

"Okay, I'm getting up."

I pull back my covers and see Oscar sound asleep beside me. He is not allowed to be in my bed because of my bad allergies, but I don't care.

Oscar is my Boston Terrier dog, but he's not black like most of them. I think he's actually called a "Red" Boston Terrier, but he doesn't look red at all. When he curls up on the couch to sleep, he looks just like a glazed chocolate donut. I've had him since he was a tiny little puppy. He would be my best friend if I didn't have Maria. Oscar and I do everything together. I sometimes even sneak him down to the beach. Mom says he's a turd dog, especially when he chews a hole in her brand-new quilt. He's so sweet though. I am his favorite person.

My dad's friend, Nick, was going out of town and asked us to keep Oscar for a few days. Well, back then, his name was Dr. Pepper because he looked like the soda, but I thought that name was stupid. Luckily for Oscar, Nick never came back to pick him up.

I'm Kimberly Ruth Favre, but everyone calls me Kimmy. They got Kimmy from my dad's name, Jimmy. His real name is James, but he likes going by Jimmy. I hate being called Kimmy. I'd much rather be called Kimberly or Ruth or even Kimbo, for that matter, but Kimmy...it's too much like my dad's name. Blah!

Before you even ask, no, I am not related to that famous football player. However, if I were, I'd be rich, and I could demand everyone call me by my real name.

I love my middle name, Ruth. I was named after my grandmother, Ruth Patterson, my mom's mother. Grandma Ruth died in Hurricane Camille back in 1969. I never got to meet her, and Mom doesn't really remember her much.

Every once in a while, Mom will take me to Gulfport to see her father, Grandpa Eugene. He lives in this place that is like a nursing home but for people who can still do stuff for themselves. He has a tiny little room with a twin bed and his own bathroom. He keeps his room extremely clean. I'm pretty sure you could eat off his bathroom floor if needed. When you walk into Grandpa Eugene's room, the smell of bleach smacks you in the face. I always draw a picture before seeing him so he can hang it on his wall. He has at least twenty of my pictures displayed in his room right now! I am his only grandchild, and he loves me a lot.

Grandpa Eugene only talks about Grandma Ruth if I bring her up. He told me that Grandma Ruth was very hard-headed like me. When Hurricane Camille was getting ready to make landfall, my mom's whole family decided to evacuate their home in Bay St. Louis, Mississippi, and go inland to ride out the storm.

Once the family got settled in with Grandpa Eugene's brother, Ruth decided she needed to go back and look for her cat. Grandpa pleaded with Grandma not to return to town, but she refused to listen. This cat of hers was like her own child. Grandma had found it as a kitten and had to bottle-feed it.

While they were evacuating, the cat got out of its crate and ran off. Grandma was devastated. So that is why she went back for it. No one really knows what happened after that, but they found Grandma's dead body in the neighbor's yard when the water receded. They think she might've drowned.

Hurricane Camille created the worst flood that the Mississippi coast had ever seen. Well, that's what I learned in Mississippi history class in fifth grade.

Guess where they found the cat? Up in a tree in the front yard of Grandpa and Grandma's house. It was alive! Grandpa has said that the cat lived to be twenty-two years old. He treated it like a baby because he knew how much it meant to Grandma. Grandpa has always told me the cat was a miracle, just like me.

I am used to hurricanes. How can anyone be used to hurricanes, you ask? Well, when you are born and raised on this Mississippi coast, you just kind of learn how to deal with them. I live in the same house where my mom grew up in Bay St. Louis, Mississippi. We all call Bay St. Louis

BSL for short. After Hurricane Camille, Grandpa Eugene was able to fix up the house and live in it until he went to his new home in Gulfport. I had always lived in a trailer until we moved in here. Grandpa was proud to give us the house. He said I deserved so much more.

Some people say BSL is paradise to them, but I'm afraid I must disagree. We have a lot of visitors to our town during the summer. They clog up the beaches with their giant umbrellas and smelly sunscreen. I can't stand the smell of that spray sunscreen stuff, and these out-of-towners seem to bathe in it. And they sure like to eat! You might as well forget going to the bay to eat a meal in the summertime. These people come in large groups and take up the whole restaurant.

Sometimes, on Sunday afternoons, my dad takes me and Maria to my favorite restaurant, Cuz's, and gets us some seafood nachos. That's the only day of the week they sell them. It's so much food that Maria and I will split them.

So, like I said, I've always lived in BSL and dealt with these summer travelers. Just like hurricanes, I'm pretty much used to them as well.

I was born in New Orleans at the LSU Hospital. I was supposed to have been born in Gulfport, but I came super early. My mom and dad were at my dad's parents' house in New Orleans for a cookout, and my mom went into labor. I wasn't supposed to be born for another three months, so it was a surprise when my mom's water broke at the cookout. I was born the very next day. Mom tells me it was the hottest day of the summer, July 3rd, 1997.

I spent a long time in the hospital before I could come home. I had a lot of complications. The doctors were not sure if I would even survive. They told my parents that I might not be able to live a normal life. Well, look at me now! I am almost thirteen years old and living my best life.

I'm probably not as smart as my friends at school though. I have to go see different teachers for extra help during the school day. I don't like having to go to those classes because it makes me feel dumb, but the teachers are really nice and help me with my reading.

I spend a lot of time in those special classes away from my friends. I wish I were as smart as Maria. She gets straight As and always helps me with my homework. I am so lucky to have her as my best friend. And did I mention that she only lives three houses down from me? We ride the bus to school together every day. Sometimes, when the weather is nice, which is pretty much all the time except when a hurricane is coming, our moms will let us walk.

Did you ever hear about Hurricane Katrina? I was a Hurricane Katrina refugee for a while. That hurricane came through in 2005 when I was just eight years old. It completely destroyed BSL! I remember coming home months after the hurricane and seeing my house for the very first time. I didn't even recognize it because all the trees in our front yard were naked. Their leaves had been stripped right from their branches. It was the strangest thing I had ever seen. Of course, I was only eight and hadn't seen much in my short life.

My dad returned after the hurricane and worked on our house to make it livable again, while mom and I stayed in a hotel in Hattiesburg. We were really poor during that time. My Grandpa Eugene would send us money so we could buy groceries. Thank goodness we didn't have Oscar yet. We probably would've had to give him up for adoption since my mom could barely keep me fed.

After we got settled back in our house, Maria's family moved in down the street. She told me her parents got a good deal on the house at the time, but it needed a lot of work. Maria spent most of her time at my home while her parents worked on their house. That's when we became best friends. And to make things even better, our moms started working together at the casino in town after it got rebuilt.

The casino was another fatality of Katrina. I've heard that the old casino was found seven miles upstream on the river somewhere after the hurricane. It was a complete loss. I'm glad they rebuilt it because my mom makes good money there as a cocktail waitress, and Maria's mom does pretty well cleaning people's rooms at the hotel.

I'll be turning thirteen this summer and am super excited to finally become a teenager! Maria is already a teenager. She turned thirteen in February. She had a huge celebration. It was way bigger than any birthday party I've ever seen.

Maria's family is from Mexico. They moved here for a better life before Maria was born. Her sister Ashley was born in Mexico. Sometimes, when my mom and dad are working, Ashley will come over and babysit me. Maria always comes with her. They try to teach me how to speak Spanish, but I'm not very good. Maria's mom barely speaks English, so I have to speak Spanish to her when I go to their house. Maria's dad is pretty fluent in English though. They all laugh at how I say the words. They tell me I sound "country." Whatever that means.

"Are you ever getting up? It is almost eleven o'clock, and I have to go to work!" Mom is still yelling at me. I decided to snuggle with Oscar for a few more minutes and must have dozed back off.

"Yeah, I told you I was!" Ugh! What am I going to do until Maria gets here? I guess I will pick up my clothes from the bathroom so Mom will stop yelling. I get up and put on a clean outfit.

As I open my bedroom door, I smell a heavenly scent in the air. "Mom, did you make bacon?" I ask as I walk into the kitchen.

"Sure did Kimmy. I wanted to fix you a good breakfast before I left. I probably won't be home tonight since I am working a double, and your dad will be over at the shipyard until late this evening. Nanny and Chas are out of town, so Ashley will be coming over later to spend the night or stay until your dad gets here."

I give her a puzzled look while I make a bacon and biscuit. "When did Nanny and Chas leave? I just talked to them on the phone two days ago, and they said nothing about going out of town."

Nanny and Chas are my dad's parents. They also stay with me sometimes when my parents are working late or out of town. I absolutely adore them. They are both retired teachers and have helped me a lot with my schooling. They even pay for me to have a tutor during the school year. They know how important education is and want me to have the very best.

"They are taking their sailboat out for a few days since the weather is predicted to be nice. The weatherman said it was perfect for the beachgoers this morning if you, Maria, and Ashley want to head to the beach later, but only if Ashley goes with you." I roll my eyes as she is talking.

"Mom, I am almost thirteen, and Maria is already thirteen. Don't you think we can go to the beach by ourselves? It's only a couple blocks that way," I say as I forcefully point in the direction of the beach.

"Kimmy, you are all I have, and I just don't want anything to happen to you."

Mom turns away to start putting up the breakfast. She never fixes breakfast, so I'm still thrown off by that. Maybe she got a lot of tips last night at the casino. "One more thing Kimmy, please don't bother Mrs. Hernandez. You know she is pregnant with her seventh child right now and needs her rest."

Yeah, that's right. Maria's mom has six kids and is getting ready to have number seven. Maria likes coming over to my house to get some peace and quiet from her younger siblings. She has two little brothers and one little sister who drive her crazy, and she is getting ready to have another little brother soon.

I told Maria that she could move in with me when the new baby comes if her mom doesn't care. We can sleep head to toes in my twin bed. That is where my head is at one end of the bed, and her head is at the other end of the bed. The only problem is when one person has stinky feet, and you have to smell them all night long.

Maria never has stinky feet. Even though she is like me and doesn't like to wear shoes, she keeps her feet clean. I, on the other hand, have been known to forget to scrub my feet from time to time, and Maria will remind me of it.

"Okay, Mom," I say, giving her another eye roll.

"Kimmy, if you roll your eyes at me one more time, you'll be grounded for a week, and you definitely won't be getting any beach time! I'll call Nanny and Chas to pick you up and make you go sailing with them. And I know how much you hate it out there on the sound."

I wouldn't say I hate the Mississippi Sound. I just hate the seasickness I get on their sailboat. I went with them last summer, and they had to bring me back the very next day because I wouldn't stop throwing up. Chas said my face was so green that I could have passed for a stowaway frog on the boat. I guess it was pretty bad.

"Nah, I'll pass. Sorry about the eye-rolling. I'm just ready to be able to do things on my own."

"All right, Sweetie, Ashley will be here soon. Have a good night. I'll see you later!" Mom kisses my forehead, grabs her purse, and heads out the door. Her perfume lingers in the air after she leaves.

My mom, Nina Patterson Favre, is such a beautiful lady. Her makeup always looks perfect, and she exercises like it's going out of style. She has this cute little tattoo on the back of her neck that you can only see when she puts her hair in a ponytail. I know she's had a busy night at the casino when she comes home wearing a ponytail. I'm not sure what the tattoo means, but it must be something special to her because she always says, "I'll tell

you someday," when I ask. I hope to be just like her when
I grow up.

CHAPTER 2

Knock, Knock, Knock.

"You're here!" I shout as I run to the living room. I open the front door and screech like I haven't seen her in ages. "Yay! I'm so glad you're here! I was getting ready to die from boredom." Maria jumps up and down and gives me a big hug. We spin around and do our secret handshake. "Where's Ashley?" I ask as I look down the street.

"Oh, you know, she's on the phone with her boyfriend," Maria says as she walks into my house.

"I can't believe we didn't get to hang out yesterday. I wanted to take Oscar for a walk down to the park, but my mom wouldn't let me go by myself, and my dad was at the shipyard as usual." I roll my eyes just thinking about it.

"Why didn't your mom go with you?" Maria asks.

"She said she had to take care of some business," I tell Maria as I use air quotes. "Is your mom feeling any better?" I ask as she kicks off her flip-flops.

"Yeah, I guess she is. That's what happens when you are on your seventh pregnancy, and you're forty-something years old. I'm constantly telling her she is way too old to be having babies. She says that God keeps blessing her and Daddy, and until the blessings stop, the babies will keep coming."

Maria's family is Catholic. My mom says they don't believe in birth control. I'm not sure what that means, but I know that until Mrs. Hernandez starts using birth control, Maria will keep getting siblings. Maria loves her siblings, but she sometimes wishes she was an only child like me.

My mom says Maria's family is interesting. I just think they are hardworking people who love kids and God. Maria's father, whom I call Mr. Hernandez because I don't know his first name, works as a card dealer at the casino. He works the night shift so Mrs. Hernandez can work days cleaning the hotel rooms. Mr. Hernandez stays home during the day and watches Maria's younger siblings. He's kind of like a stay-at-home dad but works at night. I know he must always be tired of watching all those kids. It makes me tired just sitting in their living room for fifteen minutes while trying to watch TV. It is nonstop screaming and chaos. I still don't know why they keep having babies.

Mrs. Hernandez says she really likes cleaning hotel rooms because you never know what you'll find left behind. She says, "We find, we keep, you lose and weep," which I think is her version of "finders keepers, losers weepers."

Maria has two older siblings, Ashley, who is seventeen, and Alex, who is sixteen. Alex cuts grass with a local company here in BSL. He started working for them when he was fourteen. He makes a lot of money. At least that's what he says. He's so annoying though. I only talk to him when I have to. He always has these older guys with him. They're cute, but Alex is not. Ashley, on the other hand, looks like a supermodel. She has long, thick, black, shiny hair that goes all the way down to her butt. She is probably the most beautiful person I have ever seen in my whole entire life. Ashley just graduated from Bay High School and plans on going to college at Loyola in New Orleans in the fall to become a lawyer. Ashley is super smart, just like Maria. My mom said the college is giving her money to go there. I heard them talking about Ashley getting a "full ride" to Loyola, but I'm not sure what that means. When Ashley turns eighteen, she wants to get a job at the casino like my mom to make some extra money. My mom has been talking to her boss about hiring Ashley. But for now, Ashley just babysits me and her siblings.

Ashley has a boyfriend, Jason, who is a white guy. Her parents do not like him because he is white and doesn't go to church. He is older than Ashley and works at the marina that is connected to the shipyard where my dad works. My dad says Jason is a pretty good guy and has tried talking to Mr. and Mrs. Hernandez about him. I think they don't like Jason because they think he will be working at the marina for the rest of his life like my dad does at the shipyard.

My dad hasn't always just been a boat mechanic at the shipyard. When he was younger, he went to school to become a certified mechanic and started his own business. He used to have a boat repair shop and worked very hard to get his business up and going. When Hurricane Katrina came through, his shop was destroyed, and he had no insurance.

Times got really rough for Dad after he lost his shop. He started drinking a lot of beer and coming home drunk. I also think he was spending too much money at the casino. One time, I overheard Mr. Hernandez talking about my dad being at the casino all the time and wondering how he could afford to lose so much money when he didn't even have a job. I had a hard time understanding exactly what he was saying since it was in Spanish, but I pretty much got the gist of it.

During those tough times, Dad and Mom would fuss and fight all night long. I spent a lot of time with Nanny and Chas after Katrina when Dad was trying to "figure things out," as Chas would say. They would take me shopping, out to eat, and buy me anything I asked for, which wasn't much.

They even bought me my first computer when none of my friends at school had one.

After a while, Dad decided to start working again and found a job at one of the only surviving shipyards in New Orleans. Now, Dad works all the time and is never home to fuss with Mom anymore, which is good for me, but I do miss seeing him. Dad will come home late at night and leave early in the mornings. He is always off on Sundays to take me and Maria out to lunch after she gets out of Mass. Since mom works late on Saturday nights, she will sleep in while we go out.

My dad is a hardworking man, but he tends to forget things. It's like he can't focus on getting certain things done, whether it's around the house or working on boats. He used to always have someone else's boat in the driveway working on it, but that all ended when mom had to call the police once when a customer of his got mad because dad had not fixed his boat right. Dad and this man were screaming at each other in the driveway. He called my dad some terrible names and said he would take his boat to a real mechanic who was trustworthy. I know my dad is a good boat mechanic, but sometimes, he gets sidetracked and isn't able to finish a job.

"So, what are we going to do today?" I ask Maria as she plops down on the couch. Maria always makes herself at home whenever she's at my house.

"As soon as Ashley gets down here, we can take Oscar to the beach. He would absolutely love that! I bet he's been pinned up in this house all week." Oscar jumps up on the couch with Maria when he hears his name. "Shew wee, Oscar, you're a bit stinky! I guess it's nothing a little saltwater can't fix."

Oscar has horrible allergies, just like me, and has to take a pill every day. Mom and Dad had him allergy tested a few years ago because he wouldn't stop scratching. We found out he's allergic to almost everything. So, he takes his pill every morning in a piece of cheese, which he is also allergic to, but the cheese helps to get the pill down, and the pill helps to make him less itchy. So, I guess it's worth it.

"Maybe you can help me give Oscar a bath today when we get back from the beach?"

Maria looks at me like I'm crazy. "Really Kimmy? That's not what I had in mind for today."

About that time, Ashley walks in wearing the cutest outfit ever. Her silky-smooth hair is pulled up in a ponytail high on her head, with it dangling on her shoulders. Maria looks a lot like Ashley. She has long, straight black hair but is short like me. Maria is also very pretty, but not as pretty as her sister.

"Hey, Chicas! What's on the agenda for today?" Ashley asks. Ashley has never complained about hanging out with me. I think my parents pay her well and also give her money for food.

"My mom said we could go to the beach if you go with us. Then, maybe we could stop at Cuz's for a snack. Oscar can sit out on the patio with us while we eat."

Ashley looks around the living room at my baby pictures hanging on the wall. "Did your grandpa put these pictures up here?" Ashley asks while examining them.

"I guess, I don't know, they've always been up there as long as I can remember." I jump up to see what she is looking at.

"Um, yeah, we can do the beach thing and Cuz's later. Jason seemed upset on the phone when I was talking to him a few minutes ago. I kind of think he might be hot for a girl who works down at the marina. Maybe we're not right being together," Ashley says as she glances in my direction.

Ashley seems very distracted. She is not even looking at Maria and me while she is talking. She is just rambling on about Jason. Blah, Blah, Blah. I look at Maria and roll my eyes. She does the same back to me.

"So, I guess it's a beach day with the Osc?" I interrupt Ashley's rambling.

"Sure. Has your mom said anything else about getting me a job at the casino?" Ashley finally turns around and looks at me.

"I heard her talking to her boss on the phone the other night about it. She couldn't remember your birthday, but I told her it was soon. It's June twenty-third, right?"

Ashley shakes her head. "Twenty-second, but close enough." Ashley is ready to get a real job at the casino.

"You know, Ashley, there are other places to work around here too. I see those help-wanted signs everywhere these days. I think even Cuz's had one a while back."

Ashley slings her long black ponytail over her shoulder like a model and says, "I know, but I would make so much more money at the casino serving drinks. And, maybe, I would finally meet a hot, young, Catholic guy who is rich enough to make my parents happy."

I look at Maria and bust out laughing. We both laugh until we cry while Ashley stands there staring at us. "Ok, come on, silly heads. Let's get ready for the beach."

CHAPTER 3

This is the first summer my mom has allowed me to wear a bikini to the beach. Since I am almost thirteen, I am old enough to show off my belly around others who aren't family. Maybe, just maybe, I will get a boyfriend this summer. Whenever I take Oscar to the beach, some cute guys talk to me and want to pet Oscar. Ashley is always going on and on about how much fun it is to have a boyfriend, all the stuff he buys her, and how he is the best kisser she's ever had.

I think Ashley and Jason have done "it," if you know what I mean, but I wouldn't dare ask her. Maria said she was asking their mom about women's stuff the other day, like how not to get pregnant. Maria said her mom just told Ashley to keep her legs crossed. I thought it was so funny that Mrs. Hernandez would say that as she is getting ready to have baby number seven. Maybe Mrs. Hernandez should take her own advice.

Maria nor I have ever had a boyfriend or kissed a boy for that matter. We will both be going into eighth grade in the fall, and most of our friends have kissed boys and done other things with them. But Maria and I are saving ourselves for the right one. I won't just date any old guy who thinks I'm pretty. It has to be the right one, or my dad will murder him. Dad says I can't date until I'm eighteen, but I don't believe him. He and Mom started dating when she was fifteen. Grandpa Eugene has always thought highly of my dad. He knows how smart he is and that he can fix almost anything. Sometimes, I think Grandpa Eugene likes my dad more than his own parents do.

We really do have a beautiful beach in BSL. The sand is white and soft on your feet and never gets too hot to walk on, unlike the sand in Panama City. We went there one year for a family vacation, and I almost got third-degree burns from just walking on the sand. I'm so glad our sand isn't like that.

Our ocean water is a little weird though. We don't have any waves, well, not big waves like Panama City. We have cute, tiny little waves. I crack up when I see an out-of-towner pull up to the beach with a surfboard strapped to the roof of their car. The only time you can surf a wave here is in the middle of a hurricane.

Our ocean water is brown too. It's not clear, but it sure is warm in the summertime. In the afternoon, when the tide starts going out, I like to lie on my back on a sandbar and let the warm water wash over my body. I will close my eyes and dream that I am grown, married, and having my own babies. I can even picture my future husband. He's tall, skinny like me, and has jet-black hair. I love black hair. I think it looks sophisticated and so handsome on guys.

As I listen to the seagulls squawk at each other, I watch the pelicans fly high in the breeze. They glide across the sky almost as smoothly as the jets from Keesler Air Force Base over in Biloxi.

The pelicans have always made me laugh. They circle around in the air until they think they have spotted a fish, and then they zoom down to the water like an airplane doing a nosedive. They make a tiny splash and pop up quickly. Then they bob around and sit there on the water like a duck. I'm not really sure if they get a fish or not, but I sure do enjoy watching them.

Sometimes, the pelicans fly high like the osprey, and I can't tell the difference between the two. The osprey usually flies solo, and the pelicans have friends they fly alongside. I wonder if the osprey gets lonely.

I hope I always live by the ocean. I could never imagine a time when I couldn't visit my pelicans. I think they are just about the coolest birds that exist!

Have I told you how much I hate my hair? It's not curly, and it's not straight. It's not blonde, but it's not brown. My hair is pretty much the color of our dirty ocean.

Sometimes, Maria will fix my hair with a flat iron. She is such a good hairstylist.

Once, we got Ashley to take us to the store to get one of those hair-highlighting kits you do at home. You know, the one you pull the hair through the plastic cap? OMG...it sure did hurt when Maria started pulling my hair through that thing! She kept poking and digging around in my scalp. I was sure I was bleeding under there. My hair ended up turning white because I think we left the bleach on for too long. My mom was so mad that she grounded me for two weeks and wouldn't let Maria come over. I learned my lesson for sure. I think I cried every day while I was grounded. But my hair looked awesome! It looked like I had spent my whole summer in the sun on the beach, but it was mid-February. I looked like one of those surfer girls you see in the movies. You know, the one that always carries a surfboard under her arm and has a totally hot boyfriend.

So, getting back to our beach, I guess it's ok. I'm sure a lot of people would die to live in a place like this, but it's pretty much all I know.

I have always wanted to take a vacation in the mountains. My mom has cousins who live in Tennessee. They live way up on a hill, and in the wintertime, you can see the mountains. That's what mom says. I've never been there, but Grandpa has shown me pictures.

Grandpa's brother and his wife used to live in Tennessee and would come to visit us when I was little. They always promised that I could come to stay with them when I got older, but Grandpa's brother died a few years ago, and his wife moved back to Mississippi, where she grew up. Mom's cousins still live in Tennessee, but she doesn't talk to them much.

"What do we need to pack for the beach?" Maria yells across the house while I get my bikini on. I check out myself in the mirror. I am so hot! I am starting to even look like a teenager. My boobs are getting bigger like Mom's, and my butt is finally filling out my bathing suit this year. Last year my bathing suit sagged off my butt like an old grandma, but not now! The boys are going to go crazy over me this year!

"I guess we need towels, sunscreen, and Oscar's toys. Don't forget we need a bottle of water for Osc too!" I holler back to Maria.

The last time we took Oscar to the beach, he drank the ocean water and had diarrhea for three days straight. It was awful! It was like his stomach exploded, and poop shot sideways out of his crate. Mom said Oscar wasn't ever allowed to go back to the beach after that happened, but I guess she forgot because she said we could take him today.

"Yeah, a bottle of water is a must! We sure don't want to have another episode like the last. We were cleaning up doo doo for days after that!" Maria says as she and Ashley both laugh.

"Oh, and don't forget the umbrella. We don't want Oscar to get sunburned again, either," I remind them. Poor ole Oscar, he just didn't know what he was getting into when he joined our family.

The walk to the beach was a hot one! I'm pretty sure it was 120 degrees on the pavement. I ended up carrying Oscar down to the beach like a baby. I didn't want his little feet to get burned. Good thing we aren't far!

Ashley trailed pretty far behind us the entire walk. She was on her phone talking to Jason, I guess. She seemed kind of upset, but I tried not to listen in. Maria said that Ashley and Jason have been fighting a lot, and she is thinking about breaking up, but I don't believe that. However, Ashley doesn't think her dad would ever let them get married.

When we finally got down to the beach, we were all soaked and wet with sweat. Lucky for us, the tide was in. Once we got set up, we jumped right in!

Ashley stayed up on the beach and kept talking on her phone while Maria, Oscar, and I played in the water. Eventually, Ashley put her phone up and came running into the water like a toddler.

"Hey, girlies! How about we go to a party tonight? My friend Joni is having a little get-together at her house, and she has invited us!" exclaimed Ashley excitedly.

"Oh, I don't know, Ashley," I cautiously reply. "Mom and Dad might get mad."

Ashley reassures me. "Girl, they will never have to know about it. We can go over to Joni's house and be back home before they get there."

"Do you think there will be boys there our age?" Maria softly asks.

"Yeah Maria, remember, Joni's brother is only one year older than we are. I'm sure he and his friends will be there. Don't ya think, Ashley?" I look around at Ashley.

"For sure! So, it's a go?" Ashley looks at us both and then glances out to the ocean. "Hey, do you see that huge boat out there? It's massive! I bet some wealthy people own it. It is so close to the shore."

I put my hand up to my forehead to shield the sun and squint my eyes. I see at least five tanned guys on the back of the boat, all with fishing poles. It looks like they are drinking something too. They start whooping and hollering when one of them gets a fish on their line. Stupid boys!

CHAPTER 4

D o you think we will ever get married, Maria?" I ask as I am peacefully soaking up as much sun as possible.

"I'm sure we will someday Kimmy, but I am not ready to do that any time soon."

"Do you think Ashley and Jason will get married?" I whisper to Maria while Ashley is off talking on her phone again.

Maria looks over at me and cups her hand around her mouth. "Don't tell anyone, but I think they are fixing to break up."

My eyes get as big as saucers as I jerk my head so hard in Maria's direction that I give myself whiplash. "Really? I thought you were just saying that the other day. I didn't think you were being serious."

Maria looks around to make sure no one can hear what she is getting ready to say. "Well, I think Ashley is in some kind of trouble, if you know what I mean. She was asking Mom about all that grown-up female stuff again. Mom told me to go to my bedroom so they could talk. I think it is pretty serious this time. Ashley was crying and saying that she was too young for this and was so stupid for letting Jason talk her into it."

I take a deep breath and let it out. "So, do you think Ashley might be...pregnant?"

Maria looks out to the ocean and then over at me. "I think she might be. I think that is why she and Jason have been arguing so much here lately."

Without hesitation, I ask, "So you really think that Ashley and Jason have had...sex? That is how babies are made, right?" Maria looks over at me like my head just fell off.

"Really Kimmy? Do you not know how babies are made?" Maria and I sit in awkward silence for what seems like an eternity.

I shrug my shoulders. "Maria, my parents have never told me anything about that," I bashfully respond. "Do you remember when I started my period last summer? My mom just went to the store and bought me a box of pads and gave them to me. The only thing she told me was that I was becoming a woman. She didn't tell me what was going on down there or when it would stop or anything. She seemed very annoyed with me that I had started my period. If it weren't for you and Ashley, I would have thought that I was dying or something. I wouldn't dare ask my dad anything. He is oblivious to our girly stuff."

Maria looks around again to see if Ashley is nearby. Ashley is still a good ways away from us on her phone. "Well, Chica, you have a lot to learn," Maria boldly states. "And I will fill you in on everything you need to know. So, where do we begin?"

I raise my eyebrows, and Maria proceeds to tell me EVERYTHING. Maria was throwing so many words at me that I couldn't keep up. I was so overwhelmed that I was only hearing bits and pieces. At one point, she said something about fertilization. I thought fertilizer was only for when the plants in the garden needed to grow. Then, she mentioned something about birth control and pills. And how a woman takes the pills, and a man uses something else. Whew! That was a lot of information all at once.

Maria made it clear that her family does not believe in birth control. So, she knows that Ashley is not taking the pills to keep from getting pregnant. Maria said that Jason is pretty smart and should know how to be safe, but she said when you are "in the moment," you might forget. Oh my!

"What do you think Ashley will do if she is pregnant?" I ask Maria.

"I'm sure she will have the baby. You know my parents are very religious, and that is the only option for us. My mom and dad can help her out if she needs anything.

I might have to come live with you so Ashley and the baby can have our room."

I jump out of my chair and grab Maria's hands to pull her up. "That would be the best thing ever! We could be like real sisters! I bet my mom would even get you your own bed!"

Maria doesn't seem as excited about this possible move as I am. She looks down at the sand and then back up at me. "I'm just sad for Ashley if she really is pregnant. She is supposed to start college in the fall and has been so excited about becoming a lawyer. I'm not even sure if Jason will marry her. He says he loves her, but I don't think he is ready to start a family."

I plop back down in my beach chair as we sit silently for a few more minutes. I notice Oscar is panting, and I move the umbrella, so he is in the shade now.

"I think Oscar might need to get in the water for a few minutes to cool off," I tell Maria. I get his favorite ball and toss it in the water. He runs like his hair is on fire and dives for it. Since the tide is starting to go out, the water is really shallow, and I don't have to worry about Oscar drowning.

"Hey Kimmy, come here. I want to talk to you," Ashley yells from across the beach and motions for me to come there.

"Come on, Osc, your playtime is over." Oscar is pretty good about following my directions. He runs over to me and shakes the water off him. Then, he proceeds to lie down and roll in the sand.

"Really, Oscar, really!" I shout. I forgot how much he loves the sand. Usually, I try to get him dried off before he does that, but I guess I was distracted. He will definitely need a bath after this today.

"So, what's up Ashley?" I say as I get closer to her. Ashley is holding her phone up to her ear.

Ashley takes the phone off her ear and puts her hand over it. "So, here's the deal Kimmy," she whispers. "Jason is on the phone. Can you tell him that I have to spend the night at your house tonight to babysit you? He doesn't believe me. Also, don't say anything about the party that we might be going to."

I don't feel right about this. I feel like Ashley is lying to Jason about something. But the truth is my mom did ask Ashley to spend the night with me tonight or stay until she or Dad gets home, and I don't know anything about this party she has been talking about. So, I comply.

CHAPTER 5

G irls, it is four o'clock already! We need to get over to Cuz's for some food. I'm starving!" Ashley says as she wakes us up from a nap.

I guess we all fell asleep, including Oscar. I roll over, expecting to see Oscar lying next to me, but he is not. He is gone! Oh my God! Where did he go? I panic at the thought of Oscar running away. How did I not feel him get up off my beach towel? I jump up and start yelling his name. Nothing.

"Where is Oscar?" Maria asks as she rubs the sleep out of her eyes.

"I don't know. When I rolled over, he was gone." I start crying uncontrollably as I am screaming his name. "OSCAR! WHERE ARE YOU?"

Maria and Ashley are also yelling for him. I take off running down the beach, and they go in the other direction. I can barely breathe as I am running as fast as I can through the sand and in the water. The hot ocean water is splashing all over my body as my legs start burning.

I feel like my heart is beating out of my chest. Is it possible for my heart to explode?

Just as I think I'm getting ready to have a heart attack, I trip over a sandbar, and my face smacks the water. I look up at the sky and take a deep breath to try and get myself together. I see a family of pelicans flying by. They look like they are so high in the sky. They don't even have to flap their wings to fly by me. Suddenly, I get a sense of calmness just seeing them. But the calm quickly comes to a halt, and the panic sets in again, and I start screaming for Oscar.

Just when I think I have lost my sweet baby Oscar forever, I see a little brown something out in the middle of the ocean on a sandbar that is still exposed. The tide is coming back in, so the water is getting deep. I take off running as fast as I can.

As I get closer, I see that it is Oscar, but I don't know if I can get to him. He is way past the pelican poles. Hurricane Katrina destroyed most of the private piers into the ocean, and only the poles survived. That is where the pelicans like to sit when they take a break.

I am yelling as I am running toward Oscar. He looks scared, and so am I. I don't want us to drown or get hurt. Luckily, our ocean isn't very deep, and I am able to stand up the entire way to the sand bar. Saltwater is splashing in my face. I am crying to the point that I am not sure if I am tasting my salty tears or the ocean water.

I finally reach Oscar and scoop him up like a baby. He is whimpering, and I am sobbing. All I can do is sit down in the water and hold him tight. I love Oscar so much. I cannot imagine losing him. I don't think I could live with myself if something happened to him. I yell back to shore at Ashley and Maria. They meet me halfway, and Ashley grabs Oscar so I can catch my breath.

"Oscar was almost a goner. If that tide would have been any higher, it would have swept him out to sea," Ashley says as I wipe my eyes with the back of my hand. They are burning like flames on an open fire from all the crying and salt water during that whole ordeal.

"Maybe we shouldn't bring Oscar to the beach for a while. We just don't have very good luck with him," I say as I try to pull it together.

"Why do our beach days always end in drama?" Maria asks while I get Oscar cleaned off. "And usually, our drama revolves around Oscar."

I think Maria loves Oscar like I do, but I know he gets on her nerves when he doesn't behave. He's kind of like an annoying little brother. You see, Oscar absolutely loves chasing the seagulls on the beach. He sometimes runs out into the water, chasing them away, but he has never gotten stuck in the rising tide. He always comes running back to me when I call him. I have no idea why he did such a stupid, idiotic thing this time! I guess it's partly my fault, too, since

I fell asleep. He is truly a turd dog, like my mom says. But I love my little turd!

"I'm super excited about Joni's party tonight! Are y'all?" Maria says as she tosses her long, silky, black hair into a ponytail.

"I guess I am. I'm kind of nervous though. Do you really think it will be fun?" I ask Maria.

"Kimmy, all parties are fun when cute guys are at them. I thought you wanted a boyfriend this summer," Maria giggles.

I don't get a chance to respond to her because Ashley groans loudly and grabs her side.

"Are you okay, Sis?" Maria asks as we stop in our tracks.

"Yeah, I just had a sharp pain in my stomach," Ashley replies, grabbing her abdomen and easing down to sit on the sidewalk.

"No, really, Sis, what is happening with you?" Maria says as she sits down and puts her arm around Ashley.

Oscar and I sit on the other side of Ashley. Oscar is still panting from his crazy ocean adventure. I try to pour some bottled water into my hand so he can drink it. He laps up every drop and asks for more.

"Girls, I am becoming a woman. When that happens, your body changes and continues to grow in many different ways," Ashley says as she leans back on the palms of her hands.

Maria and I don't say anything, but we both know what each other is thinking. I quickly change the subject because I've had enough sex talk for the day.

"Did my mom say when she or Dad would be coming home tonight?" I ask Ashley as Maria helps her up.

Ashley gazes up at the sky as she replies, "She didn't say. All she told me was that she had to work a double at the casino, your dad was working late at the shipyard, and she didn't even know if he would be home before tomorrow morning. I am shocked by all the double shifts your mom has been working here lately. She must be making a lot of money. My dad says that he sees her tip jar overflowing all night long. As soon as she empties it, he says it magically fills back up. I can't wait to turn eighteen so I can start working over there with her. I'm going to be rolling in the dough! And Jason won't have to buy me anything ever again."

Would my mom allow Maria and me to go to that party tonight? I keep worrying that she will be mad if she finds out.

"Are we going to tell my mom about the party?" I ask Ashley again.

"Nah, I don't see it as necessary, do you?" Ashley says as she waves her hand in the air.

I think about all the late nights my mom has spent at the casino and how I used to miss her when I was younger. I don't really miss her much now. I kind of like her not being home so much. Especially since I am becoming a teenager. She likes to get all up in my business and ask me questions about Maria and my friends at school. I am getting to the point that I no longer like to answer her. Plus, if I get a boyfriend this summer, I can hide him from her and talk on the phone to him as long as I want. Once again, I have to get a boyfriend first.

CHAPTER 6

I love food—most of it, actually—except for calamari. It's like chewing on a nasty old rubber band. The only way to eat calamari is to remove it from the breading, eat the breading, and throw the white ring away.

Maria says that I am wasteful. Her parents make her eat all the food on her plate before she can have dessert. I think that is a stupid rule. If I don't want all my food, I give it to Oscar and then get my dessert.

My parents have never made me clean my plate. My mom says that causes eating disorders. I'm really skinny already, and my mom pretty much lets me eat whatever I want. A few nights ago, I ate two honey buns, a brownie, and a bag of sour cream and onion potato chips for dinner. Then, I ate some tortilla chips, salsa, and leftover catfish that my mom brought home from the casino. She gets to eat for free over there and always brings me home her leftovers. The casino has some delicious food in their restaurant. Sometimes, she brings home these huge chocolate chip cookies. Mom says the restaurant workers give her free food because she is so pretty. But I know that all the cocktail waitresses get free food from the grill.

"Hey, y'all! What ya drinking? The usual?" the bartender yells at us from the bar inside as we walk up to Cuz's.

We have to sit outside on the patio because we have Oscar. "Yep!" We all yell at the same time. If people in town didn't know any better, they would think that all three of us are sisters. Except for the fact that I look completely different from Maria and Ashley, but we act so much alike, it's crazy.

They have this special drink at Cuz's called Midnight on the Beach. It's filled with alcohol, but one time, my dad asked them to make it a "virgin" for his baby girl, and they did! Ever since then, that's what I always order. It has a bunch of different juices in it that make it dark blue. I think it's mostly grape juice. I am not sure what's in it, but I know it is tasty. Maria always gets water, and Ashley gets an unsweet tea with extra lemons. "Don't forget the water for Oscar!" I holler to the bartender. "He is joining us today."

"Coming right up!" he yells back.

"I already know what I want to eat. Do you?" I look over and ask Maria.

"Let me guess, shrimp and crab bisque with a basket of toast?" Maria says as she giggles at me.

"You know it! But I might add a small salad to my order this time. I'm trying to eat a little healthier. You should too!" I say to Ashley as I look over at her. She is concentrating hard on the menu like she has never seen it before in her life.

"Well, I think I might try something different today. I'm trying to live more on the edge. Have you ever tried their shrimp alfredo? I think that would be a good change for me," Maria says as she glances up from her menu. Maria always orders the cheeseburger with ketchup only and a side of sweet potato fries. I've never seen her eat anything else there except for when we share the seafood nachos.

"I think I will have the full-size roast beef po boy with a side of mac and cheese. I also want an order of seafood swamp fries as an appetizer." My eyes almost bulge out of my head as Ashley looks up at me and then says, "How about some onion rings, too? I'm starving."

I swap glances with Maria and say, "Whatever floats your boat, Sis!" We all bust out into laughter. I bet Oscar thinks we are crazy!

The bartender brings us all our drinks and takes our orders. He has a very puzzled look on his face as Ashley orders. She usually gets the house salad with either chicken or shrimp and light Italian dressing on the side. I'm sure he's as surprised as we are about her appetite today. Maybe she's just hungry from all the swimming in the ocean we did or the running down the beach looking for Oscar. Or perhaps she really is pregnant. Time will only tell.

"Oh my God, Oh my God, Oh my God!" Ashley says while she is waving her hand over her mouth. "It's those guys from the yacht we saw out on the bay earlier, and they are coming this way!"

I look over my shoulder and spot them out of the corner of my eye. "Don't look Kimmy! They are going to see us!" Ashley squawks at me as she smacks my hand.

"Geez, Ashley, don't you want them to notice us? I'm sure if we married one of them, we would never have to work a day in our lives. And we would always be tan and beautiful," I say to Ashley as I side-eye the guys again.

Ashley looks down at her phone and slowly says, "Girls, be cool. I think they are coming up here to the patio." Ashley looks up from her phone and makes the biggest, most glamorous smile you have ever seen. She has the most perfect straight teeth, not to mention how white they are. Her teeth and her silky black hair make her a supermodel queen. If this whole lawyer thing doesn't work out for her, Ashley could most definitely be a spokesperson for just about any beauty product out there.

"Are they gone?" I look at Maria before I look over in their direction.

"Uh, no, they are coming toward our table," Maria whispers.

I freeze and make big eyes at Maria. "What are we going to do?" I ask Maria like I've never talked to a boy in my life.

Ashley replies through her grinning teeth, "Act natural, Sis!"

I tilt my head in her direction about the same time the hottest guy approaches our table. "Hey ladies!" he says. I think he might be the hottest guy I've ever seen in my whole life! He has a dark tan with muscles on top of muscles. His hair is wavy dark blonde with light streaks from the sun. It goes all the way down to his chin. His eyes are the color of the ocean at Panama City Beach. Even his swim trunks are gorgeous!

He rakes his hand through his hair, slings it out of his face, and says, "I'm pretty sure we saw you all on the beach earlier when we were out fishing."

OMG! I can't believe they saw us on the beach! I hope I wasn't doing anything stupid when they saw us.

Ashley replies very calmly, "Yeah, that was probably us. We were on the beach for a few hours with Oscar."

The hot guy looks at the empty seat next to Ashley. "So, who is Oscar?" he asks.

I pipe up and say, "My puppy! Right here, meet Oscar!"

I lean down under the table and grab Oscar. On my way up, my ponytail snags on a screw sticking out underneath the table. "Uh, I'm stuck," I mutter to myself. "Hey, can someone help me?" I call out to anyone listening.

"What's going on, Little One?" I can hear the hot guy asking.

Little One? I squint my eyes, and my eyebrows form a V. Am I really that little? Like a little sister or something? Why would he call me, Little One?

"Um, my hair is stuck on this screw under the table, and I can't get loose." I roll my eyes while talking, but nobody can see them because my head is still under the table.

Maria leans down under the table and tries to help. "Ashley is going to kill you, ya know. I'm sure you have thoroughly embarrassed her," Maria whispers to me like someone is actually trying to hear what she has to say.

I arch my neck back and try to look over at Maria. "Pish, do I look like I care? Just get me loose!" I growl at Maria.

Maria grabs the top of my head and yanks my hair off the screw. "Ouch!" I say, as I'm pretty sure she just pulled a thousand hairs out.

"Ok, you're free now, but your hair is a bust!" Maria starts laughing. "You look like a rooster that's about to crow!"

I slowly bring my head up above the table. Not knowing that the hot guy and all his friends were standing around.

"Did Little One get unstuck?" the hot guy asks me while laughing. Actually, everybody is laughing. I can feel my face turning ten shades of red right now as I want to crawl back under the table and curl up with Oscar.

"Yeah," I say as I try to smooth out the top of my hair. It is no use. I pull my ponytail holder out and shake my head.

"Wow, Little One, you've got some long hair! I bet you get lots of boyfriends with that hair," the hot guy says to me as I am now turning a hundred shades of red.

"I guess," I reply softly. I have never been so embarrassed in my life. No one is laughing now as I run my fingers through my matted-up hair. When I get in the ocean, the saltwater dries out my hair, and it gets all knotted up. Everybody is just kind of looking at me now. What should I do? I guess it's time to get Oscar out for real now.

I drag him by his collar out from underneath the table without putting my head back down there. "So, here is the culprit of this hair disaster," I laugh and say to the crowd of hot guys standing around my table.

Oscar looks up at them as they gather around to pet him. Oscar is an adorable puppy dog. He loves people and wants all the pets he can get. Apparently, the guys really like Oscar too, because they are all kneeling down on the patio goo goo and gaa gaaing over him like he's a tiny baby or something.

"You have a really cute dog, Little One," the hot guy says as he looks up from petting Oscar. His friends all nod and agree with him. It seems like the hot guys might be more interested in me than Ashley right now. This is very strange. I did not expect this, but you know, Oscar always draws in a crowd of guys whenever I take him out.

"Do you girls have any plans for later on?" the hot guy asks as he is still petting Oscar.

Ashley sits straight up in her chair and says, "Well, we were planning on going to a party at my friend's house tonight. It is supposed to be pretty awesome with lots of free-flowing kegs."

Free-flowing kegs? What is she talking about?

"Oh man, we could use a good beer bust later. What do y'all think?" The hot guy looks around at his friends. They chat amongst themselves for a minute while Ashley checks her phone. Then, the hot guy looks back at us. "I'm

R.L., by the way, and these are my friends: Keith, Ricky, Greg, and Ashton."

R.L. puts out his hand to shake mine. As I reach out for his hand, he takes hold of mine, raises it to his mouth, and kisses the top of it. What just happened? The hottest guy that I have ever met is instantly in love with me.

Just as he is lowering my hand back to earth, I notice a very interesting tattoo on the inside of his arm. It looks like a cross but has a scorpion wrapped around it. Gosh, he must be at least eighteen since he has a tattoo. In Mississippi, you can't get a tattoo without a parent signing for you unless you're eighteen. I know because last summer, I walked into the tattoo parlor by the beach and asked for a rose on my ankle. The receptionist laughed and told me to come back when I turned eighteen.

As I try to catch my breath, I manage to get out a few words. "What does R.L. stand for?" I ask as I gaze into his ocean-blue eyes.

"Well, Little One, wouldn't you love to know," R.L. says as he tosses his hair out of his eyes.

All I manage to say is, "Um, yeah." I'm such an idiot! Why do I always freeze up when I try to talk to a hot guy?

I wonder what R.L. stands for. I'm sure it's something amazing, or it could stand for something stupid and embarrassing. Actually, I'm pretty sure there's an old man at Grandpa Eugene's home who calls himself R.L. That's pretty funny!

Just as R.L. is finished with my hand, he goes over to Maria and does the exact same thing! So much for him being in love with me. He then does it again to Ashley. What's with this guy? Is he some kind of Romeo or something? But he does something different with Ashley. He takes both of her hands and presses them together, and then he kisses them. Hmm, I've never seen anyone do such a romantic thing in my life. Ashley blushes and smiles up at him.

"So, tell me more about this party tonight," R.L. says to Ashley as he steps back to his friends.

Ashley proceeds to give him the details of the party, the exact location, and who all is expected to be there. I didn't realize this was a drinking party. My mom is not going to be happy if she finds out. I'm just glad that Joni lives within walking distance of my house. That way, if I want to go home, I can.

"Well, looks like your food is coming out," says R.L. as the bartender has a crap ton of food on the serving tray. "I guess we will catch up later. It was very nice meeting you all, especially you, Oscar," R.L. says as he pats Oscar on the head. And just like that, they are gone. Well, not really gone. They just went inside the restaurant where it is air-conditioned.

The bartender hands out all the food and I let out a huge sigh of relief. "Whew, what was that all about?" I ask as I look around the table at Maria and Ashley.

"I think that's our ticket to paradise tonight," says Maria.

"It is definitely our ticket to something," I agree with Maria. "How old do you think they are Ashley?"

"Oh Kimmy, too old for you, Chica," Ashley says as she chuckles.

"But the real question is, how old do they think I am?" I say as we all bust out laughing.

"Not old enough," Ashley says with a wink and a huge smile on her face.

CHAPTER 7

We rushed home after scarfing down our food. I'm pretty sure Ashley even licked her plates. Notice I said plates and not one plate. She ate all her meal, all the swamp fries, and most of the onion rings. She WAS starving!

"I'm jumping in the shower first since it takes me so long to fix my hair," announces Ashley as we walk in the front door. "And I have to do full makeup tonight. You never know who will show up," she says as she prances through the house.

"Is Jason not coming to the party?" I ask Ashley.

Ashley nods her head. "Nah, he has to work late at the marina. We might meet up later, or he might come over here after we get back home."

Ashley seems like she wants to see Jason. Maybe they made up through text messages.

"What if R.L. is at the party?" I ask.

Ashley stops suddenly and makes a complete 180-degree turn. "What do you mean by that?" she asks me.

I raise my eyebrows. "I mean, what if R.L. and his friends show up tonight? What are you going to do?"

Ashley hesitates and comes up with a stunning reply. "I guess I'll just tell him that I am available."

I look at Maria, and we both look at Ashley as she turns around and closes the bathroom door.

"OMG! So, they did break up!" I whisper to Maria as I put my hands on my knees.

Maria plops down on the couch and puts her hands over her head. "I just cannot believe it! What about...you know?" Maria says as she rubs her belly.

"Maybe she's not pregnant. Maybe she was just really hungry this afternoon," I say as I think back to how tasty all the food was today. I could've probably eaten as much as Ashley did if I hadn't had so many butterflies in my stomach from R.L. and his friends.

I sit down beside Maria for a few minutes and stare out the window. "How do you feel about this whole party thing tonight?" I ask as I slide down to the floor.

"Oh, I think it will be loads of fun. Lots of cute guys and probably some of our friends from school will be there too. I think it's completely harmless. Just a bunch of teenagers looking for a good time," Maria reassures me.

"I guess you're right, Maria. When have we never had a good time at a party? Let's go pick out our clothes!"

I have a ton of clothes in my closet! Nanny and Chas make sure I have the best of the best. Every time they come to visit, we go over to the mall at Gulfport for a full day of shopping. Sometimes, they take me to downtown New Orleans, and we go boutique shopping. I have some really expensive pieces of clothing. I'm sure even Ashley will wear something from my wardrobe tonight.

Maria holds up a super cute tight black dress. "What do you think Kimmy?"

"Hmm, for me or for you?" I ask.

"For me, silly," Maria barks back.

"Um, yeah, if you want to get lucky tonight!" I giggle.

"I'm ready to get lucky. How about you Kimmy?"

I'm pretty sure I am blushing right now, but I agree with Maria. I didn't know what it meant to "get lucky" when I overheard some kids at school talking about it one day, so I asked my mom. She didn't really want to explain it to me. All she said was that it was something adults do. So, of course, I asked Maria because she knows everything. And as usual, she knew what it meant and thoroughly explained it to me.

"After meeting those guys today, I've been so excited I just can't stand it," I say as I do a full-on toe touch in the air.

Maria changes into my black dress and spins around the room. "Yeah, me too Sis. I think I am ready for one of them to take me to their yacht and rock the boat all night long!"

"Bahahaha! That was the funniest thing you have ever said, Maria!" I say as I turn to look through my closet.

"Just don't tell Ashley I said that. She is very protective over us, you know," Maria says.

I pull out a white dress similar to the black dress that Maria picked. "Thoughts?" I kick my leg up in the air again to see if I'm as flexible as I used to be.

"Nah, not white. It's too pure," Maria says as she walks over to my closet. "How about this one?" Maria pulls out a skintight red dress that was my mom's when she was younger. "It screams sex!" Maria says with a purr in her voice.

"Ok, I'll try it on. You know, my mom used to wear this when she first started working at the casino," I say to Maria.

"That means it is good luck!" Maria says back.

"What do you mean by good luck?" I question.

"Well, from what my dad has seen your mom do at the casino, it just means that it helps her get a lot of tips."

If this dress has helped my mom make money, I'm sure it will make me a lucky woman tonight. Maybe the luck of the casino has worn off on the dress. We shall see.

Ashley comes out of the bathroom wearing only a towel. I'm pretty sure her belly is sticking out. I'm not sure if it is from a human baby or just a food baby. Ashley is so beautiful when she isn't wearing makeup. I am just a little jealous of her beauty. If only I were as pretty as her, I would probably already be married. Haha! What a funny thought!

"Next!" Ashley says as she goes into our guest room to change. Ashley usually sleeps in there when she stays to watch me overnight. She keeps some panties and bras here, along with her good-smelling lotions and body sprays. Ashley told me I can use her stuff when she is not here, but I don't. I wouldn't want her to come back and it all be gone, so I just leave it alone.

"Do you want me to do your hair and makeup for tonight?" Maria asks as she brushes out her ponytail.

"Of course I do!" I say back.

"All right, let me take a shower, and I will get myself ready while you are in the shower. I should be ready by the time you get out."

"Sounds good! Don't forget to shave your legs. Actually, don't forget to shave everything!" I snicker as I shout to Maria.

I stand in front of my mirror, admiring my changing body. My hips are getting bigger. My waist is getting smaller. And my boobs, whew wee, are at least three times the size they were last summer. I push up my boobs in my sexy red dress and make them look like they are popping out the top. I bet Ashley has a bra I could borrow to make them look that way all night long. I pucker my lips like I'm going to get a kiss. I lean toward the mirror and practice kissing myself. I stick out my tongue and act like I'm French kissing a boy. Oh my, this is really getting me going. I am most definitely ready for my first kiss tonight!

CHAPTER 8

D o you want cat eyes or regular eyes?" Maria asks as she moves closer to my face to apply my eyeshadow.

"I don't really know. What do you think?" I ask as I imagine which would look best.

"I guess let's try some cat eyes tonight."

When Maria says cat eyes, she just means putting a little eyeliner past where it should go. It's really nothing fancy.

"I wonder if R.L. and his friends will show up tonight?" I ask Maria as I think about kissing myself in the mirror earlier.

"Nah, they're too mature for a little high school party," Maria says as she steps back to look at her final product. "Perfecta! You look absolutely gorgeous! Go check yourself out Kimmy."

I walk over to my mirror and don't recognize the person looking back at me. "OMG, Maria! You're right, I am so beautiful. I don't even look like myself!" I step back, completely stunned. "Now for the hair."

As Maria starts flat ironing my hair, she tells me what Ashley explained to her while I was in the shower. Ashley told her that this party might get a little wild and not to let anybody take our panties off. And if either of us feels uncomfortable at any time, let Ashley know. I'm really starting to get excited. I've never been to a party with kegs before. What happens at these parties? Do people really get wild and crazy? I guess I'm about to find out.

"Should we eat dinner before we go tonight?" I ask Maria while she sprays my finished hairdo with some of Ashley's good-smelling perfume.

"Doubt it, we shouldn't be hungry. They will probably have chips and snacks there."

Hmm...I think to myself. Chips and snacks sound pretty good, but I'm not so sure this is that kind of party.

Ashley busts into my room. "Jason just texted and said he might get off work early tonight." She rolls her eyes. "He's going to ruin my night of fun! He is always doing that crap! That's why I am over him."

Ashley stands in my doorway, looking like she is ready to serve cocktails at the casino. Her hair and makeup are perfect. She went with the cat eyes too! Ashley's skin looks like it has been kissed by the sun. Her cheeks are slightly pink, and her lips are rosy red, but I notice that her eyes look bloodshot, like she's been crying, or maybe she just got too much saltwater in her eyes like I did today.

Maria stands up and takes Ashley's hands. "You know he loves you very much, Ashley. That is why he wants to see you. I'm sure he has missed you here lately since he's been working so much."

Ashley doesn't say anything back. She just lets go of Maria's hands, turns around, and heads back to our guest room.

"Was she about to cry?" I softly say to Maria as she sits back on my bed.

Maria looks at me and then quietly says, "I don't know what is going on with her right now. I think she loves Jason, but she wants to live her life as a normal teenager and not be tied down to anyone. She is getting ready to head off to college in the fall and wants to be independent. Jason sometimes treats her like a baby, and she doesn't appreciate that."

"But Maria, he treats her like a princess and buys her everything she wants!" I interject.

I cannot believe that Maria and I are having such an adult conversation about things.

"Kimmy, we don't know what happens behind closed doors though."

"You're right. I guess it's really none of our business either," I say back to Maria as I drop my head down.

"What time did Ashley say we were leaving?" I ask Maria as I swiftly try to change the subject.

Maria looks lost in her thoughts and then says, "Uh, Ashley said we would go over to Joni's around eight o'clock. She said teenager parties don't usually start until around nine or ten, but we will need to be home by midnight, so we don't get caught, if you know what I mean."

The thought of getting caught by my parents suddenly makes my stomach hurt. I would be grounded for the rest of the summer—no trips to the beach, no time with Maria, and definitely no lazy afternoons. I would be made to do chores from sun up until sundown and probably get sent out on the boat with Nanny and Chas until I puked myself straight. Ok, I have to stop thinking about that and focus on having some fun tonight. What's the worst that can happen?

CHAPTER 9

H ey, Chicas! We are leaving in ten minutes!" Ashley shouts down the hall.

It is only seven-fifteen, but I guess Ashley is getting bored watching TV in my living room. Maria and I have been primping in front of the mirror for over an hour now, and we look absolutely fabulous! My cat eyes are perfect, and her lips are to die for. My hair looks like I just walked out of the salon, and Maria looks like she has a hot date with my skintight black dress on. But Ashley, my beautiful Ashley, looks like she just walked off the cover of a magazine. Maria and I look like evil trolls compared to her. Ashley's beauty is definitely in a different ballpark. She told my mom that she wanted an interview at the casino as soon as she turned eighteen. They will hire her on the spot if she looks like this in the interview.

"How do I look?" Ashley asks as she stands up and spins around my living room, holding her hand out like her prince charming is about to kiss it.

I guess she is still thinking about our little run-in with R.L. this afternoon when he kissed all our hands. That was strange, but I kind of liked it too. I've never had a guy talk to me like he did today. I feel like he showed true interest in my feelings and wanted to know my thoughts. Maybe the hand kiss is like a direct connection to my brain. It was like he was connecting to my thoughts or something. That was the weird part.

"You look amazing, Sis!" says Maria as she grabs Ashley's hand and pretends to kiss it.

"Do you really think so?" Ashley questions us like we weren't being truthful with her.

"You are always beautiful, Ashley. Even when you don't have any makeup on and have just eaten ten pounds of food. Your beauty is like none other!" I say as I bend over to pull my boobs back up into my dress. I don't have much there, so I want to make sure I show it all off tonight.

Is it wrong to want to be someone else? I envy Ashley's looks and her popularity with the boys. I have never liked the way I look. I am super skinny with frizzy, dishwater blonde hair, and the boys seem to only like me when I have Oscar around. I have always struggled in school. Sometimes, people make fun of me when I can't read something. I don't know what I want to be when I grow up. Ashley and Maria are very smart! Like I've said before, Ashley is going to college soon to become a lawyer.

She has always been good with her words and speaking to others, whereas I stutter when I'm nervous and sometimes can't think of the right words to say. And Maria, she talks about becoming a doctor one day and a veterinarian the next. She will be whatever she wants to be.

I take Oscar for a quick walk before we leave. He keeps sniffing the air like something is there, but I can't seem to see anything. The sun is still up even though it's nearly eight o'clock. It doesn't take long for me to start sweating. Summers in BSL are always scorching hot! I also think I got a slight sunburn at the beach today.

We have a fenced-in yard, so Oscar doesn't have to be on a leash. Suddenly, Oscar stops dead in his tracks. Then he barks his loudest voice! So that you know, Oscar never barks unless something is seriously wrong or he suspects someone is hurt.

"Oscar, what's going on?" I quietly say as I look around the yard. I don't want to talk too loud in case someone is within earshot of me.

"Come on, let's go back in!" I am nearly talking in a whisper now. Oscar is pretty good about listening, but for some reason, he is not obeying me right now.

"Oscar, get up here!" I say sternly. He still doesn't listen. "Get up here right now, Oscar!" My teeth are gritted together, and I can feel my cheeks getting hotter by the second.

I march down my front steps and walk over to Oscar. He is still standing and growling at the air. When I get up to him, he jumps when I touch him. What on earth is going on with him? He sure is acting strange!

I scoop him up, look around the yard, and out to the street. I don't see anything at all, but Oscar certainly sensed a disturbance. When he realizes he is safe in my arms, he gives me a sloppy kiss with a huge smile on his face. Hopefully, I won't smell like a dog tonight after carrying him. I think I will use some of Ashley's perfume to freshen up my dress.

As I tell Maria and Ashley how strange Oscar was acting outside, Maria starts laughing and says that Oscar must have seen a haint. *Bahahaha!* Oh lord, I hope Maria doesn't say that in front of my mom, or she'll start painting everything blue and put up one of those silly-looking bottle trees in our front yard. Poor Oscar, he just can't catch a break. It's a good thing he is staying home tonight and can protect the house from that haint.

Our walk over to Joni's was uneventful. Our neighborhood is considered one of the safest places in BSL. I technically live in the historic district of town. Most of the houses in my district survived Hurricane Katrina because of the seawall that had been built. I really like to look at all the colorful homes. I call them Easter egg houses because of their different paint colors. Some are pink, others are yellow, and my favorite is a two-story lime green house that sits a little off the road with tall palm trees scattered throughout the yard. It is the color of key lime pie and looks like a movie star lives there. My mom told me about a movie that was once filmed in BSL, and they used that house as a backdrop in one scene. Now, old man Chism lives there. He is friendly but only comes outside to walk his tiny black poodle. I've heard he spends his evenings at the casino, but I don't know if that's true. He is wealthy with no wife or children, so I guess he has to spend his money somehow.

The sun is starting to set, and I am getting a little nervous about this party. The breeze is flowing through the palm leaves. They sound like someone opening a paper lunch bag only to realize they weren't hungry and then closing it back quickly. It's a sound I would miss if I ever left the ocean. I've heard out-of-towners talk about how that same sound grates on their nerves, and they just can't understand how people deal with it here. It's relaxing to me and makes me feel at home. I get a slight chill when a car passes by. I'm not sure if I'm really cold or if my nerves are getting the best of me. I'll be glad when we get there, and my mind can be at ease for a while. I guess it is the fear of the unknown that causes people anxiety because it sure does it to me.

CHAPTER 10

W hat did you say?" I yell loudly at Maria. I can't hear her over the loud music in the house.

"Let's go outside and talk!" Maria shouts over the music back to me. I can feel the beat of the music deep inside my chest.

Thump, Da, Thump, Da, Thump

I smile at some cute guys as we zig-zag through the crowd of people at Joni's house. I've never in my life seen so many people crammed into a house, and this house is enormous! I keep brushing against people's sweaty arms and damp shirts. Yuck! I guess you could say I'm a germ-a-phobe.

"Yeah, what's up?" I ask Maria when we finally get to the patio outside. The air is a little crisp, and I can smell the salty ocean in the breeze. I close my eyes briefly and try to gather my thoughts back. Taking a break from all the action was a pretty good idea. I'm wet with sweat, and my ears are ringing.

"Have you seen Ashley lately?" Maria asks in a slight panic.

"She was over there talking to Joni and some of their friends earlier," I say as I point toward the door.

"I haven't seen her for a while, so I was just wondering." Maria looks around like she's about to say something, then stops. "Let's just go back in and enjoy the party, I guess."

Back in the house, kids are hollering and carrying on around the drinks. We walk over to see what all the commotion is about.

Do it, do it, do it!

The crowd chants as Ashley holds a long hose to her mouth, and another girl pours a beer into a funnel attached to the top of the hose. I watch as the beer goes down the tube into Ashley's mouth, and she chugs it until the funnel is empty. She throws the funnel to the floor, and beer runs down her chin. The crowd cheers loudly when she is finished. I am in complete awe of what I just saw. So, this is what teenagers do for fun at parties?

"Should we try it?" I say as I look over at Maria, who has a huge smile on her face.

"Really, I can't believe you just asked me that, silly." Maria smacks my shoulder and starts walking toward her sister. "Let's at least get something to drink."

She grabs my hand and pulls me over to the drink table. "What shall it be Kimmy?" Did Maria just ask me if I wanted alcohol? I don't know what to say. Should I get a beer, liquor, or just a soda? I'm so confused.

My parents always told me never to start drinking, or I might end up like my mom's uncle, Randy. He was a severe alcoholic who was never able to hold down a job. He got really drunk one night and went on some kind of rampage. He ended up driving his car the wrong way down a one-way street in the French Quarter and hit a mother and her child head-on, killing both of them. My mom says he will see the same four walls for the rest of his life.

"Should we? Do you think we will get in trouble? I am only twelve, and you're just thirteen. I'm pretty sure you have to be twenty-one to drink alcohol in Mississippi."

Maria grabs a red cup, fills it with beer from the keg, and hands it over to me. "Girl, live a little. Opportunities like this don't come around very often for us, and we might as well enjoy ourselves."

I am shocked at what Maria just said. She is always the one who will whoa me back when I try to do something dumb. And now, she is the one wanting to be stupid and try alcohol. But you know what, if Maria thinks it's ok, then what the heck!

"Thanks! Just don't let Ashley see us drinking this."

I take my first sip of beer and almost throw up! Why do people like drinking this? It seriously tasted like dirt and pee mixed together. I don't know what pee tastes like, but I imagine it tastes just like this beer.

"This is some nasty stuff!" I say as I snarl my face into a frown.

"I think it's pretty good! You know, my dad has let me try his cervezas at home. He will make me go get them out of the fridge and then tell me to take one sip to make sure I didn't poison him. Then he grins like an opossum and chuckles when I take a sip. I didn't like it the first time I tried it either, but my dad said it is an acquired taste. Now I actually kind of like the way they taste."

This is something I did not know about Maria and her family. I had no idea that her dad drank beer. I'd probably have to drink beer, too, if I had to watch those kids of his all day long.

"So, your dad is ok with you drinking beer?" I yell in Maria's ear as the music starts thumping again.

"I wouldn't say that. He knows it is illegal for me, but it is kind of a tradition in my family."

I'm really not sure what she means by tradition, but I don't want to look stupid and ask. "Acquired, you say, does that mean it tastes better when you drink more of it?" I'm pretty smart with my vocabulary, but sometimes I have to double-check what words mean.

"Yeah, that's right! So, after you drink this first cup, the next one will taste a little better. It probably won't taste good to you until you've been drinking it for a few years though."

I sip on my cup of beer until it is gone. I decide to try another one. I make my way through the crowd to the keg. I am already starting to feel a little funny. I don't know if I like this feeling. My legs are tingling. My eyes are heavy but relaxed. My feet are gliding on the floor, guiding me along the way.

I pour myself another cup full of the nasty stuff. I turn around quickly to get back to Maria. *BAM!* I slam smack dab into a chiseled chest of steel. At the same time, I lose my balance, and my beer flies up in the air!

"Little One! Is that you?"

In a dazed state, I look up. "R.L.? Oh my God, I'm so sorry! I had no idea you were standing behind me!" Geez...if this afternoon wasn't embarrassing enough with my hair getting stuck under the table, now I have spilled my beer all over the place and all over R.L.

"It ain't no thing but a chicken wing! A little beer never hurt anybody. Let's get you a refill." He grabs my cup out of my hand. My grip was so tight that I barely let it go on his second attempt.

"Don't be shy, Little One. I'll make sure nobody puts anything in this."

I watch him closely as he goes over to the keg and refills my cup. My mom has told me stories about people spiking drinks at the casino with date rape drugs then taking them upstairs to the hotel and having their way. I don't know how she knows that, but she is careful to watch her customers and make sure none of them get taken advantage of.

R.L. hands me my cup back and winks. "See ya around!" he says as he walks away.

When I finally get back over to Maria, she is talking to some guys who look like they might be our age. "Hey! How's it going!" I say as the music gets louder. The guys nod their heads. They look really familiar, but I'm not sure how I know them.

"I'm Kimmy!" I try to yell over the music. They introduce themselves to me, but I can barely hear them. All three are so cute.

"Do I know you?" I ask the cutest one whose name is Kylan. He said to call him Ky for short, but he doesn't look like a Ky to me.

"Um, yeah, Kimmy, don't you remember me?"

Hmm, I think for a minute, but I still can't remember how I know him.

"We went to the same summer camp at the middle school last year. I can't believe you don't remember me. We were placed in a group together during that idiotic square dance class they made us take. We were partners!"

I rack my brain, and then it comes to me. "Oh yeah, I remember you. You stumbled over your feet and fell when we were doing the do-si-do. You took me down with you. Yes, I remember that now like it was yesterday! Everybody laughed, including me. But you twisted your ankle and had to be carried off by the camp counselors. I never saw you again after that."

Kylan looks down at the ground, my cup of beer, then back up at me. "That's because I broke my ankle and had to have surgery two days later." How embarrassing! And I thought I was a total klutz.

"Well, looks like you're doing good now!" I say back, not knowing what to say. "So, what grade will you be in next year?" I ask Kylan, as I can tell he wants to change the conversation.

"We will all be freshmen over at the high school. What about y'all?" He points to me and Maria.

"Eighth grade. I am getting ready to turn thirteen in a few weeks, and Maria is already thirteen." I smile my biggest smile when I think about becoming a teenager. I touch my cheek and then my lips. I am pretty sure that they are going numb. My tongue is starting to feel like a brick as I take my last sip of beer.

"That's cool. I'm fourteen and getting ready to be fifteen in August. I am hoping to get my hardship license soon. My parents work in New Orleans, and we live so far out that the bus no longer comes by my house. My older brother had been taking me to school, but he starts college in the fall and is moving to Tennessee."

Did he just say Tennessee? Wow! I've never heard of anyone going to college in Tennessee. "I have family up there! From what I've been told, it is such a beautiful place." Did I just miss the fact that he said he will be getting his driver's license soon? That could be fun!

My thoughts are starting to get cloudy, but I'm really feeling good about myself. "How did you hear about this party?" I ask Kylan as Maria and one of his friends walk out to the patio. Now, it is just Kylan and I standing by ourselves next to the outside French doors. Well, we aren't really by ourselves. We are jam-packed into Joni's sunroom with probably a hundred other people, but no one else is paying us any attention, so it's like we are all alone.

"My brother is friends with Joni and Maria's sister, Ashley. My friends and I are just tagging along until we have to go home at midnight. My parents said we could come hang out for a few as long as we were back home later."

I wish my parents were like Kylan's. My mom would be having a cow right now if she knew I was at this party.

"Wanna drink?" I ask Kylan as I motion toward the kegs and drink table.

"Sure! Sounds fun!"

I guess I could have one more beer before we go home. What's one more gonna hurt? Right?

CHAPTER 11

I open my eyes, and the room is pitch black. Where am I? How did I get here? Why is everything moving around me, but I am lying perfectly still? I think I'm in my bed because I'm pretty sure I can hear Oscar snoring. I pat next to me in my bed and feel a body. I make my way to their head and touch their long hair. Ah, it's Maria. I sigh. Ok, so we must be home in my bed, and it must still be night outside. Why is my head hurting so bad? What happened to the party? And Kylan, what happened with him? I drift back off to sleep and have the best night's sleep of my entire life.

"Oh God! Oh God! Oh God! Maria, I'm about to be sick!" I jump up, crawl over Maria, and race to the bathroom. I make it to the toilet and hit the floor with my knees. I raise the toilet seat and am very thankful that I cleaned it a couple of days ago. I start uncontrollably gagging. I close my eyes, and the room is spinning even more. What is going on? I feel like I am on the outskirts of a merry-go-round, and it is getting faster. I must jump off and get my footing, but it is too late. I hang my head even lower in the bowl and start heaving up everything I have eaten in the last three days.

After about twenty minutes of gagging and coughing and heaving, it finally stops. I stretch out on the cold tile floor only to feel my body break out in a ferocious sweat. I fan my face with my hand, but it isn't working.

Oh No! Here it comes again! I hang my head in the toilet and let it flow out of my mouth. Not much came out that time except for stomach acid, so it should be over with. My teeth start chattering, and my body starts to shake. I lie down again, only to realize now that I am completely naked. Where are my clothes? Why are they not on my body? Well, I can't worry about that right now. I have to rest so I don't throw up anymore.

When I wake up, I am freezing. I am pretty sure the thermostat is set to the Arctic. Why am I so cold? I am not sure that I can even stand up.

"Maria! I need you!" No response. I crawl over to the linen closet and raise myself up with the doorknob. Whew, that was hard work. I grab a towel and wrap it around my body. Then, I get a washcloth and wet it in the bathroom sink. I slap it to my forehead and lean against the sink for a few minutes until I can get enough strength to walk to my room.

As I cross the hallway, I notice something strange. The living room light is on, and I see Oscar lying in his spot on the couch, all snuggled up with his blanket. If Oscar is on the couch, then who is snoring on my floor?

As I open my bedroom door, I realize it must be getting close to morning because I can see the sunrise peeking through my black-out curtains. My bedroom is still very dark though. I walk over to my bed to find the dress I was wearing last night balled up on the floor. I feel my way to my chest of drawers and pull out some panties and pajamas. At least I'm not naked anymore. I crawl back into bed and close my eyes.

"Kimmy! Hey Kimmy!" I hear Maria calling my name, but I can't respond. Am I dead? Then I feel someone pushing on my shoulders, shaking me back and forth in the bed.

"Wake up Kimmy! You have to get up! Your mom will be home soon and..." Maria stops mid-sentence. I can finally open my eyes and roll over to see Maria sitting straight up in my bed.

"I'm awake. I don't feel good," I say in a groggy, raspy voice.

"Kylan is on your floor!" I jump up like someone lit a match under my butt.

"What?" I say in a loud whisper. I swiftly roll over and turn on my lamp on my bedside table. Sure enough, Kylan is sound asleep in the middle of my floor. "Oh my God, Maria. How did he get there?"

"Do you not remember?"

"Remember what?"

"Remember what happened last night?"

"Um, If I remembered what happened last night, then I would know why Kylan is asleep on my floor and why I was naked when I woke up to puke my guts out this morning."

I really don't remember anything. I laid my head back on my pillow, trying to rack my brain of what happened last night. The last thing I could think of was dancing with Kylan and getting close to him. Almost close enough to kiss him. I remember going to the keg several times and holding Kylan's hand, making him go with me. I remember having to pee like fifteen hundred times at Joni's house, and that's about it.

"No, Maria. What happened?" I roll my head off my pillow only to realize that my headache is back with a vengeance.

"Well, let me fill you in, Sis."

Maria proceeds to tell me about how I had like eleventeen beers last night and acted a complete fool in front of all of Ashley's friends. She says that Kylan is in love with me and wouldn't leave my side. He even called his mom and asked if he could stay with a friend who was having a hard time. That friend was me, apparently. Kylan was afraid that someone might take advantage of me, and he wanted to make sure that I made it home safely. So, when I started crawling on my hands and knees out the patio, Kylan got his brother Ken to take us all home. Maria then tells me that Kylan and I were kissing in the back seat of Ken's Expedition, and his hands were all over me.

"Well, isn't that interesting," is pretty much all I could say to Maria.

"Yeah, I'm not really in the mood for talking about it anymore. We were way too young to be doing that last night, and I don't ever want to do that again until we are of legal age. That was so stupid of us!" I can hear the anger in Maria's voice. "Now, we need to figure out how to get Kylan out of here without your mom seeing him."

That's when I hear the front door close and footsteps in my living room. "She's home!" I say to Maria in a highly panicked whisper. "We have to hide Kylan because the first thing my mom will do is come check on me to make sure I'm okay."

I jump out of my bed and tiptoe over to Kylan, who hasn't moved an inch this whole time Maria and I have been talking. I sit next to him for a second and admire his attractiveness. Does Kylan really like me like a girlfriend?

I get closer and give him a gentle tap on his shoulder. "Hey, Kylan, you need to go hide in my closet, like now!" Kylan raises up and doesn't even question what I am saying. He crawls his way to my closet and closes the door.

Just as I get settled back in my bed, my mom opens my bedroom door. I make sure my eyes are tightly shut. I can feel her presence near my bed. I don't move. I don't even breathe. Then, I hear my door shut back.

I let out a huge sigh of relief. "That was a close one, Maria. Now, how are we going to get Kylan out of here?" I ask Maria as I lie on my back and stare up at my ceiling fan circling round and round.

"I don't know Kimmy. We are really in a predicament this time."

We lie in my bed and don't move or speak for at least ten minutes. Then, at the exact same time, we roll over, facing each other.

"Did you really puke your guts out this morning?" Maria asks with a giggle.

"You have no idea!" I respond as I roll my eyes at her.

Maria and I both agree that since it is only a little after 6 a.m., we should just close our eyes for a little bit and try to get some rest. I open my closet door and see Kylan sitting under my clothes in complete terror. I reach out to touch his face to calm him, and he grabs my hand.

"I had a great time with you last night, I think," Kylan says as he pulls me into the closet with him. I just now realize that he has no shirt on and is only wearing his boxers. "What happened last night?" he asks.

"I have no idea, but Maria does. She filled me in a little bit. I think we both had a great time last night. From what Maria said, we really hit it off at Joni's party. And I'm pretty sure we both had too much to drink as well."

Kylan puts his arm around me and pulls me closer to him. His body is warm and smooth. I put my hand on his chest and feel his muscles. I could get used to this.

"From what I can remember about last night, Maria is right. Will you stay in here with me while I try to remember everything that happened?"

I grab a blanket off my shelf and cover us up. I cuddle up closer to Kylan and immediately drift off to sleep.

I feel Kylan's rough fingers brushing my hair off of my forehead. His hands feel like he's been building houses for years. I wonder how they got so rugged and callused. Then I feel his soft lips kiss my cheek. Am I dreaming? This could not possibly be happening to me!

"I've liked you since summer camp last year, but I didn't know how to contact you. I was too embarrassed to ask my friends to get your number after I got hurt. I had always hoped we would run into each other somewhere. I had even thought we might have a class together in high school, but I wasn't sure I could wait that long. I never imagined that I would see you at Joni's party last night, but I'm sure glad I did."

Is he talking to me, or is there someone else in my closet? I open my eyes and look up at him through the dark. "I'm really glad too," I manage to say in my softest, sweetest voice. My throat is a little sore from being so sick earlier, but I'm sure it will go away as soon as I get to drink some water.

"When I closed my eyes earlier, I'm pretty sure I saw a glimpse of everything that happened last night. And I liked what I saw." Kylan spoke to me like he was talking to an angel. I must still be asleep and dreaming.

"Gosh, I'm so sorry Kimmy. I bet I sound like such an idiot. I just can't believe that last night happened, and I am sitting in your closet right now. I guess it's kind of funny. Would you mind if I kissed you?"

Oh no! I can't let him kiss me right now this second. My mouth still tastes like puke, and I'm sure my breath is reeking. But what should I tell him? If I say no, he will think I don't like him. If I say yes, he will be totally disgusted by me.

"I got really sick this morning in the bathroom. I think all that beer I drank last night came back to haunt me," I giggle when I say this, hoping he will know that I want to kiss him, but it is in his best interest to wait until I have brushed my teeth.

I immediately change the subject. "What's your plan for getting out of my house today? My window is at least six feet off the ground, so it would be a pretty hard fall if you jumped out. I sure don't want you to break your other ankle." Kylan snickers and looks down. I can feel my face getting hotter too.

"Doesn't your mom usually go to bed for a while after she gets home from work?"

It took me a minute to think about his question. My brain is a little foggy still. "You're right, she does. She will take a shower and then go to bed. My best guess is that she will sleep until noon. Then, get up and head back over to the casino around two o'clock for another double. What time is it right now?"

Kylan pulls out his phone and looks down. "Oh no, it's dead. I think we took a bunch of pictures last night. I'll be curious to see what's on here when I get it charged up."

I smile back at Kylan, but deep inside, I'm concerned about what might be on his phone. I guess it is too late now to worry about. The damage has already been done.

I crawl out of my closet and tiptoe over to my bed, where Maria is sound asleep. My alarm clock says eight-sixteen. I think I will get up and see if Mom is in her bedroom yet. I tell Kylan to stay put, and I head out my door.

It is really quiet in my house. I hear my mom talking on the phone in the kitchen. When I get there, I see that she is making herself some toast. I grab a bottle of water from the fridge. I don't know who she is talking to, but she quickly hangs up.

"Hey Honey, you're up early this morning." She brushes my hair out of my face and pats my head.

"Yeah, I couldn't sleep. Maria is still asleep in my bed." I'm hoping she doesn't ask me any questions.

"Do you know when Ashley left? She's not in the guest room. The bed is made and all." Mom asks as if she knows we were up to no good last night.

I hesitate and respond, "Pretty early, I think. I didn't hear her leave." Shew, maybe I dodged a bullet.

"Well, she forgot to lock the front door when she left. She must've been in a hurry. Has Oscar been out yet?"

Ashley didn't forget to lock the door. We forgot to lock it when we got home last night. Ashley wasn't with us. I have no idea where she went after Ken brought us home. Maybe Maria knows.

"Uh, no, I haven't taken him out. Maybe Ashley did before she left." I know that's not true, but I can pretend, right?

"Can you please take him out? And Kimmy, did you have an upset stomach in the night? Someone threw up all over the toilet in the hall bathroom." Oh no, I forgot to clean up my mess.

"Yeah, I guess I ate something that didn't agree with me. I'll take Oscar out and clean up the bathroom."

I rush out the door with Oscar so fast it makes me dizzy again. It is already hot outside. I look at the thermometer on the side of the fence, and it says eighty-eight degrees. It's gonna be a scorcher! I hang outside for a few minutes, trying to figure out how to get Kylan home. Even if he can get out of my house, he still needs to get home. I don't have any money for a cab, and he lives too far away to ride my bicycle. I have no good ideas. Maybe Maria will know what to do. She always knows what to do.

I finally make it back in my house. It is really quiet again. My mom has gone to bed, and Oscar jumps back on the couch to take a nap. I run to the bathroom to clean up my mess and brush my teeth. Now, if Kylan wants to kiss me, my breath will be fresh and clean. His won't be, but I don't care at this point. He's probably already seen me naked since I had to strip off my dress and throw it on the floor so I could get in the bed. Maybe he doesn't remember it, and if he does, I hope he liked what he saw.

I open the door to my bedroom. It is still pretty dark in there. Maria is sleeping, and I guess Kylan is still in my closet. I check my phone only to find that I have seventeen missed calls all from the same number. I don't know the number, so I decide to get in the closet and call it back.

"Hey Kylan! You still alive?" He must've gone back to sleep because he was pretty delayed on his answer. "Do you know this number? It has called me seventeen times." I show him my phone.

"Wow, you have one of those new smartphones! That's so cool!" I hand him my phone so he can closely examine the number.

"Yeah, my grandparents, Nanny and Chas, gave it to me for Christmas. They always make sure I have all the best stuff." I smile, and he takes a closer look.

"Oh my gosh, that's Ken's number. How did he get your digits? He must be calling to check on me to make sure I made it through the night without being taken advantage of." He looks over at me and winks. "I should probably call him back."

CHAPTER 12

D ude, it sounds like you're in a pretty damn good bind!" I hear Ken say to Kylan as he laughs hysterically on the other end of the phone.

"Um, yeah, any suggestions would be much appreciated at this point. I am currently sitting in Kimmy's closet with Maria sleeping in the bed and her mom down the hall taking a nap. At least we hope she is sleeping." Kylan reports back to Ken.

"Well, man, I'll tell it to you like this. Women will always get you into trouble no matter how old they are. I can come over there right now and get you, or you're going to have to walk your ass over to the Welcome to Louisiana sign with your thumb stuck out."

Oh my, Kylan's brother is pretty tough on him. If I ever had a younger sibling, I'd probably be a butthole to them as well.

"Ok, I guess I'll just jump out her window and hope I don't break my leg," Kylan says back to Ken in an annoyed way.

"All right, man, chill. I'll come park down the road a ways and walk over to her house. Just tell me which window to come to, and I'll help you down. We sure don't want to end up in the hospital again over this silly girl."

Who is he calling a silly girl? Did Kylan tell his family about me already? Nah, his phone's been dead.

I feel like my life has changed drastically over the last twelve hours. I went to my first teen party, drank my first beer, and had my first kiss, I think. And I'm pretty sure I've got my first boyfriend. Surprisingly, Kylan really does seem head over heels in love with me! I'm such a lucky girl. I guess you could say that I "got lucky" last night in a PG kind of way.

Kylan hands me the phone to explain to Ken which window is mine. I give him a very detailed description of the outside of my house. He remembered it as being one of the only salvageable houses after Katrina.

"And don't worry about Oscar. He never barks unless he sees a ghost or something strange going on. Which is usually never," I tell Ken, but I suddenly remember Oscar barking at the air last night before we went to the party. Maria said he probably saw a haint, but I've never seen or heard about any ghosts in our neighborhood.

However, there is this ancient graveyard named Cedar Rest Cemetery that has some awfully creepy above-ground graves that are caved in. I'm pretty sure you can see the caskets inside of them if you look close enough. But I'm too chicken to look. I'm afraid I might see a dead body. The last time I went to that cemetery was on a school field trip to look at the angel carvings in the trees. Those carvings are amazing! My teacher said the angels would keep the demons below and protect our town from evil. I'm not so sure that a carving in a tree can do all that, but I do like to admire them every time we drive by one.

With his voice shaking, Kylan looks over at me and says, "Do you think this will work?"

I take a deep breath. "I sure hope so. I'd really like to see you this afternoon without a cast on," I say as I giggle. Did I just ask him out on a date? What do kids our age do for dates? I'm sure neither of us have any money, and I know my mom won't let me go anywhere with him unless Ashley goes with us. But Mom will never know if she's not home, right?

Kylan leans over and wraps his arm around my shoulder. I lean into his chest, and all my cares and worries seem to fade away. I'm still not sure that I'm not dreaming. I pinch the side of my leg just to make sure.

"Why'd you do that?" Kylan asks.

"I'm so afraid that I'm dreaming. This all doesn't seem real," I say as I look into his eyes.

"Do you want it to be real?" Kylan says back to me as he brushes his fingers against my cheek.

"Yes, yes, I really do. You're everything I've ever dreamed of. I just don't want to wake up, and it all have been a dream. Even so, it would be an amazing dream."

Kylan turns my head toward his and tries to get as close to me as possible in my closet. "I know you went and brushed your teeth because I smelled your minty toothpaste when you climbed back in here. I popped a piece of gum while you were out talking to your mom. Can I kiss you now?"

How can I deny that? My heart is racing, my palms are sweaty, and all of a sudden, I feel warm inside and out. It's about to happen. I'm going to get my first kiss. Well, at least the first one that I can remember. I never answer Kylan. He just sits there looking at me. At least, I think he's looking at me. It's pretty dark in this closet. I turn my body completely around so that I'm facing him. I lift my arm, so my hand is resting on his shoulder. I feel one of his hands move to my waist and the other to my face. Then he moves his hand from my waist to the other side of my face. It's really going to happen. I wrap my arms around his neck. We both lean in at the same time. I feel the warmth of his breath on my face. He kisses my cheek first. Then he makes his way to my mouth. I push my lips out toward his, and it finally happens! Our lips move in sync with each other like dancers in a ballet. It feels so good. It feels so natural. My body is humming, and I'm starting to feel tingly all over. This is the magic moment I have always dreamed about. He opens his mouth a little, which in turn causes mine to open. I feel his tongue brush up against my lips. Our lips lock back together. I push my tongue out gently, and it enters his mouth. I can feel his hand start to move down my body and rub my back. Then he moves his hand over my boobs on the outside of my shirt. Everything is absolutely perfect!

Tap, Tap, Tap!

We both jump, and I'm pretty sure we just slung spit all over my closet.

"Hey, Kimmy. Open up!"

It's Maria. Whew, I was afraid my mom was on the other side of my closet door. I crack open the door. "What's up?" I say to Maria. My face is red hot, and my lips feel like they're on fire.

She snickers, "What are y'all doing in there?"

I probably look like a deer in headlights when I answer her. "Nothing, why?" I respond, knowing that I will be giving her all the juicy details as soon as Kylan leaves.

"Well, someone keeps knocking on your window, and it's scaring the crap out of me!"

I pause until I can gather my thoughts. "Ken, it's Ken here to get Kylan. Open my blinds, Maria, so that he can see us."

Maria opens the blinds as Kylan and I crawl out of my closet. My clothes are all bunched up, and Kylan still isn't wearing a shirt or pants. I grab his clothes and toss them over to him.

"Here, you might need this," I say with a huge smile on my face.

"Pants, yeah. Shirt, nah, you keep it. I'm sure it's already hot as hell out there."

Did Kylan just tell me to keep his shirt? What am I going to do with it? Does this mean we are boyfriend and girlfriend? Should I ask him? I don't know what to do! But I do know that the next few minutes are a make-or-break for me. They will determine how the rest of the summer will be for Maria, Kylan, and me.

"Ok. So, you're going to climb up on my desk, open my window, and gently make your way to the ground. Notice I said gently. Let's just hope that Ken is feeling strong this morning." I take a deep breath and slowly let it out.

Kylan turns his shirtless body around and looks at me like he might never see me again. "Kimmy, please promise me that if something happens and we get caught, you will try your best to contact me. Maria, you have my number in your phone. Kimmy, so do you. I put it in both of your phones last night in case we got separated. I'm being serious. I've never done anything this crazy in my life. Here's to many more crazy times together!"

Kylan puts his hands around my waist and pulls me into him. He gently kisses me on the lips. He cups my face with his hands and says, "Call me later as soon as you wake up. I'll definitely see you this afternoon!"

He kisses me again, turns around, and then proceeds to climb out my window. And just like that, he is gone. I climb up to make sure he made it down safely, and he did. As I shut my window, I see Kylan and Ken walking down the road. Ken has his hand around Kylan's shoulder like he's giving him the third degree. I bet Ken wonders where Kylan's shirt went. Little does he know everything that just happened.

Maria grabbed my arm and helped me off my desk. "OMG, Kimmy! You have to tell me everything!" Maria is grinning from ear to ear.

"Well, we kissed for a long time. Until you knocked on my closet door and scared the bejesus out of us!" I say as I shove her shoulder.

"I'm sorry, I was terrified that whatever Oscar barked at last night was outside your window."

I laugh, thinking back to how spit flew out of our mouths, and I had to wipe my face with the back of my hand.

"Did anything else happen?" Maria asks as she winks at least fifteen times at me.

"If you count him touching my boobs, then yes! Well, he touched them through my shirt, but it felt really good." *EEK!* I can't believe that I am sharing this with Maria. I never in a million years thought that I would be the one to kiss a boy first.

"I guess you could say we were making out, Sis. And it would have kept going if you hadn't interrupted us!" I say through my teeth.

"Hey, I didn't interrupt you, Ken did. It's all his fault, so blame it on him."

I stood still and pondered what she had just said. "Yeah, but I'm sure glad he did interrupt us because I'm not sure how much longer I could have behaved myself in that closet all alone with Kylan, if you know what I mean." I wink back at Maria.

"Well, I have something to tell you," Maria says as she twirls around my room.

"What?" I say to her, as I know she is up to something.

"Do you remember Kylan's friend Peyton, who was with him at the party last night?"

I seriously have to think hard about this one. I don't remember much about the party, but I think I remember Peyton. He was really cute too.

"Um, maybe, why?" I raise my eyebrows to Maria as she sits down on my bed.

"Well, you better sit down for this one." She grabs my arm and pulls me to the bed. "Last night, while you and Kylan were dancing like two crazy people, Peyton and I went outside to get some fresh air. We talked for a long time, and then he kissed me! Not just once, but for at least thirty minutes! We made out like it was going out of style. We probably would have kept going if you hadn't crawled out to the patio saying you were dying."

I busted out laughing, and Maria just smiled. "Did I really do that?" I asked sheepishly.

"Uh, yeah, you did."

I think for a moment, then say, "So you're telling me that you were the first of us to kiss a boy? I thought I had won that game." I snap my fingers and fall back on my bed.

"Oh Kimmy, you did win that game. You were kissing all over Kylan while you two were dancing. That's why Peyton and I went outside to talk, so we didn't have to keep looking at you two."

Bahahahaha! Finally, I have the first kiss bragging rights.

"So, are you going to try to meet up with Kylan later?" Maria falls back on the bed beside me.

"Of course I am! I am in love with him!" I close my eyes and realize that my head is still slightly swimming.

"Don't you think you're rushing into this whole love thing a little too fast?"

thing a little too fast?"

I look over at her like she's crazy. "No, absolutely not! When you know, you know!"

CHAPTER 13

Are y'all still in bed? I'm leaving for work. Come on and get up. Oscar needs to go out." I hear mom talking, but I'm not sure I'm conscious yet. "Kimmy, are you ok in there? It is almost one o'clock in the afternoon!"

Yes, I'm conscious now, but I don't want to open my eyes. I'm afraid that she might start asking questions again, and I'm just not in the mood to produce any answers. I'm pretty sure we also pulled the whole party thing off last night. And Kylan, oh sweet Kylan. If Mom had any idea what transpired over the last twenty-four hours, she would probably strangle me right here, right now.

"I hear ya. I think we stayed up way too late last night." My eyes are still closed. My blackout curtains are really doing their job today. I take a deep breath and hold it until she says something.

"I tried calling Ashley to make sure she is coming over tonight to stay with you, but her phone went straight to voicemail. I reminded her yesterday that I needed her for tonight as well. When y'all get up, can you make sure she knows? Send me a text when you talk to her."

I give my mom a thumbs up. "Sure thing, Mom," I groggily say back.

She eases the door back shut, and I roll over to see Maria smiling. "You ready to go have some fun?" She says in a slightly creepy tone with her eyes still closed.

"I'm not sure that I can handle any more fun tonight. My fun meter is pretty much pegged for the next few days. Especially if alcohol is involved."

I rub my stomach, remembering how violently ill I was just a few hours ago. I'm pretty sure I have what is called a "hangover." I've heard my mom talk about her customers having hangovers and ordering the hair of the dog. When I first heard her talking about that, I thought she really meant dog hair, like plucking one of Oscar's hairs out and putting it in a drink. Yeah, that was a pretty stupid thought on my part.

"My mom says that if you have a nasty hangover, you should go and get the exact same drink you had the night before that gave you that hangover. Supposedly, it will cure you!" I look over at Maria and smile back.

"So, you're saying you need some beer for breakfast, Kimmy?" Just thinking about drinking a beer makes me want to vomit in my mouth.

"Uh, I was just kidding, maybe."

I ever so gently raise myself in the bed. I prop myself up with my elbows. "I can't do it, Maria." I fall back into my pillow.

"You really are hungover, Chica! You know, you were hilarious last night. You made a good impression on Kylan too," Maria says with sarcasm as she laughs.

Oh, Kylan, my sweet boy. I still can't wrap my head around his kind heart and soul. How was I lucky to run into him last night at the party? And Maria hooking up with Peyton? What are the odds?

I push myself up again and am successful this time. My head is pounding. My stomach is still a little queasy, but I'm alive, and that's all that matters. I roll over and plant my feet on the floor. I look down and see my mom's red dress still on the floor beside my bed. How did Mom not see it when she came into my room a few minutes ago? Oh yeah, because it is pitch black in here. I knew I got those curtains for a reason. I look over at my phone on my nightstand: no missed calls and no text messages. I would guess that Kylan is still in bed, although he did tell me to call him when I get up. I'm sure he's waiting for my call. I better take Oscar out first.

The air outside is so thick you could cut it with a knife. I look over at the thermometer. It's ninety-two degrees and probably ninety-five percent humidity.

Sometimes, Oscar gets distracted. He just keeps sniffing at everything. He will take a few steps and sniff some more. Just when you think he is getting ready to do his business, he catches another scent. Dad says he is "reading the newspaper." I chuckle, thinking about Oscar sitting on the toilet reading a newspaper and trying to do his business while wearing old man glasses.

"Come on, Osc. Let's go back in before we die from heat exhaustion." Whew, I was only out there for five minutes, and the back of my shirt is already wet.

"Hey! You startled me!" Maria jumps up off the couch in my living room.

"Who on earth did you think was coming through my door?" I say to Maria as I shuffle Oscar back into the house.

She grins. "All that talk about haints last night kind of got me thinking. This house has been here for a very long time, and didn't your grandmother die here?" Maria asks, knowing good and well that my house isn't haunted.

"She did, but I'm pretty sure she wouldn't want to bother us."

Maria leans down and snuggles her face with Oscar's. "I've just had a really strange feeling ever since we woke up this morning. Like something's not right."

I look around the room to make sure we are alone. "It's not right, Maria. We both kissed boys last night, and I'm pretty sure by this evening we will both have boyfriends. Speaking of boys, have you talked to Peyton today?"

Maria sighs, "Nah, I'm waiting for him to call me. We left the party so abruptly last night that all I said when we got in the car was call me, and I had to holler that out the window. I hope he heard me. I know he has my number because I put it in his phone."

Maria seemed a little worried that Peyton wouldn't call her, but if I were a betting person, I'd say he was still asleep in his bed like we were until about twenty minutes ago.

"How about I go fix us a big breakfast to take our minds off these boys?" I love cooking breakfast. My mom always keeps eggs and canned biscuits in the fridge. And if I'm lucky, I will also find some leftovers to heat up.

"That sounds great! I can help!" Maria says excitedly.

I end up making us some double omelets with mushrooms, onions, bacon, and cheese. Maria likes jalapeños in hers, and I like Cajun seasoning on mine. Nanny taught me how to make omelets when I was around five years old. I hated eating eggs until I realized you can mask their taste with other stuff. Maria and I like to think that we are sophisticated eaters. Not many kids our age would eat the things we do, but that's how we were raised.

"When do you think I should call Kylan?" I look over at Maria, who is fanning her mouth from the heat of the omelet.

"I thought we were trying to get our minds off these boys Kimmy?" Maria squints her eyes at me.

"Well, I just can't stop thinking about him. He is such a gentleman. I am still wondering if it all was just a magical dream." I stab my omelet with my fork and look up to see my dad standing in the kitchen doorway. I look back at my omelet only to realize that my dad is standing in the kitchen. Did he hear our conversation about the guys?

I slowly look up like I didn't see him two seconds ago and hope he's not actually there. Maybe this hangover has got me seeing things now. Nope, he's really standing there. Act surprised Kimmy.

"Dad! Why did you have to sneak up on us like that? OMG! Can't you warn us before you barge in here on our fancy breakfast?" Dad rolls his eyes at me and shakes his head.

"Kimmy, oh, how I've missed you too." My dad is a pretty cool dude, but he would strangle us just like Mom would if he knew about last night and especially about Kylan sleeping in my room.

"I'm just home for a few. I'm going to shower up and head over to pick up Jason. I ended up sleeping at the shipyard last night. I was involved in getting everything cinched up on a sailboat and lost track of time. When I realized how late it was, I figured Nanny and Chas would already be in bed, so I slept on the cot in the office."

Sometimes I feel sorry for my dad. He has to put up with my and my mom's attitudes, and all he ever wants to do is make more money so we can be happy.

"What are you two girls doing this afternoon?"

I look at Maria and try not to laugh. "Oh, nothing, I'm sure. We might take Oscar for a walk, but that's probably about it." I just lied. Oh well, he'll never find out.

"Ok, that sounds like a good plan. Just promise me you won't get into any trouble with that old turd dog."

I look down at Oscar, who is intently watching my fork. "We won't!" Maria and I both reply with huge smiles on our faces. Dad shakes his head and goes off to take a shower as Maria and I clean up the kitchen.

"Whew, that was a close one, once again," I whisper to Maria. "Let's get all this cleaned up and go outside to call the boys."

I wipe my hands on the kitchen towel and realize I left a cup on the table. "Crap, I forgot a cup." I grab the cup, but it slips out of my hand and flies across the room. Maria and I both freeze in our tracks as we watch water spray from one end of the kitchen to the other. It's like it is happening in slow motion. Then, I remembered something. I remember that last night, when I was getting a cup of beer, I turned around and ran into R.L. I still can't believe he actually came to the party. I bet he thinks I'm a loser now.

"Kimmy, what is it with you throwing cups across rooms?" Maria asks as we start laughing so hard I have to grab my side.

Chapter 14

I'm really nervous about calling Kylan for some reason. I have butterflies in my tummy, and my palms are super sweaty. I don't know why I'm so nervous. Kylan is such a sweet boy who would never want to be mean to me, but I'm still worried that he will stop liking me for some reason.

"Hello?" Kylan says from the other end of the phone.

"Hey, it's me, Kimmy." Did he not know it was me?

"Oh hey, Kimmy! I was wondering when you would call. My phone has been charging, and I haven't had a chance to put your number in yet. I wasn't sure this was you, but I'm sure glad it is!"

Ok, everything is cool, I think to myself. "I had a good time last night with you and this morning," Kylan says, as I can tell he is smiling by the tone of his voice.

"I did too, from what I can remember." I laugh and realize how dumb that sounded. "So, you want to meet up later and hang out?" I ask Kylan, but I'm afraid he will say no for some reason.

"Of course I do! Peyton stopped by a few minutes ago and was talking about Maria. Maybe I can get him to come too. Actually, Peyton just got his driver's license today. I'll just see if he can come pick me up, so I don't have to bother Ken."

"Oh wow! I had no idea that Peyton was sixteen already," I say to Kylan.

"Yeah, he was held back in third grade and has an early summer birthday. I think he might've even started school a year late too. I don't really know. All I know is that he is sixteen, has a driver's license, and access to a car."

"So, where do you want to go?" I ask Kylan, relieved knowing that I'm pretty sure he likes me. "Keep in mind that wherever we meet up, it has to be close to my house because Maria and I will be walking." I hope he doesn't say the park around the corner. It's so lame, and only little kids go there with their stay-at-home moms.

"I'd love to go down to the beach this afternoon, then maybe grab a snack from somewhere downtown. What do you think?"

That actually sounds pretty perfect to me. "Yeah, that sounds great!" I say to Kylan without trying to sound too excited.

"Ok, how about we meet at the marina by the ramp in about an hour?" An hour? I haven't even had a shower yet. OMG, how am I going to get ready so fast?

"How about an hour and a half? Maria and I just got up, and we have to get ready. Since the days are getting longer, we should have plenty of sunlight left. As long as I'm home by dark, I should be fine. My mom just left for work, and my dad will be heading back to New Orleans soon, so they'll never even know."

Did I just sound like I don't want my parents to know I'm hanging out with Kylan? I hope he doesn't think that.

"Oh, ok. Sounds like a plan! I'll see you soon!"

"Ok, bye!" I reply and quickly hang up my phone.

"Maria, go get in the shower! The boys are meeting us in an hour and a half down at the marina." I shout across the house. Oh crap! My dad is still here, I think. I hope he didn't hear that. Nah, I'm sure he's in the shower.

Maria comes running to my bedroom. "What did you say? I couldn't hear you because I was talking to your dad." Oh no, now my plan is spoiled.

"Did he hear me?" I whisper back to Maria.

"I don't think so. I didn't hear what you said, so I'm sure he didn't either. By the way, have you heard from Ashley yet? Your dad was asking if she was staying again tonight because he really needs to finish up a boat and that your mom was working a double again." I ponder that for a second.

"We better tell him yes even though we don't know for sure because if not, he will call Nanny and Chas, and we won't get to see the boys at all. I'm sure Ashley will be here soon. She's probably at your house recovering from last night." Maria and I both laugh.

"I think I'll run home for a few minutes and shower over there so you can go ahead and start getting ready. I'll be back in about an hour."

Maria leaves and I shew my dad out the door so I can start getting ready. I take a long hot shower and try my best to remember some details from last night. It's all very foggy still. I'm not sure if I will ever remember what happened, but I know that whatever did happen has changed my life for the better.

It takes me a while to get ready. I am being very particular about my hair and makeup today. Although, I know that when I get to the beach, the wind and salty water will turn my hair into a hot mess. That's why I have decided to wear my hair curly today. I never wear my hair curly to school because I'm afraid the kids will make fun of me. I have some amazing beach waves in my hair, but most of the girls at school wear their hair straight. And when I say straight, I mean they flat iron every single inch of their hair. Mine looks really good like that, but not when going to the beach. Maria is so lucky. Her hair is naturally straight. All she has to do is blow dry it and brush it out. Her hair always looks perfect, just like Ashley's.

I slip on my new bikini and meticulously decide which cover-up to wear. I have one Nanny and Chas bought me in the spring that makes me look like a teenager. It is black with little white flowers all over it. It's pretty sexy if you ask me. I think I'll wear that one.

Knock, knock, knock!

That must be Maria. Has it been an hour already? Wow, time sure does fly. I run to the living room and open the door with so much force that it flies back and hits the wall.

"Hey! Are you excited or something?" Maria asks with a worried look on her face.

"I guess I'm just a little nervous about seeing Kylan today." I look down, embarrassed, as I feel my face turning red.

"So, Ashley wasn't at home, and she hasn't been there since yesterday afternoon when she came over here," Maria says with a slight tremble in her voice.

"What do you mean, Maria?" I turn my head to the side like Oscar does when he's trying to understand what I'm saying.

"I don't know Kimmy. My mom is really worried because when she calls Ashley, it goes straight to voicemail. That's not like Ashley to have her phone turned off. She's always on it, talking or texting with Jason and her friends. My dad just left for the casino, and my mom has all the kids. She's sending Alex out to see if he can find her."

I can tell that Maria is very concerned. "Oh, don't worry, Maria. I'm sure she's at Jason's or something. Maybe she lost her phone last night at the party. From what I can remember, it got pretty wild over there before we left."

Maria grins and shakes her head. "Yeah, I'm sure she's fine. She's probably sleeping off a hangover somewhere like we did today or like you did." Maria giggles.

"Did your mom call Jason?" I ask.

"No, she didn't want to bother him since he's probably at work. I promised my mom that I would keep my phone charged and report back to her every hour or so until she hears from Ashley."

Maria is very mature for her age. Maria's parents have always treated her like she's much older than she actually is. I guess it's because Mrs. Hernandez keeps having babies, and Maria is one of her older children now. I sometimes feel like her parents depend on her a little too much, and that's why she likes being at my house. She knows she can relax when she's over here and not worry about cleaning up after anybody except for herself.

"Did I tell you what Kylan said about Peyton?" I ask Maria, trying to change the subject.

"No, what did he say?"

I smile. "He said that Peyton was asking about you and that he just got his driver's license today! Can you believe that? You're dating a guy who can drive! That's the most awesome thing I have heard in a long time!"

Maria gasps and puts her hand over her mouth. "Kimmy, Peyton didn't say anything about that last night. Maybe he didn't want me to know in case he failed his test today. I had no idea that he was even sixteen already. I thought he was still fifteen. Maybe he can come pick us up?"

I raise my eyebrows and smirk. "I already told Kylan we would walk down to the marina, but maybe he can bring us back home."

Maria winks at me and twirls around. "That sounds fantastic!"

CHAPTER 15

I notice the clouds building as we walk out by the marina. "Hey, Maria," I point out to the yachts. "Isn't that the same boat we saw R.L. on yesterday?" The boat was pulled into a slip and tied up. I only remember it because of its silly name.

"*My Children's Inheritance*, yeah, I'm pretty sure that's the same boat. I don't think I've ever heard of such a stupid name for a boat," Maria says as she squints her eyes to focus on the boat.

"I feel sorry for their children if that's the only thing they get when their parents die," I say to Kylan as he laughs.

"Well, at least they get a million-dollar yacht out of it. I'll probably only be stuck with my dad's old canoe and that crusty fishing boat he bought from the grumpy sailor man years ago. That's the kind of luck that I have." We all laugh and keep walking.

Then, I notice several guys coming out from the cabin on that yacht. I quickly look the other way so they don't think we are staring at them.

"OMG! Maria, that's R.L.'s friends. I remember seeing them at the party last night." Maria jerks her head to look. "Don't look!" I sternly whisper back to her. "Remember, I made a fool of myself last night, and I don't want them calling us over to talk about it."

"Oh Kimmy, don't worry. I'm sure they don't even see us."

"Hey! There's the little drunk one! How's the hangover!" One of the guys on the boat shouts and points at us. They hold beer cans up in the air and toast each other. I am so humiliated right now. Kylan puts his arm around my shoulder to shield me from them. We start walking so fast that we are almost running.

We finally make it down to the beach just in time for it to start sprinkling. Of course, this would happen of all the days for it to rain. The one day that I finally get to go to the beach with a guy, it has to rain.

Kylan looks at me and winks. "You gonna melt?" he asks.

"As mean as she is, she'll be the last one to melt," Maria pipes up. Kylan looks over at her in surprise.

"She's not mean to me. Maybe it depends on who she's with at the time."

Kylan leans over and kisses me on the forehead. "Is this real?" I look up at him and ask.

"Of course, it is real. Why wouldn't it be?" Kylan says with sincerity in his voice.

"All of this just seems too real to be true." I can feel the blood rushing to my face now. "I just mean that me and you and Maria and Peyton. She's my best friend, and he's your best friend. We all are like one big happy family."

Maria and Peyton are ahead of us as we walk down the beach. "Aren't they so cute holding hands?" I ask Kylan.

"Yeah, but not as cute as us!" he says back with a huge grin on his face.

"Hey guys!" Kylan shouts to Maria and Peyton. "Do y'all want to go sit under the pavilion until the rain stops? I see blue skies over there, so it shouldn't last long."

We all run over to the pavilion and huddle up on one of the picnic tables. Kylan has his arm around me, and Peyton has his arm around Maria. I wish this moment would last forever. I feel so comfortable in Kylan's arms. I look over at his tanned arm that's sitting on his lap. I grab his hand with mine and intertwine my fingers with his. He pulls me closer to him. I look up into his deep brown eyes. His eyes are so dark that you can't even see his pupils. It's pretty mesmerizing. He moves his hand from my shoulder and places it gently on my cheek.

"I was afraid I was dreaming too, until I saw you walking down the steps at the marina a few minutes ago. At that moment, I knew you had come to see me, and I didn't just have a nasty hangover," Kylan whispers in my ear.

Then he leans in and softly kisses me on the lips. I can feel his tongue against my teeth. I open my mouth, and his tongue slips inside. If I were standing up, this would definitely be a foot-popping moment. You know, like when a girl gets kissed by a handsome boy in a movie and fancy music starts playing, then suddenly, her foot pops up behind her. Well, that's just it. If only I were standing up.

He slowly pulls away from me and smiles. "We're going to have fun this summer, aren't we?" Kylan says to me as he leans in for another kiss. I want to answer him but don't want to stop kissing him. I pull back slightly from him just enough to utter the words, "You bet," and then we go back to doing what we were doing.

I feel like we've been kissing for thirty minutes straight when we realize that Maria and Peyton are gone. We stand up and look all around, only to realize that the rain has stopped, and they are in the ocean. How on earth did we not hear them get up? I guess you could say we were caught up in the moment.

"You wanna get in?" I ask Kylan as I start taking my cover-up off.

"I'll go anywhere you want to go as long as I get to be with you," Kylan says back. OMG! Isn't he just the sweetest guy ever?

As Kylan starts to take his shirt off, I can't help but watch. He looks like one of those lifeguards over at Panama City Beach. You know, the ones who spend hours beyond hours in the sun to the point that you're not sure if their skin can get any more tan. Well, that's Kylan. He has a tan year-round.

Actually, if I remember correctly, he said his dad was Puerto Rican, and his mom's family was originally from Cuba. He said his mom is half-white because his grandfather, who was a white man from the United States, married a Cuban refugee a very long time ago. None of Kylan's grandparents are alive anymore. I remember him telling me that this morning when we were talking in my closet. I mentioned how Nanny and Chas live in New Orleans and asked where his grandparents live. That's when he told me that they were all dead. I told him about how my grandma Ruth died. He said that his grandfather died in Hurricane Camille too, and his grandmother died when Hurricane Katrina hit New Orleans. She didn't actually die from the hurricane. She had a heart attack and couldn't get to the hospital. He said his mom cried for days after she passed away.

"Hey, y'all, wait for us!" I yell out to Maria and Peyton as Kylan and I run toward the water. I'm so glad I didn't flat iron my hair today. It's flying all over the place and will probably be all matted up before the day is over.

Maria and Peyton turn to look at us and take off running toward the pelican poles. "I guess they don't want to hang out with us losers," Kylan says as he sits down in the surf. "Looks like the tide is going out. Look how shallow it is out there where they are. I bet you could just about walk all the way out to Ship Island with such a low tide."

I look beyond Maria and Peyton and notice a family of pelicans flying toward the shore. I sit down beside Kylan and lean against his arm's warm, wet skin. I can taste the saltwater in my mouth and feel the warmth of the sunshine over my body. I look at him, and he looks back at me.

All of a sudden, he gets a mischievous look on his face. The next thing I know, I am flat on my back against the sandbar. Kylan has me pinned down, tickling me to the point I almost pee myself.

"I was hoping you were ticklish," he says as he leans in to kiss me. We roll around in the water as I uncontrollably laugh until my side hurts with pain. "Maria was right. You're pretty salty too," Kylan says as he licks his lips after a kiss.

"I'm not salty. That's the ocean water you're tasting," I say in my defense.

"There's only one way to tell," Kylan says as he cups his hands around my face and gives me the biggest sloppiest kiss there ever was. "Yeah, you're pretty salty," he says as I shove him off of me.

"Well, you're not too far behind me," I say as I slap him on the shoulder.

We both roll over and lie flat on our backs in the ocean. The water is just low enough that we stretch our arms without having to worry about a wave hitting us in the face.

"Can I tell you something?" I ask Kylan.

"Of course, always," he replies.

"This is my most favorite thing to do. I like to come out here and dream about my future. I watch the pelicans fly high overhead and hope that they don't drop a poop on me. Then, I continue dreaming. It kind of clears my head to do this."

At that exact moment, a family of pelicans fly directly over us. "Don't open your mouth," I say to Kylan as I glance over in his direction.

"Why'd you have to say that? Now I am smiling. What if it gets on my teeth."

I giggle. "Eww, gross! I'd never kiss you again!"

We lie there for what seems like an eternity. I close my eyes and picture Kylan and I as grown-ups with little kids running all over the beach. I feel his finger reach over for mine. "You're right Kimmy. This is pretty amazing. All my cares and worries are completely gone. Not that I had any, to begin with, but I do feel like I can think more clearly now. I'm not sure if it's the water helping or if my hangover is finally wearing off. But I do know that this is a pretty cool feeling. I can't believe I've never thought to do this before."

Kylan rolls over and touches my bare midriff. My stomach jumps. "Did I scare you?" he asks.

"No, I just wasn't expecting it. It actually felt good." He works his way up to my chest and then my face.

"Oh, the things we're going to do together this summer. I can't wait!" Kylan says as he kisses my cheek.

What is he talking about? Should I be concerned? Should I be excited or nervous? Kylan is almost a year and a half older than me. I'll be thirteen in a couple of weeks, but he'll turn fifteen when school starts in the fall. Is he too old for me to be dating? What will my mom say when she finds out I have an older boyfriend who is getting ready to be in high school? Should I whoa him back? Is this relationship moving too fast? Nah, I think we're just perfect for each other.

CHAPTER 16

Y'all, it's getting late. We should probably head for a snack," Kylan hollers at Peyton and Maria as they are huddled together out by the pelican poles. Peyton raises his hand and gives us a thumbs-up.

"What do you think they are doing out there?" I ask Kylan.

"Well, you and Maria are best friends. I'm sure you will find out later." How does Kylan know that girls tell each other everything?

"What if she doesn't tell me?" I ask him as we start to walk out of the ocean.

"I'll make you a deal. If Maria doesn't tell you, I'll give you twenty dollars," Kylan says as he gives me an exaggerated wink.

"You're pretty confident about that, aren't you? I bet you don't even have twenty dollars to give me if I won the bet."

Kylan stretches out his arms and yawns. "So now, you're betting me that I don't have twenty dollars to give you if you win my bet? I had no idea you were such a gambling girl. So, If I lose the bet and have to give you twenty dollars, what are you going to lay on the line saying that I have the money?"

I stopped in my tracks. Ok, I'm super confused now. Did I just make two bets back-to-back with Kylan? He can tell that I am completely lost in his words. See, this is part of the reason why I sometimes have a hard time in school. My mom says my processor is a little slower than others, but I'm not really sure what she means by that.

"All right, all betting aside, if Maria doesn't tell you, I will beat it out of Peyton tonight when he's at my house."

Whew, an embarrassing moment was averted. I really did not want to ask him to explain it to me. I'm so glad he realized that I was getting confused. I feel so comfortable already around Kylan. I feel like he understands me and my feelings even though we've only been hanging out for a little less than twenty-four hours.

I brush all the sand from my swimsuit and watch Kylan as he dries himself off with his towel. He has such a muscular body for such a young guy. He stretches his arms up over his head and shows off his happy trail as his swim shorts slide down on his hips. This girl, Jessica, who was in my seventh grade class at school, told me that a guy's happy trail leads to his privates, and a guy's privates make a girl happy, so that's why it's called a happy trail. I don't think I ever told Maria about that.

I think Kylan is probably the hottest guy my age I have ever seen. How did I not notice this last year at summer camp? Maybe I wasn't mature enough to realize it, or maybe he was nerdy. He did break his ankle while we were square dancing. I mean, come on, who breaks their ankle while doing an old-timey dance? The hottest guy in the world, that's who.

I pat myself dry with my towel and hope my swimsuit dries by the time Maria and Peyton make it to shore. If not, it's going to look like I wet myself through my swimsuit cover-up. I hate looking that way.

Maria and Peyton take forever to make it to the shore. They were way far out there! "What took y'all so long?" I ask as they slink out of the water.

"No reason. We were just watching the waves," Maria says.

I snicker, "Yeah, yeah, that's what they all say." Maria slaps my arm, and I can see her face turning blood red. "Y'all want to go get a bite to eat?" I ask everyone.

Maria looks at Peyton and then at me and Kylan. "Peyton has offered to drive us over to the Rum Kitchen if you guys want to go." Slight panic sets in. My mom would kill us if we went across town over to Hwy 90 with a guy who just got his driver's license today.

"Um, maybe you should check in with your mom first," I tell Maria.

"Oh, crap! What time is it?" Maria shoots me a look.

"It's almost six o'clock," I say to her as I look down at my phone.

"Ugh, I missed my five o'clock phone call to her. I promised I would call her every hour until I heard from Ashley. I don't have any missed calls on my phone. Maybe Ashley called her. Ok, give me a minute to call her, then we can decide."

Maria walks away and leaves me with Kylan and Peyton. I look over at Peyton's stomach and notice that he doesn't have a happy trail like Kylan. I wonder what that means. Does that mean that he hasn't hit puberty yet? He has a few pimples on his face, so I'm sure he's started puberty. Peyton is a pretty attractive guy, but not nearly as attractive as Kylan. I really did get lucky with Kylan.

As I'm getting lost in my thoughts again, I turn around to see Maria throwing her arms up in the air as she talks in very fast Spanish on her phone. It sounds like her mom is really pissed. I would love to go to the Rum Kitchen with the guys, but I don't think that would be a good choice for us today. I hope that Maria doesn't have to go home right now. I'm not done hanging out.

Maria slams her phone shut and runs over to where we are standing by the pavilion. "My mom is so mad at me! She said I have to be home in one hour, no exceptions!" Maria starts rubbing her eyes and crying. "Ashley has still not come home, and Mom can't reach her. She finally called Jason, and he hadn't talked to Ashley since yesterday. I wanted to tell Mom about last night's party but knew we would be totally busted. I wanted to say that Ashley is probably at someone's house sleeping off a hangover, but I didn't. What should I do?"

Maria looks over at me, sobbing. Peyton puts his arm around her and starts rubbing her back. "It'll be fine, Maria. We can hang out again tomorrow. Remember, I have my license now and can come see you whenever you want," Peyton says to Maria.

We all stand around in silence for a few minutes. I wrap my arms around Kylan's waist. He turns me toward him and puts his hand against my cheek. "I'm sure Ashley is fine. We'll get Maria home safely, and maybe we can hang out at your house for a while."

I stare up at him and lay my head on his chest. "That sounds great!" I mumble into his chest.

"How about we all grab something from the Snack Shack and eat over at the park by Kimmy's house?" Kylan asks us. "It would be quick and easy, and then we can walk Maria home."

I raise my head off Kylan's chest and look over at Maria, who is in a full-on embrace with Peyton. Maria nods her head yes and looks up at Peyton. "How's that sound to you?"

Peyton kisses Maria on the forehead and says, "Only if that's what you want to do, Maria. I'll take you home right now if you want to go, but I'd love to grab some food and eat at the park with you."

Maria looks over at me. "I'm pretty hungry, so let's do that, then I'll head home," Maria says with tears in her eyes.

The food from the Snack Shack isn't nearly as good as Cuz's, but it's pretty tasty, nonetheless. We all get their special *Cheeseburger in BSL* with a side of fries. Surprisingly, Kylan pulled out two twenty dollar bills and paid for all of it. He is such a gentleman!

"I've been doing a little lawn maintenance for the people down the street. They're really rich. They have a huge house and about twenty-five acres of land in the bayou. I guess you could say I'm their lawn boy," Kylan says as he smirks.

"You're a pretty cute lawn boy if you ask me!" I say to him as he shoves the change in his pocket.

"Oh, come on Kimmy, you're gonna make me blush."

We head over to the park around the corner from my house. As we eat our food, we try to remember details from the party last night. Peyton said that he remembers a few things, like when I got up on the table and danced.

Then, Kylan had to climb up on the table and get me down. Kylan's memories from last night are somewhat like mine, foggy and sparse. He remembers things that I don't, and I remember things that he doesn't. And Maria, somehow, remembers everything but doesn't want to share. I think we thoroughly embarrassed her last night. Oh well, at least she's the only one who can remember. The rest of us remember last night as pure bliss.

As we start to walk down the street towards Maria's house, we notice several cars in her driveway. It's hard to tell from such a long distance, but I see Alex's truck along with three others. I wonder how strange it is to see so many cars over there. Maria's mom and dad share a car, and Alex is the only other person who lives there with a vehicle.

"Who all is over at your house?" I ask Maria with a concerned look on my face.

"Looks like Alex and his friends. They probably all worked today and are getting ready to leave. But usually, they park over at Froogel's and carpool. I'm not sure why they are all over here unless they are looking for Ashley." I don't see her parents' car in the driveway. I guess Mr. Hernandez is at work.

As we stop at the corner of Toulme and Easterbrook, I look over my shoulder to see the dreaded Cedar Rest Cemetery. This has to be the creepiest cemetery I have ever seen. I grab Kylan's arm and squeeze it tight. "Let's walk a little quicker, please," I say to him with a slight tremble in my voice. We pick up the pace until we are standing in front of my house.

"Maria, are you okay with walking the rest of the way by yourself? I don't want your mom to be suspicious," I say in a whisper. "We will stand here in my yard and make sure you get home, all right?"

Maria looks back at me while she is hanging tightly onto Peyton. "Sure, but promise me you will watch the entire time."

I nod to her. "I promise," I say.

Maria and Peyton hug and kiss like they will never see each other again while Kylan and I turn our heads. I can hear Peyton saying something to Maria, but I can't quite make out his words. I guess it's really none of my business anyway.

"Hey Kimmy, I'll call you later," Maria says as she starts to walk away.

I wave bye to Maria and turn back to Kylan. "Where's Peyton's car?" I ask, puzzled. "Don't y'all need to go get it before it starts getting dark?"

Peyton spins around on his toes. "Oh crap, Kylan! I hope it's still there!" Kylan and I laugh.

"How about you run downtown and get it, then drive back over here to pick me up?" Kylan says to Peyton. I think that's a great idea! That would give us a few minutes of alone time without Peyton or Maria today.

"Y'all gonna make me walk past Cedar Rest by myself? I thought y'all were my friends." Kylan looks at me, and I look at Peyton.

"Yeah, it is pretty scary over there. We can walk you to the corner just past the cemetery if you want us to. Do you need me to hold your hand?" Kylan says jokingly. Peyton turns around and shoots us his middle finger. Kylan and I bust out laughing.

As we watch Maria safely go up the steps to her porch, Peyton rounds the corner by the cemetery and is finally out of sight. "I guess I will go let Oscar out. Do you want to come in or wait outside?" I turn my head to look at Kylan.

"You know what, I'm going to play it safe this time and wait out here. I sure don't want to risk getting stuck inside your closet again," Kylan nervously laughs.

I run inside to get Oscar. I can tell he's been sound asleep on his bed because his floppy gums are pushed so far up his face it looks like he is smiling. I open my front door, and Oscar bolts off my steps so fast it looks like he is flying. He runs up to Kylan like he's known him his entire life. He is jumping up on Kylan's legs and licking his hands. Come to think about it, this is the first time that Oscar has met Kylan. Oscar is acting like Kylan is his long-lost best friend. I guess what they say about dogs knowing a good person when they see them is true.

"Oscar, get off of him!" I yell.

"Awe, it's fine. He's so cute. I wish my dogs were this friendly. They live outside and guard the property. They don't even act like pets. They're more like workers. Except for one, Suki," Kylan explains. "My dad got these two white Great Pyrenees puppies when they were only five weeks old. We named one Suki and the other Buddy. Dad said if we don't touch or pet them, they will become guard dogs, and we would never have to worry about thieves. Well, I broke that rule first because they looked like big cotton puffballs. I ended up sneaking the girl dog into my bedroom at night and kept her in my bed until she was too big for me to carry out every morning. As she got older, she would lay on the porch right in front of the door on the mat and whimper until someone would let her in. It got to the point that my dad had to put her out in the garage so we would stop babying her." Kylan continues to pet Oscar.

"So, what happened to Suki?" I ask.

"Nothing. She's still alive and well. She makes her rounds every day. She's actually very smart. My dad will feed her a big breakfast at our house. Then, she will go over to our neighbor's house, the rich ones, and act like she's starving until they give her a bowl of scraps. She has made a path between our house and theirs where she goes back and forth so much. Then, she comes back and waits for us all to get home. She's the most loyal dog a family could ever ask for."

"My mom calls Oscar a turd dog because he is always getting into mischief. I love Oscar though. He likes to sleep under the covers in my bed when I sneak him into my bedroom at night. I guess you can say that Oscar is pretty loyal too. He's kind of like a brother to me since I don't have any siblings," I explain to Kylan.

I put Oscar back in the house so we can have a few minutes of peace and quiet before Peyton returns. I sit down on the porch, and Kylan sits beside me, as close to me as he can possibly get. I thought he was going to sit on me by accident. He puts his arm around my shoulder and pulls me even closer. The sun is starting to set, and I can hear the tree frogs beginning to tune up. I'm still in my damp swimsuit, and I feel a slight chill in the air.

"So, what are we?" Kylan asks. I turn my head to look at him.

"What do you mean, what are we? I'm Kimmy, and you're Kylan," I say back to him, realizing after I had already spoken that that's not what he meant. I look away, thinking about how much of an idiot I am sometimes.

"I guess I am officially asking you to be my girlfriend. So, what do you think?" Kylan says with a slight look of worry in his eyes.

I look at him for a few seconds, examining every feature of his face. I then look off in the distance and see the palm tree in the front yard swaying with the wind. The salty smell of the ocean lingers in the air as I sit here, thinking about how perfect of a moment this is.

"Of course," I softly reply to him.

Kylan leans in, seals the deal with a gentle kiss, and says, "This has been the best day ever."

CHAPTER 17

*S*CREEEEEEEEEEEECH!

"OMG! What is my mom doing here?" I say to Kylan as my mom pulls into my driveway, literally on two wheels. Without hesitation, Kylan's hand flies off my shoulder as he scoots as far away from me as possible. I can feel my heart skip a beat. Suddenly, my palms are sweaty, and my stomach feels like I just did fifteen flips in a row on the trampoline.

I look over at Kylan, and his eyes are as big as saucers. He goes to stand up. "There's no point in leaving now. We're totally busted." I drop my head down between my hands and mutter. "She's never going to trust me to do anything again. I'm so sorry, Kylan. I don't know what to do," I say in pure shock as my mom jumps out of her car and slams the door.

"Kimmy! Get in the house right now!" she yells as she is nearly running down our sidewalk to get to me as fast as she can. "Who are you?" she says, pointing to Kylan. "And why are you here? Never mind, it doesn't matter right now. Kimmy, get in the house, and you," she says, pointing to Kylan again. "You need to leave immediately! Do I need to call your mom?"

I am completely stunned by the way my mom is acting. What is going on with her? Yeah, I know that I have a boy sitting on the porch beside me, but at least we are on the porch and not in the house in my bedroom. Geez.

"No, ma'am, I'm so sorry. I know I shouldn't be here. My friend is on his way to pick me up right now," Kylan says to my mom, then drops his head down. "I'm so sorry, Kimmy. I really am," Kylan whispers to me as his eyes start to fill with tears.

"I'm serious, boy, you need to get out of here! We have some major family issues going on right now, and you are definitely not our family." Mom jerks me by my arm, pulls me up the steps, and into the house. I don't even get to say goodbye to Kylan.

"Oh my God, Mom! You just completely humiliated me!" I yell as she slams the front door behind her.

"Sit down on the couch and don't move," Mom orders me while she runs into the kitchen. Then silence...I don't even hear her moving around the kitchen. Where did she go? Did she run out the back door? Do I smell cigarette smoke in the kitchen? Mom hasn't smoked in years. I can't believe that she yelled at me in front of Kylan for absolutely nothing. Maybe she is having a midlife crisis.

"Ahhhhhhhhh! I can't believe this has happened!" I nearly jump out of my skin as my mom screams at the top of her lungs from the kitchen. "She's here, Jimmy. Kimmy is here. She was sitting on the front porch when I pulled up. Some boy was sitting with her. I don't know what was going on with them, but I will address that later. Right now, I need you here with me, with us."

I hear my mom whisper some things to my dad on the phone, but I can't tell what she is saying. I'm pretty sure something is wrong, but I don't know what. I get up to look out my living room window to see if Kylan is still sitting on the porch. No, he's gone. My heart sinks. I guess Peyton made it over here. I sit back on the couch and pet Oscar. He is curled up like a chocolate donut on his little bed. He is oblivious to anything around him right now except for his snuggles from me.

Mom comes back into the living room and starts pacing back and forth from the window to the kitchen and then back to the window.

"Mom, what's wrong?" I softly ask, hoping she won't yell at me. She looks over at me and starts crying. "Is it Grandpa Eugene? Is he ok?" I ask. My mom drops her head and shakes it. Tears are streaming down her face. She slowly walks over to where I am sitting. My heart starts beating faster. I sense that Mom is in terrible pain. I know she is hurting just by the look on her face. She sits down beside me and places her hand on my knee.

Mom clears her throat and tries her best to speak to me in a shaky, weak voice. "Grandpa Eugene is fine. I actually talked to him this morning on my way home from work." I breathe a sigh of relief. I love my grandpa so much and miss him more than Mom knows.

"Kimmy, I have some terrible news." Mom puts her head in her hands and shakes it back and forth. She pulls down her ponytail and rakes her hands through her long, silky hair. She takes a deep breath and slowly releases it. "I wanted to wait until your dad got home, but I can't wait any longer, or you might find out from someone else, and I don't want that to happen. I really don't know the best way to say this." Mom takes another deep breath. "It's Ashley. They found her, but it was too late. She was already gone Kimmy."

"Mom, what are you talking about? What do you mean by gone?" She never responds. I look over at my mom. Her face is blackened by mascara from where it has been running down her cheeks. I have never in my life seen my mom this upset. I understand what my mom said, but I cannot comprehend.

Then, all of a sudden, it hits me like a ton of bricks. I feel my heart completely stop beating. My mouth goes dry, and I can't speak. I try to squeak out some words, but they are trapped deep inside of me. I open my mouth, but nothing comes out. What is wrong with me? Is my body shutting down? I hear no sounds. My vision is blurry, and my eyes are burning as they start filling up with tears.

Mom and I sit in silence for what seems like an eternity. Just as I think my body is starting to die, I consciously remind myself to take deep breaths. In my head, I can hear Mrs. Heather, my school guidance counselor, telling me to calm my body.

Close your eyes and take five slow breaths Kimmy. Exhale your breath quickly like you are blowing out the candles on your birthday cake. One...two...three...four...five...

I can feel my heartbeat starting to slow as I release my fifth breath. I look over at my mom, who has her head on her knees with her hands on her ears. She is softly humming a familiar song and rocking back and forth. I feel my voice in the back of my throat finally come to me.

"Mom? What happened?" Mom slowly raises her head and looks over at me. Her eyes are red and swollen like she's been stung by a thousand bees. Her face is blotchy and soaked with tears. She moves closer and wraps her arms around me. She presses her cheek against mine and gives me the tightest hug I can ever remember having from her. She squeezes me so tight that I can barely breathe.

"She was in a wreck. They found the car down in a ravine off of I-10 in the swampy area between the Pearl River and Slidell." Mom stops and takes a deep breath. "She was on the passenger side. No driver was found. They think the driver walked away to get help, but no one knows yet. Ashley had already passed by the time someone arrived."

I look over at my mom in complete shock. What did she just tell me? I must have misunderstood her. All I can say to her is, "What?"

I look at Mom. She looks over at me. I start to sob. I'm not sure what is going on right now. My Ashley, she's gone. The tears come streaming down my face like someone turned on the kitchen sink. I can't stop. I feel like I'm going to hyperventilate. I remember to breathe, but that's not taking away the pain in my body. My heart is aching, my body is uncontrollably shaking, and I'm pretty sure I'm going to throw up.

"Baby, I'm so sorry." My mom strokes my head like she did when I was an infant and couldn't go to sleep. She moves my hair out of my eyes so she can see me looking at her. "I know that Ashley was like a big sister to you. She was like a daughter to me and your dad. We loved her just like she was our own child. I am devastated Kimmy."

All I could think about was my best friend and how much she was hurting right now. "Maria, I have to go be with Maria, Mom!" I jump so fast up off the couch that Oscar lets out a strange yelp. I must've scared him.

"Oh Kimmy, I know you want to be with her, but right now is not a good time. Maria's family needs some time to grieve and process everything before we barge in on them."

"But mom, you don't understand! Maria was just with me all afternoon. I've got to go see her. We are best friends, and I want her to know that I am here for her." Mom looks at me like she knows she can't tell me no right now, but she also knows that we need to give the Hernandez family some space.

"Listen, Honey, let's wait until your dad gets home. He is on his way right now. I am going to start working on a lasagna to get my mind off things. We can take it down to them later tonight. They have a huge family with many mouths to feed. They are going to need a lot of food over the next few days. And with Mrs. Hernandez being pregnant, she won't be cooking any time soon," Mom says as she stands up and walks over to the living room window. She moves the curtains out of the way and raises the blinds. I can tell that she doesn't really know what to say to me, and I definitely don't know what to say to her right now.

Mom turns toward me in a daze. She has a solemn look on her face. She opens her mouth to speak but closes it as if she has changed her mind on what she will say to me. Then she opens it again. "Why don't you go call Maria and see if she answers her phone. Let her know that we will be down later. Also, let her know she is welcome to come here whenever she wants. I told Mr. Hernandez when he called me that Maria can stay with us during this time if they need her to." I nod my head and slowly turn to go to my bedroom.

"Kimmy, wait." I stop in my tracks. "Who was that boy with you on the front porch earlier?" Oh no, what do I say? As if things couldn't get any worse, they just did. Should I tell her about the party? And how we all got drunk last night when Ashley died? Oh my God, I can't get my thoughts sorted out. I start to panic. My heart starts beating faster and faster to the point that I just might pass out. Then I see Kylan in my head and think about what a wonderful day we just had together. I immediately feel tingly all over just thinking about him.

"His name is Kylan, Mom. I guess he's my boyfriend. He's a perfect guy too. I'm so sorry, Mom, that he was over here this afternoon. I promise he didn't come in the house. He wanted to just hang out with me on the front porch. He's the nicest guy I have met in my whole entire life.

Mom, I really think he might be the one. You know what I mean?"

Mom drops her head and pinches the bridge of her nose with her thumb and fingers. She shakes her head and looks up at me. "Kimmy, don't you think you're a little too young to have a boyfriend? How old is he?" Mom looks at me, but I can tell that her thoughts are elsewhere.

"He's fourteen and will be fifteen in August. He'll be a freshman when school starts back. We actually met at summer camp last year. He's the kid who broke his ankle while we were square dancing. You have to formally meet him and talk to him. You will see what I mean."

Mom takes a deep breath and lets it out. "Honey, I will need to talk to your dad about all this boyfriend business. In the meantime, only Maria is allowed over here. No boys for now. I'm going to go call Nanny and Chas. They were out on the boat when I tried to call earlier and couldn't hear what I was saying. I'll be in the backyard if you need me."

I start down the hallway and realize I am terrified to call Maria. What should I say to her? I know that she is my best friend, but how do I handle this type of grief? All of a sudden, I feel so distant from Maria. We've only been away from each other for a little over an hour, but so much has happened in that short period of time. Do I act like everything is fine? Of course not!

My hands start shaking, and I feel like I'm going to throw up again. Why am I feeling this way? Maria and I tell each other everything. I know she would be here for me if I ever needed her. I have to put my fears aside and do the right thing.

I close my bedroom door. I pick up my phone but place it back down on my nightstand. I crawl into my bed and pull my covers over my head. I can't believe what is going on. I roll over and scream at the top of my lungs into my pillow. *AHHHHHHHH!*

I close my eyes and picture Maria and her family in the living room of her house. They are all crying right now. I can feel it. I cannot imagine what they are going through. Why did this have to happen to Ashley?

I gather my thoughts and decide to rehearse what I am going to say to Maria when I call. I've never had anything like this happen to me or my family. Is there really anything someone can say to make things better when someone dies?

"Kimmy, is that you?" A familiar yet deeper voice than Maria answers the phone.

"Yes, it's Kimmy. Who is this?" I ask the person on the other end of the phone.

"It's me, Alex. Maria is in the bathroom taking a shower. She told me to answer her phone only if you or some kid named Peyton called her." I'm surprised Maria trusted Alex with her phone. Maybe she really wanted to talk to me.

"Um, hey Alex. Can you have her call me when she gets out?" There is a long pause on the other end of the line.

"Kimmy, do you know what has happened?" I look around my room to try and find my answer. Suddenly, I burst into tears. I cannot respond to Alex. "I guess you heard. Yeah, I'll tell her you called."

Just as I get ready to hang up the call, words come to my mouth. "Alex. What should I say to Maria when she calls me back?" That was probably not the best thing to ask Alex right now. He just lost his sister too.

"Kimmy, just tell her you're sorry, and you love her. That is all she needs to hear right now." And with that being said, Alex hangs up the phone.

CHAPTER 18

I open my eyes to realize I've been asleep for over an hour. For a moment, everything seems completely normal, like nothing has happened. I look at my ceiling fan and try to catch its rhythm. Minutes have already passed, and my mind is clear. Was all this with Ashley just a dream? I wonder. Then it hits me. My best friend's sister is gone, and my life will never be the same. Why must our minds be so mean and play such nasty tricks on us?

I lean over to check my phone. No missed calls and no text messages. Hmm...that's strange, I think to myself. I wonder if Alex passed along the message to Maria about me calling.

I can hear my dad talking to my mom in the living room. I smell the heavy scent of lasagna lingering in the air. I don't want to get up. All I want to do is lie here in my bed and pretend that nothing has happened when I know good and well that all our lives have just been turned upside down.

Buzz, Buzz...Buzz, Buzz...

Oh man, who is calling me? I don't feel up to talking right now. The only people I want to hear from are Maria and Kylan.

Buzz, Buzz...Buzz, Buzz...

I roll over to grab my phone from my nightstand. It's Maria. I instantly feel anxious. I can tell my pulse is starting to speed up. I take a deep breath, then slowly answer, "Hello?"

"Oh, Kimmy! What are we going to do? I told you I knew something was wrong. Ashley and I had a strange connection where we could tell when the other was in danger. We were kind of like twins. I just knew she was in trouble, but I didn't know what to do or who to tell. I got so caught up in the party last night and Peyton today that I pushed those feelings to the back burner. If only I had acted instead of being so selfish."

I'm not sure what to say back to Maria. I thought she would be crying like I've been doing all evening. Instead, she seems angry with herself.

"Maria, I'm so sorry this has happened. It's not your fault. Please don't think that it is. My mom is making a lasagna for your family, and we will be coming over soon. Is there anything I can do to help you feel better?"

Maria doesn't say anything. I look down at my phone to make sure our call is still connected. It is. I patiently wait for Maria to say something. She never does. I sit in silence.

"Maria, are you ok?" She still doesn't respond. Did I say something wrong? This was what I was afraid of. Sometimes, my words don't match my thoughts and feelings. This was one of those times.

"I'm here Kimmy. I don't know what to say. That's why it took me so long to call you back. You're my best friend, but I have so many huge emotions going on right now that I just don't know which ones I need to express. I'm sorry. I hope I didn't scare you. I'm not mad at you. I'm just angry at whoever did this to my sister, our sister."

My mom often reminds me that everything happens for a reason. We may never know what that reason is, but God does, and he is always in control of all our lives, no matter how big or small. Nanny says that we will have many friends throughout our lives. Most will last for only a season, but very few will last a lifetime. Maria is one of those lifetime friends. Even though her cultural heritage is completely different from mine, we are friends for life. Nothing on this earth can tear us apart.

"Maria, can I tell you something?" I ask because I really don't know what else to say right now.

"Of course, Kimmy. You can tell me anything," Maria replies.

"I was terrified to call you this afternoon when my mom told me about Ashley. I didn't know what to say. I've never talked to anybody who just lost a family member.

Then, when Alex answered the phone, I was relieved to have more time to think about my words. But that didn't help. I mean, is there really anything you can say to someone to make them feel better?"

I take a deep breath and slowly let it out. "I even asked Alex what I should say. Then, I realized how stupid that was. Maria, I know that I will never have a blood sister. I don't know what I would do if something happened to you. I just cannot imagine going through life without you in it. I will always be here for you, as I know Ashley was always there for both of us. She was like the big sister that I never had. I always felt so fortunate to have her in my life."

I can hear Maria crying on the other end of the phone. I also hear a lot of commotion in the background at her house. Kids are screaming. Mrs. Hernandez is yelling. I start crying again too. My eyes hurt so bad that it is painful to feel the tears welling up. I can't understand why God had to do this.

"Can I come live with you Kimmy?" Maria solemnly asks in such a low whisper that I can barely hear her.

I pause and listen to all the chaos in the background before I respond to her. I know she gets extremely frustrated with her younger siblings. "Of course, you can. My mom told me that she told your dad you could stay over here if you needed to. Do you think your parents will let you come stay here for a while?"

"I think at this point in our lives, they're not really going to care what I do." Maria has a tone to her voice that I've never heard before. It is a very hollow tone, yet slightly annoyed.

"I'm going to get up and go check on the lasagna. Get your stuff packed and be ready when we get there. I'll go talk to my mom about you staying over. If anything changes, I'll text you. Have your phone nearby. Love you, Sis. See you soon."

As I hung up the phone, I realized I needed to call Kylan and tell him what happened. I wish I knew more details to give him, but I won't know much until after we visit the Hernandez family.

I pick my phone back up to call Kylan, and it starts vibrating right there in my hand. It's Kylan calling me. He must've known I was thinking about him.

"Hello?" I say once again, like I don't know who is on the other end. Is that normal? Does everybody answer their phones like that even though they know who is calling them because of caller ID?

"Hey Kimmy. I heard the news about Maria's sister, Ashley. I'm so sorry. You know my brother, Ken, was good friends with her. They went all through high school together. He's pretty upset." I can hear the sympathy in his voice.

"Thanks, Kylan. I was picking up my phone to call you when you called me. How did Ken find out about Ashley?" I ask because I think it's really strange that people already know about this. We just found out like an hour ago.

"Ken has been helping at the fire department downtown for a while, and they told him about the accident when he went in this evening. He just called my mom a few minutes ago. Ken was told that Ashley was completely unclothed in the car, and no one else was around. They are already suspecting foul play."

I sit in pure astonishment. All I can do is blink my eyes. Foul play? What does he mean by that? I thought it was an accident. Unclothed? What? Neither my mom nor Maria said anything about that.

"Kylan, I don't know what you're talking about. I haven't heard any of that. All my mom told me was that she was found in the passenger side of a car and had already passed when someone found her. Do you think that is the truth about her not having any clothes on?"

I'm not sure that I want Kylan to answer my question. I grit my teeth at the thought of having to share this information with Maria. I close my eyes and anticipate what Kylan is getting ready to say next.

"Gosh Kimmy, I figured you knew that. I'm so sorry to be the one to tell you. Yes, she was in the car without any clothes on. Ken said they couldn't even find her clothes. They also think she might've been dead before the wreck. Apparently, it looked like Ashley had been strangled to death, and someone wrecked the car to cover it up."

Things just went from bad to worse. What should I do? I can't tell my mom all of this. I wonder if she knows and just doesn't want me to know. Should I tell my mom about the party? It might help find out who did this to her. I just have so many thoughts running through my head.

"Oh Kylan, I am so heartbroken right now. I don't know what to say." I feel the tears coming back to my eyes.

"You don't need to say anything at all Kimmy. I'm sorry that I even told you. I just figured you already knew about how they found her. Do you think your mom hates me? She seemed pretty mad this afternoon."

I'm not really sure how to respond to him right now. I am still completely stunned by what Kylan told me about Ashley. I can't wrap my head around everything right now, and he wants to know if my mom likes him. Really? I can feel my blood starting to boil. Is he really that insensitive?

"Let me tell you something, Kylan. My family is very distraught right now about what just happened to Ashley. She was like a sister to me and a daughter to my parents. What you just told me has completely blown my mind. I was just starting to accept the fact that Ashley had been killed in a car accident, and then you have the nerve to tell me all this. And to top it off, you ask if my mom likes you or not. Who cares if my mom likes you! KYLAN!! I've had enough for now."

"But, Kimmy, I just—"

"BYE KYLAN! I'M DONE!"

Oh my God! What just happened? I can't believe I just hung up on Kylan. He really pissed me off though. Why would he want to act like my best friend's sister didn't just die or, better yet, was murdered? Maybe Mom was right. Maybe I'm too young to have a boyfriend.

I throw my body back on my bed and tightly shut my eyes. I try to block this day out of my mind, but I just can't stop thinking about what Kylan told me. Why would someone want Ashley dead? She would never hurt anyone. And why was I so mean to Kylan?

Buzz, Buzz...Buzz, Buzz...

Geez...It's Kylan again. What does he want now? Can't he give me a little space? He's such an insensitive jerk! I can't believe I ever thought he was such a gentleman!

Buzz, Buzz...Buzz, Buzz...

I don't want to talk to him right now, but I think back to the events of earlier today. Our alone time together when we were lying in the ocean. The warm breeze blowing through my hair. The way Kylan's face turns red when I catch him looking at me. The gentle touch of his hands on my body. The softness of his lips when they were on mine. His hard, tanned body was on top of mine in the surf as he tickled me until I was numb all over. And the way he insisted on paying for all our lunches today when he definitely didn't have to.

Buzz, Buzz...Buzz, Buzz...

"Hey, Kylan. Maybe I just overreacted. I'm so sorry, I really am. I have so much going on in my head right now that I can't decide how I need to think or act."

Crickets. Just when I think that Kylan is going to hang up on me. I finally hear his voice on the other end of the line.

"I'm really sorry too, Kimmy. I shouldn't have said anything about what Ken told me. Who knows if it's even true? I don't want it to be true, but that's how I received the news. I should've thought about how my words were leaving my mouth before I opened it. And the reason why I asked about your mom is because I really like you Kimmy, and I want to be able to see you again. I'll be driving soon, and I want to take you out on a date, but I know right now is not the right time to discuss all that. Will you please forgive me?"

I take a deep breath and slowly let it out. "I will forgive you if you promise to forgive me for yelling at you a few minutes ago. I...I...I just don't know what to do." I rub my eyes and feel the tears coming back. "I want to scream at the top of my lungs and let it all out, but I also just want to crawl up under my covers and hide from the rest of the world. My eyes hurt so bad from crying all afternoon that I can't even see straight. Everything is blurry, and I want to run away. I wish you could come hold me right now, lie next to me in my bed, and tell me everything will be fine."

How could I ever stay mad at Kylan? I truly think he is the love of my life. I feel a sense of peace when I am near him. Is this normal? Is this what love feels like? But I am definitely too young to experience love like this. Maybe it's just lust that has overcome me.

"You know, if I were allowed, I would be right there with you. Close your eyes and pretend that I am lying next to you, holding your body against mine. Now, wrap your arms around your body and hold yourself really tight."

I do as Kylan says. I can almost feel his presence next to me. If only we were older, we would be lying beside each other in my bed. All my cares and worries would be gone just knowing I have Kylan all to myself.

"It's working," I tell him. "The only thing that would be better than this would be for you to really be here, but I know that's not possible right now."

"Can I come see you tomorrow? I just can't stand the thought of being away from you," Kylan says. "Maybe I can formally meet your parents and hopefully cheer you up a little. How's that sound?"

That sounds fantastic, but I'm not sure that's such a good idea. I can't tell Kylan that though. I don't know if my mom will ever allow Kylan over here with everything going on. The only way that I'll be seeing him is to sneak out of the house. Hey, that's not too bad of an idea. At least we could get some alone time.

"Sure, I'll ask. I've got to go. We are taking some food over to Maria's house. I'll call you back later when I get home. Oh, by the way, can you call Peyton and let him know about Ashley? I don't want Maria to have to explain everything to him."

Without hesitation, Kylan responds, "Of course, Babe! Is there anything else I can do? I want you to know that I am here for you and also for Maria."

Babe? Did he just call me Babe? Whew...that just took my breath away. I know I'm his girlfriend, but does he think I'm so hot that I'm also a babe? My heart is melting.

"I just need to get through the next few days. Please be patient with me. I'm already asking for your forgiveness because I know I will be difficult to deal with. I'll call you later. Bye."

I hang up the phone before Kylan even gets a chance to say goodbye. I jump up off my bed and straighten out my clothes, run my fingers through my hair, and open my bedroom door to face the world. At least now I know that I won't have to do this alone.

CHAPTER 19

Hey Sweetie. I thought I was going to have to come wake you up. Are you about ready to go see the Hernandez family? I just took the lasagna out of the oven, and your dad is getting cleaned up."

I think about how sad everyone at Maria's house will be. I'm scared that I might start crying when it's not appropriate. I am hurting so much, but I know that Maria's family is hurting even more. I'm not very good with my words, and I am always nervous about talking to people in tense situations. And I know it will be very tense over at Maria's.

"No, I'm not ready to go down there. Mom, can I ask you something?"

"Of course, Kimmy," Mom replies as she wrinkles her forehead.

I study her face and think carefully about my words. "Is there anything I should know before we go to Maria's house?" I don't want Mom to know I talked to Kylan and what he told me. "Have you found out anything else about...you know...what happened to Ashley?"

Gosh, I really didn't want to ask her that, but I want to see if she will tell me anything else. I don't want to tell Maria what Kylan told me if it's not true.

"Kimmy, please sit down." Oh no, here it comes. All of a sudden, I, for real this time, think I'm going to throw up. I walk over to the kitchen table and pull out a chair. I gently rest my elbows on the tabletop and place my chin in my hands.

"I've noticed that you are starting to mature in more ways than one, and I want to treat you more like a teenager than a child." Mom sweeps her hair out of her face and looks around the room. "So, what I am about to tell you is very disturbing, but your dad and I think you should know."

I'm not sure what my mom can say that will upset me more than I already am, but I have to act surprised when she tells me what she's about to say. I really wish Kylan hadn't told me what Ken heard at the fire station.

"We think something terrible happened to Ashley. It's more than just a car wreck. When they found her in the wrecked car earlier today, she wasn't wearing any clothes. And her body...her body was beaten and bruised to the point Ashley was nearly unrecognizable. The police are looking for a suspect. Until they find someone, we must be cautious and watch out for each other. With that being said, I don't want you going anywhere without someone with you. Nanny and Chas are coming tomorrow to stay with us for a while to ensure you are safe when your dad and I are at work."

My heart just sank. Mom has heard what Kylan told me. I was afraid of that. I will just act like I don't know anything. It's probably best that way.

So much for seeing Kylan anytime soon. Nanny and Chas will probably make me go out on that godforsaken boat for days at a time where there will be no cellphone service. But wait, Maria wants to come and stay here. Maybe that will be my way out of any boat trips.

I decide it is probably in my best interest not to ask any more questions about Ashley. I don't want to seem like I am suspicious or anything. So, I change the subject.

"Um, Maria wants to come stay with us for a while. I was thinking she could have Ashley's room. But if Nanny and Chas are coming, she will need to stay with me, right? You know, my bed is tiny. Do you think we could get another bed for my room or at least some kind of mattress she can sleep on so we won't be smashed up against each other?"

Whew, all that just flew out of my mouth like a lightning strike in the bay. Mom looks at me, puzzled. "This has never been a problem before, but I'll see what your dad and I can do. Maybe we can run by the store after we visit with the Hernandez family."

"Mom, Maria is a teenager, and I'll be one soon. We need our own spaces, you know."

Mom nods her head. "Of course, Honey, of course. Now, go get yourself ready so we can leave before the lasagna gets cold."

Typically, we would walk down to Maria's house since she is just a few doors down from ours. But my dad decides we should drive since there might be a killer on the loose. Not a word was spoken in the car on the very short ride to her house.

I am so nervous that the palms of my hands, soles of my feet, and armpits are soaking wet. I'm sure glad I put that extra deodorant on before we left. My Spanish has greatly improved over the last few months. Maria has been teaching me so many words and phrases that I plan on being fluent in Spanish by the time I graduate high school. I think it's so cool that all the children in Maria's family are bilingual. Maria's dad speaks excellent English, but Maria's mom is still hard to understand. Her sentences are incomplete, and she often forgets to add an "s" to the end of certain words. I try to speak to her in Spanish, but she says my accent isn't proper. Oh well, I'm a work in progress.

My dad parks the car on the side of the road. Our street is pretty narrow, so if a vehicle is parked on both sides, it turns into a one-lane road. As we cross the street, we hear the kids screaming inside the house. I pity poor Maria for having to deal with that crap all the time. I completely understand why she wants to come stay with us. Not only does she need some alone time, but she also needs some quiet time.

Mom grabs my hand with hers and pats the top of it. "Now, Kimmy, this is going to be very hard. If you need to cry, it's fine. I will probably be crying too. It is always ok to express your emotions when something like this happens. Please don't be afraid. Just be yourself when we go in here. I promise you we won't stay long. Maybe you can help Maria gather her things while your dad and I talk to Mr. and Mrs. Hernandez."

I realize that no words can describe how I feel right now, so I don't say anything back to my mom. I just nod and grab her hand tighter. My dad puts his arm around my mom's shoulder, and we walk up the steps to their house.

I pause for a moment on the last step and think about how much I miss Ashley. This will be the first time I have stepped foot into Maria's house, knowing that Ashley will never walk through this doorway again. I sniffle my nose as I feel the tears welling up again. I try to think about something else, but I can't. Kylan crosses my mind for a moment, but I am quickly reminded about what I am getting ready to face.

Ding, Dong...Ding, Dong.

Ding, Dong...Ding, Dong

Before I can even gather my thoughts, Mr. Hernandez opens the door. I jump as I am startled by the creaking door. I take a step back, hoping he didn't see me do that. I look up at Mr. Hernandez and see the tears in his eyes. I've never in my life seen a grown man look as sad as Mr. Hernandez does right now.

"Hello Nina," Mr. Hernandez says to my mom as she steps up and hugs him. "Nice to see you Jimmy," Mr. Hernandez says to my dad as he shakes his hand. "And Kimmy, you are growing up way too fast, just like Maria." I nod to Mr. Hernandez, unsure of how to reply, so I don't. "Please come in Favres. We welcome you into our home for such a solemn occasion."

As I step into Maria's house, I see two of her younger siblings running around the living room fighting over a toy. Alex is sitting on the couch with Mrs. Hernandez, looking at pictures. Mrs. Hernandez is crying and holding her belly. She looks like she is about to pop! I haven't seen her in a few days, I guess.

I can smell a variety of food as my dad hands me the lasagna to take to their kitchen. I place the dish on the kitchen table beside about twenty other dishes. I see casseroles, tamales, breads, fruit, and cakes galore. There is also an assortment of sodas, bottled water, and fruit juices on the counter. Hopefully, they can freeze some of this food for later.

As I am lost in my thoughts with all this food, I don't even notice Maria standing beside me. I turn toward her, and she grabs me for a hug. I can feel her melting in my arms. "I'm so sorry," I mutter to her. "How are you doing?"

Maria looks at me and shakes her head. "As good as can be expected at a time like this. My mom though, I'm afraid she's about to go into labor. She's been having contractions all evening since I got home. This baby is not ready, and neither are we. I'm so worried about her."

I'm not good when it comes to talking about babies being born. I have no idea how that happens or what goes on when it happens. I know I've seen things in movies about it, but it's probably totally different in real life. Maria, however, has been in the room with her mom when her last two siblings were born, and she is planning on being there when this one is born too.

Maria's family doesn't believe in going to a hospital unless you are really sick, hurt, or dying. Mrs. Hernandez has had all her babies at home. My mom thinks she is crazy for that because of everything that can go wrong without a doctor. Mom probably worries because of how I was born so premature and required a lot of help at birth. Mrs.

Hernandez always has someone there called a midwife, but all they can do is help deliver the baby.

"Did you talk to your dad about coming to stay with us?" I ask Maria, as I'm not quite sure what else to say right now.

"He groaned for a minute but said that was fine as long as I was home for the wake." The wake? What is she talking about? Does that mean she has to be home every morning when she wakes up?

"So, your dad wants you home pretty early every morning?" I ask. Maria's eyebrows almost cross as she looks back at me.

"No Kimmy, a wake happens when someone dies. The family of the person who died has a huge gathering at their home the day or so after they die, and everybody comes to mourn with them. They bring tons of food, pictures, money, and gifts for the family. They also tell stories about the person who died. Usually, the dead body is there too. But Ashley won't be there for her wake. They are doing what's called an autopsy on her body to determine how she died."

I stand there without words for a moment. I've never been to anything like that before. I don't think I have ever gone to a funeral. I remember when people died during Katrina, but I was too young to go to the funerals.

"So, will they have a funeral too?" I ask Maria as she straightens up and starts organizing the food on her kitchen table.

She mumbles under her breath, "Pastas go together. Casseroles come next and go beside the tamales. Desserts go way over there. I just have to get this all fixed."

"Maria, are you ok?" Maria looks up from what she is doing.

"What Kimmy? This food is such a mess over here. I'm not sure that Mom and Dad will be able to sort through all of it on their own. Did you say something about a funeral?"

I'm afraid that Maria is about to have a major breakdown. Maybe I shouldn't ask any more questions. Their culture intrigues me, and Maria has always been excited to share it with me. But maybe this is not the best time to ask.

"Yeah, Ashley's funeral will be in a week or so. My dad said the autopsy would take a while. In our culture, we have the wake immediately in hopes that the family can get enough money from family and friends to pay for the funeral. By the time the funeral gets here, the family has grieved and is ready to celebrate the dead person's life. Oh, and her funeral will be at Our Lady of the Gulf Catholic Church. You know that big church over by the beach?"

I notice that Maria is now taking two plates out of her cabinet and filling them with food. "I hope you're hungry because we need to start eating on this food. Mom said for us to make sure to take a bunch of it to your house tonight and come tomorrow for lunch and dinner."

As she starts piling the plates higher and higher, I realize that she's putting food on there that I've never seen before in my life. "What is all that stuff?" I ask her as the food keeps getting taller and taller.

"Oh, don't worry, it all tastes good. And since we are going to your house, we can throw it away if we don't like it. Your parents are cool like that. Mine would make me clean my plate before they would let me leave the kitchen table. I remember one time my dad had Alex sit at the table for two hours after dinner because he wouldn't finish his guacamole. By the time he ate it, it had turned brown and looked like baby poop. I told him that he should've just toughed it out, pinched his nose, and ate it. But no, he had to be stubborn. That was the first and last time he ever did that. I guess he learned his lesson."

Wow! I knew her parents were strict about food, but I had no idea they were that bad. I consider that nearly child abuse. Maria says the key to staying out of trouble at her house is to take out small portions of food and eat it all. She said that her mom always makes enough for there to be seconds.

Maria looks around to make sure she got us a little bit of everything. "How about a whole plate of desserts just for us?" she says as she puts plastic wrap around our plates. "Should we fix your parents a plate?" Maria asks as she grabs a donut and takes a huge bite out of it. "Here, eat the rest of this," she says as she hands me the donut.

Maria is acting strange. I feel like she's nervous about something, but I'm not sure what. I guess if my sister had just passed away, I would be acting weird, too.

"Um, I'm not hungry right now, but I'll eat it. Your parents would be pissed if we let it go to waste." I take a bite of the donut. OMG! This is the best donut I've ever had in my life!

"Where did these donuts come from?" I ask Maria with half the donut hanging out of my mouth.

"These are Buñuelos, Mexican donuts. They are super sweet and probably very fattening. We're skinny, so we can eat these. My mom and dad, however, probably shouldn't," Maria says as she giggles.

"Are we fixing a plate for your parents?" Maria asks as she goes to get more plates out.

"Nah, let's hold off. I'll let them know about the food before we leave." I think my parents would feel strange if they took food from Maria's parents. My mom was adamant that the Hernandez family had enough food to feed all the hungry mouths. Since Maria is a Hernandez, it's probably ok that we got some food.

Maria puts the extra plates back in the cabinet. I think she knows my parents won't be taking any food home.

"Is your stuff packed?" I ask Maria as we start walking toward her living room with our plates full of food.

"You know it!" she says with a little spunk in her voice. "I packed nearly my entire bedroom into my mom's huge suitcase. Do you remember that time those people stayed in the casino hotel and left a bunch of luggage? The hotel staff contacted the owners of the luggage, and they said that they were flying out and couldn't take all their stuff, so they just left it there. The casino offered to ship it to them for a fee, but they declined. They said to keep it. So, my mom was able to get one of the large suitcases and everything in it."

I had to think hard about that one. "Oh yeah, I remember. Do you remember all the bizarre things from that suitcase?"

"I do! It had some Christmas decorations, a ton of cotton balls, and like fifty of those old-timey film canisters with used film in them. It was kind of like they robbed a Dollar Tree or something," Maria says as we walk right past everyone in the living room, not even paying attention to what they are doing. I'm kind of glad we did that. I need to get my mind off of things for a few seconds.

"Did anyone ever get that film developed?" I ask Maria as we open her and Ashley's bedroom door.

"No, I think my mom threw all that junk away. She was afraid of what she might see in the pictures. You know they say a picture is worth a thousand words. I'm not sure my mom even knows a thousand words in English. So, it was probably for the best."

And just like that, it all hit me again. As I look around the room, I can feel my eyes starting to burn, and tears start streaming down my face. I see Ashley's bed perfectly made. All her perfumes are neatly lined up on her dresser. I look at the posters on her side of the room. Then, I notice her hairbrush. It looks like she had just brushed her hair and laid it down with a ponytail holder beside it. Everything was untouched from the last time she was here. Her headboard is covered in pictures of her friends, us, Oscar, and Jason.

"Jason," I say to Maria. "Where's Jason?" Maria suddenly stops what she is doing and starts looking nervously around the room. Her eyes are darting back and forth from me to the ceiling back to me and then to her window. I feel like something is majorly wrong.

"He's not allowed over here. My dad thinks he had something to do with the car wreck. He is planning on talking to your dad to see what time Jason left work last night. I just overheard my parents talking. That's all I know."

I don't think Jason would ever want to hurt Ashley. She was his world, and he absolutely adored her and everything about her.

"Really, Maria? Your dad thinks that?" I say with astonishment in my voice.

"I don't know Kimmy. Something was going on between them yesterday, remember? Ashley was lying to Jason about going to that party. And she was mad when he told her he was getting off work early. Ashley was so worried that he would show up at the party and ruin her night."

I thought hard for a minute but couldn't recall seeing him at the party. My thoughts are still pretty fuzzy from last night though.

"Kimmy, I don't want to talk about it anymore. That's between my parents and the police now. I know that I will probably never see Jason again. And as far as I'm concerned, I'm totally fine with that."

CHAPTER 20

The past few days have been such a blur, to say the least. Maria has practically moved in with us. She keeps going over to her house and bringing loads of more stuff to mine. She says that she can't stand the thought of sleeping in the same room where Ashley last slept before she died. I agree with Maria. Every time I have to go into their bedroom, my palms get sweaty, and my heart starts beating faster. It is kind of like Ashley's presence is still there. I can almost smell the scent of her favorite perfume.

Maria told me that her mom plans to turn their bedroom into a nursery for the new baby. Mrs. Hernandez said she wants all of Ashley's things boxed up and taken to the Goodwill in Waveland. She told Maria and me to take what we wanted, and the rest will be donated to someone who needs it.

It just makes me sad to think that Ashley's things will be put in a store, and anyone can go buy them. I told Maria we could box all her stuff up and take it over to my house. Then, when we are ready, we can go through it all, keep what we want, and decide what to do with the rest. Maria liked that idea. So, that's our plan. When Maria gets all her stuff moved over, we will start working on Ashley's.

It has been almost a week since they found Ashley. My mom, dad, and I all went to Ashley's wake. If I didn't know any better, I would have thought we were celebrating something joyous. People were laughing, the adults were drinking alcohol, and kids were running around outside and playing just like any other summer cookout.

Maria's uncle brought over his flattop grill. All the men gathered and cooked about a hundred pounds of chicken and steak fajitas. While the men were cooking, the women all sat around in a circle and told stories of childbirth and all kinds of gross stuff. Maria and I excused ourselves from the circle early on when we realized that we had absolutely nothing to share and really didn't want to hear about our body parts getting stretched out in more ways than one.

Do you want to know the best part of the entire wake? Kylan and Peyton got to come. Since Maria's family considered this a social event, Maria got permission to invite the guys. It turns out that Peyton's dad works at the hotel check-in at the casino and already knows Mr. and Mrs. Hernandez. They weren't friends, but Peyton said his dad knew who they were, so he came and brought the guys.

So, after we dodged out of the women's circle, we were able to get the guys away from the men's barbeque bonanza and into Maria's house, where we could all talk. I have barely spoken to Kylan since he told me everything Ken had heard. I was kind of mad at him for telling me that. We still don't know what happened to Ashley. Maria said the autopsy report should be back sometime in the next few weeks.

I couldn't kiss Kylan at the wake, because so many people were around. I really wanted to kiss him, and I know he wanted to kiss me too, but I definitely didn't want to get in trouble. I wouldn't even let him put his arm around me. He tried to hold my hand, but I told him it was not appropriate. I hope he didn't think I was being mean.

Before the wake was over, everyone was called to gather in the Hernandez family's backyard. Mr. Hernandez spoke some words in Spanish, and I understood some of what he was saying. He thanked everyone for coming, and then we formed a circle in their yard, held hands, and prayed. My mom came over and stood beside me to hold my hand, and my dad stood beside Kylan and held his hand.

I'm glad I had my mom by my side because this is when things got terribly sad. Mr. Hernandez asked everyone in the circle to take turns and each say one word that described his daughter. Thank goodness my family was near the start because I'm not sure that I could have thought of a word if I had been at the end.

There were about six people in front of me, but I had my word before we even got started. Mr. Hernandez began with his word for Ashley, "Hija," which means daughter in Spanish. The next few people said smart, intelligent, gentle, and kind.

Then it was my turn. My heart started beating faster and faster, and my throat felt like it was filled with a hundred cotton balls. Everyone was looking at me, and I didn't know what to say. Then it came to me...beautiful...I always thought that Ashley was the most beautiful person I had ever seen. With her long, silky black hair and perfect complexion, Ashley was beautiful inside and out, and that's exactly what I said.

After my turn passed, I bowed my head and cried. The heat from the tears streaming down my face was unbearable. I didn't want anyone to see me crying, so I kept my head down.

I have no idea what everybody said after me. I guess it really doesn't matter because I know that Ashley was an amazing person who didn't deserve to die so young. Kylan told me afterward that he didn't know he would have to say something about her. He said he barely knew her, but he knew she was responsible because she helped take care of me and Maria, so that's what he said.

When the wake was over, I guess you could say we all went our separate ways. Mom had to get back to work, and Dad headed to the shipyard. Kylan went over to Peyton's to spend the night, and Maria and I went to my house and watched a movie with Nanny and Chas. I don't think any of us spoke two words to each other the rest of the night, not because we were mad but because we were simply mourning Ashley's death.

The next day, Nanny promised to take Maria and me over to Gulfport to do some shopping. For one, we both needed a nice dress for the funeral. Also, Nanny said that retail therapy always makes everyone feel slightly better. Nanny said it wouldn't cure us from our sadness, but it would take our minds off things for a little while.

Gosh, was she right! We truly had a great girl's day out. We got sophisticated black dresses for the funeral and matching purses to go with them. Nanny even took us to the nail salon to get a mani and pedi. Nanny also insisted that Maria and I get new swimsuits and cover-ups since we now have boyfriends. Nanny said that all ladies need at least two swimsuits for the summer. She said to always have a dry one on hand for when you need to change. No one wants to walk around in a wet swimsuit all day.

We ended our day with a late lunch at the food court. Nanny and I both got orange chicken, rice, and an egg roll from the Chinese restaurant. Maria had to be different and get a salad from the Fresh Garden. She said she was watching her figure. Nanny and I thought that was funny because she already looks like a beanpole. I'm glad we ate lunch after trying on all those clothes. I'm not sure that anything would have fit me after all that Chinese food.

We stopped in Pass Christian at Robin's Nest on our way home. Nanny wanted to get something special for Maria's mom. We were able to find these beautiful wind chimes made from shells and sea glass. They will look lovely on Mrs. Hernandez's front porch. Their sound reminds me of the bay on a warm summer day.

As we were crossing the bridge from Pass Christian to Bay St. Louis, I saw a long line of pelicans flying high above the water. I closed my eyes as I thought back to the last day we spent with Ashley. It was nearly perfect. The sun was shining so brightly on the water that it looked like a million sparkling diamonds. I could see Ashley lying on the beach with her black sunglasses on that took up half of her face while Maria and I splashed around in the surf. Ashley's hair was pulled up into a high ponytail on top of her head, and Oscar was right beside her.

For a moment, it seemed like all was fine with the world. I could feel the sand between my toes, the warm breeze in my hair, and the taste of the salty ocean water. Then, I opened my eyes and realized she was gone.

I looked over at Nanny driving the car but noticed she had her Bluetooth thing in her ear, and she was talking on her phone. How did I not hear her? Did I just get caught up in a daydream again? Why couldn't it be real? Why did I have to snap back to the ugly reality of what has happened? I sit and shake my head back and forth until I am almost dizzy. I throw my head back on the headrest as I squeeze my eyes together so hard that I can feel my eyelashes on my cheeks. Then, I remember that I have to breathe.

One...two...three...four...five...

When I open my eyes again, I see Cedar Rest Cemetery approaching us on the right. I immediately look away. I can't stand the thought of going to a funeral, especially when it's for my best friend's sister.

I look back at Maria. Her fingers were moving a mile a minute. "Who are you texting?" I ask her.

She glances up at me and then back at her phone. "Peyton," Maria says with a smile on her face.

I turn back around in my seat and face the front. Thank goodness we are past Cedar Rest now. I notice several cars in my driveway as we turn down my road. One is my mom's car, and the other two are unfamiliar. Why would my mom be home right now? She should be at work. And who do the other two cars belong to?

Nanny parks us on the side of the road in front of my house. She is still talking on her phone as Maria and I get out of the car. Maria looks at me, and I shrug my shoulders. About that time, a police officer comes out my front door and steps down on the porch, followed by my mom and another police officer.

"Thank you, Mrs. Favre. We appreciate all your help with this ongoing case," says the female officer to my mom.

Maria and I continue to walk up to my house. My mom turns toward me. "Kimmy, this is Officer Jane. She will be coming back tomorrow to talk to you about a few things."

I immediately freeze. I feel like the world has just stopped. I see the officer put her hand out to shake mine, but I can't move. I jump as I feel Nanny's hand on my shoulder.

"I'm so sorry, Officer Jane. She's been going through a lot since everything happened. We've been shopping all day and are pretty tired. Kimmy, say hi to Officer Jane, then you and Maria head into the house," Nanny says as she gives me a nod.

I put my hand out and shake with the officer. Her grip was so firm she almost broke every bone in my hand. Ouch!

As Maria and I step into my living room, I suddenly feel like I'm going to throw up. Why does the officer want to talk to me? What is she going to ask me? Have I done something wrong? Why couldn't she speak to me right now?

I look over at Maria, then down at Oscar. No words can describe the knot I have in my stomach right now. As if I didn't feel bad enough already, now I have to wait and see what the officer wants to question me about.

The rest of the evening was uneventful. I barely spoke a word at dinner. Mom went back to the casino, and Nanny heated us up some frozen baked ziti. I guess Dad is still at the shipyard. He's had to miss a lot of work this past week, so he's been working almost every night. The last time I saw him was at Ashley's wake. He will have to take off again for Ashley's funeral.

My dad gets paid hourly, so he doesn't get paid if he doesn't work. And if he doesn't get paid, my mom gets furious because she will have to work double shifts to pick up the slack.

Dad used to get paid by the job, but something terrible happened when he was trying to rush and get it done. He thought he had a starter fixed on a boat. But when the owner got it out on the bay and turned off the engine, it wouldn't start back up. That guy was stranded and had to call a tow boat to get him back to the marina. It also ended up causing damage to the boat, and he sued my dad's boss. It was pretty ugly. I'm surprised my dad didn't lose his job over it. After that incident, Dad's boss wanted him to slow down and take his time. That's why he is paid hourly now and spends so much time at the shipyard.

Chas put Maria's new bed together today while we were out shopping. It fits perfectly in my bedroom. At least she won't have to sleep on the blow-up mattress anymore. I'm pretty sure Oscar's toenail poked a hole in it because this morning, when we woke up, Maria was on the floor, and her mattress was as flat as a pancake.

My day ended with a sweet call from Kylan and a funny bedtime story from Chas. I love that my granddad is such a good storyteller. Even though I'm almost a teenager, I'll never be too old to enjoy his stories.

As I close my eyes, I realize how fortunate I am to have such an amazing family. It pains me to think about not having Ashley in my life anymore. No one will ever be able to fill the void that she left in my heart. But I'm thankful for all the love and support my family has shown to me, Maria, and the Hernandez family.

I open my eyes and look over at Maria, who is staring up at the ceiling. "Can't sleep?" I ask her as I roll over on my side.

"I don't think I have slept since Ashley left us. I'm just really glad that your parents are letting me stay over here for now," Maria says as she yawns and pats Oscar on his head. Oscar is in his usual chocolate donut formation with his nose tucked into the covers.

"Hey Maria, what do you think the police officer will ask me tomorrow?"

Maria hesitates. "I'm sure it's something about Ashley. Just promise me, Kimmy, that you will tell the officer the truth. Don't hold back any details. We want to find out who did this to her. Maybe there is something you can remember about the party or some clue you can give that would help the officer solve the case."

I lie here and feel my stomach start to tense up again. I'm not sure if I will get any sleep tonight. "Why haven't the police talked to you yet? Why do they want to talk to me first?" I say as I have a million thoughts going through my head right now.

"My time is coming Kimmy, and I remember a lot from that night. Way more than what I have told you. I'm just waiting for the right person to tell it to. I didn't want to say anything to you, but my interview with the police is at nine o'clock tomorrow morning. Mom didn't want me to tell anyone. She just told me to be there and be ready to answer a lot of questions."

I stare off into the darkness of my bedroom and try my hardest to remember more about that night, but I just can't. It is like there is a hole in my brain, and I can't recall any specific information about Joni's party. And what memories I do have are already starting to fade.

CHAPTER 21

*B*eep, *Beep, Beep...Beep, Beep, Beep...Beep, Beep, Beep*

"What's that, Maria?" I say as I sit straight up in my bed. I'm pretty sure that I just fell asleep an hour ago.

"Sorry Kimmy. That's the alarm clock that I brought from home." Maria yawns. "Mom said that I need to get up and take a shower this morning so I will be clean for my interview with the officer."

I roll over to check my phone. I've been putting it on vibrate before I go to sleep at night, so if Kylan texts me, it won't wake up Nanny and Chas. Sure enough, I have four text messages from him. I pick up my phone to read them.

Hey beautiful, call me when you get this. (9:08 pm)

If you see this before you wake up, call me. (10:15 pm)

> *I really need to talk to you.* (11:26 pm)

> *I guess you are still sleeping. Call me as soon as you get this. I need to talk to you before your interview with the police.* (6:37 am)

I sit and stare at my phone, unsure of what might be happening. "Maria, Kylan needs me to call him now! I think something has happened," I say in a panic.

"What? What do you mean?" Maria groggily replies as she sits up in the bed and props herself up with a pillow. "It's only seven-thirty. Do you think your Nanny is awake?"

I look up at the ceiling and lie very still. I don't hear anybody stirring in the house. My blackout curtains are super dark, and I know Nanny and Chas have the same ones in their room.

"I'm not sure. I'll go sit in the closet and talk to him. Why don't you go ahead and get in the shower? I'll fill you in when you get out," I say to Maria, as I really don't want her to hear me talk. I don't know what Kylan is about to tell me, and I don't want Maria getting upset this early in the morning, especially right before her interview with the police.

Maria gathers her stuff, chooses an outfit, and heads for the bathroom. I tiptoe into my closet and gently close the door. I don't want Nanny to think that I'm awake yet, or she will come in here. It's not that I don't want her to come in here. I've just got to have some privacy when I talk to Kylan.

I look down at my phone in the dark closet. It lights up the whole space. I can feel my heart pounding pretty hard against my chest. I'm worried about what Kylan is about to tell me. I touch his name to call him and take a deep breath.

"Hello?" Kylan answers.

"Hey Kylan," I whisper. "I got your messages. I just woke up," I quietly say, as I still am not sure anyone can hear me.

"Can you talk for a minute?" Kylan asks with a slight hesitation in his voice.

"Of course. Well, actually, I'm in my closet. Maria just went to take a shower, and I think Nanny and Chas are still asleep, so I'm trying to be super quiet so nobody comes in."

There is silence on the other end of the line. Kylan finally speaks. "They got a suspect in custody last night. Ken was working at the fire station and said it came over the radio. He called my dad, and I overheard the conversation. My dad confirmed what Ken told him, but he said it's not public knowledge yet, so we can't discuss it. I didn't want you to go into the interview today without knowing this."

Something is different about Kylan right now, but I can't figure out what it is. "So, what am I supposed to do? This completely changes everything, Kylan. When do you think they will tell the public?" I ask.

"Dad said the police will contact Ashley's family first, and then it will be on the news. I'm guessing it will be on there today at noon, if not before. You don't need to do anything right now. I probably wouldn't say anything to Maria this morning. Let her parents tell her," Kylan insists.

That just doesn't sit right with me. Maria is my best friend, and I tell her everything. Why would he not want me to tell her?

"No, I'm telling her. She needs to know. She won't speak a word of it to anybody, though. She has an interview with the police at nine o'clock this morning. Maria told me last night that she remembers everything about the party and will be sharing it with them today. I'm sure her parents already know or will know by the time she gets back to her house."

I hear Kylan sigh on the other end of the phone. "Ok Kimmy, but make her promise that she won't tell anyone about this."

I don't understand why Kylan is being so secretive about this. "Did Ken say who the suspect is?" I ask.

"No, he didn't know last night. All he knew was that someone was taken in for questioning. I'll text or call you if I hear anything else. I have to go. I can hear my dad coming down the hallway. We'll talk later." Then, the line went silent.

Hmm...that was interesting. So, how am I going to break this news to Maria? I crack open my closet door to see if anyone is in my bedroom. Whew, thank goodness, it's empty. I crawl out of my closet, afraid my creaking floorboards will give me away. I stand up and walk on my toes back to my bed, slide under the covers, and close my eyes.

"Hey Kimmy, I'm getting ready to leave." I open my eyes and see Maria standing in my doorway. I must've fallen back to sleep.

"Ok, oh, wait! I have to tell you something." I sit up in my bed and motion for Maria to come sit down. She closes the door and eases down on my bed, careful not to wrinkle her skirt.

"I talked to Kylan. Ken heard last night that they have a suspect. The person was brought in and questioned. Kylan said Ken didn't know who it was or anything about the person. Please don't tell your parents. The police will be talking to them."

Maria looks at me like she's about to break down. I scoot over next to her and put my hand on her back. She bows her head, and tears drip from her cheeks.

"I'm so sorry. But maybe this is the answer we've been looking for. Hopefully, they have the person in jail who hurt Ashley, and we won't have to worry anymore," I say to Maria. She stands up and walks over to my mirror to check her face. "You still look beautiful. Here, take some tissues and dry your eyes."

Maria pats her face dry and looks at me over her shoulder through the mirror. "I'm telling them everything! I'm not holding back anything from the other night. I saw a lot, and I remember every single detail. I hope you do the same when you talk to them later. I'm so angry right now I could spit. I pray that whoever did this to Ashley rots in hell!"

Maria has always been a pretty even-keel person. I've rarely seen her get upset or mad. The angriest I've ever seen her was a few years ago when Alex was taunting us about playing with dolls and saying we were too old. Then he ripped one of the heads off the doll, and Maria lost it on him. She took off running toward him like a football player making a tackle. She knocked him down so hard he hit his head on the floor, then she started pounding her fists on his chest. Mr. Hernandez had to pull her off of him. It was actually kind of funny at the time. Other than that, I've never seen Maria so upset until right now.

"You might want to take some deep breaths before you head out. Try not to hurt anyone between here and there. Come on, I'll watch you walk home. You can never be too careful."

I walk through my living room, wondering where Nanny and Chas are. I know they aren't still asleep. As I open the front door, Oscar leaps up over the steps and bolts toward the fence. I look up and see Nanny pulling weeds from my mom's flower bed, and Chas is trimming the trees on the side of the house.

I hug Maria as she waves goodbye to Nanny and Chas. "Call me as soon as you're done. And please don't say anything about what Kylan told me. I don't want to get him in trouble."

Maria stares at me, and then she winks her right eye. I know that is her sign for ok. I watch as Maria starts down the sidewalk toward her house. I decide to walk out to the road to make sure she can get in her front door. I see the police car already in her driveway.

While Maria is gone, I take a shower and get ready for my interview. I'm not sure how much information I will be able to remember, so I found my sketch pad that I got for Christmas last year and started making some notes.

1. *We spent the day on the beach.*

2. *Ashley lied to Jason about going to a party. Actually, she had me lie to him, too.*

3. *Oscar ran away, but then we found him.*

4. *Ashley's stomach hurt as we were leaving the beach.*

5. *We had lunch at Cuz's, where we met some surfer dudes. They were hot! Ashley ate a ton of food.*

6. *We went home and got ready for the party.*

7. *Maria fixed my hair and make-up.*

8. *Ashley was mad at Jason for ruining her plans.*

9. *The party was wild. I woke up in my bed with Maria by my side and Kylan on my floor.*

10. *That's all I can remember.*

I think I will give the police this piece of paper, then I won't have to talk. Yeah, that's a perfect plan. I'm sure they will get enough information from Maria that they won't need to talk to me.

Since I haven't heard from Maria yet, I figure it's time to go see what Nanny fixed for breakfast. I look down at my phone, and it's already eleven o'clock! I guess I need to be thinking about lunch instead.

I walk out of my room and smell a heavenly aroma. I think Nanny is fixing my favorite meal, sauerkraut and smoked sausage! She's never fixed that for my lunch. That's always a dinner dish for us.

"Just as I suspected, Nanny! My favorite!" I say as I give Nanny a big hug. "But why are you fixing this for lunch? Don't we usually eat this for supper?"

Nanny leans down to check the cornbread cooking in the oven. "Almost done," she says. "I thought you might need something to cheer you up, and Chas and I are taking you and Maria out for dinner tonight. Our treat!"

Oh wow! This is a big deal! When Nanny and Chas are here, they always cook our meals. They say it's healthier and much cheaper to eat at home.

"What's the occasion? I mean, why are we going out tonight?" I ask, not sure of what she is going to say.

"Well, let's just say it's an early birthday present for you. I know your big thirteenth birthday is coming up next week, and we just wanted to start celebrating it now. If you want, you can invite that little boyfriend of yours to come too," Nanny says as she smiles and pinches my cheek.

I'm completely blown away! "Hey Nanny, do you think Maria's boyfriend, Peyton, could come too? He and Kylan are best friends like me and Maria. Peyton drives too!"

Nanny squints her eyes at me like she is trying to think hard about this. Then she grins. "I guess that would be fine, but you might want to ask Chas first. You know how protective he is over you girls."

My Chas never had any daughters, but he grew up with three sisters. He has always treated my mom like his daughter from the day she married my dad. At least, that's what Mom has always told me. He even calls her his FDIL. That stands for *Favorite Daughter-In-Law*. Being that she's his only daughter-in-law, we all laugh when he says it. Then, when I was born, he fell in love the very first time he laid eyes on me. He said I looked just like his baby sister Pam when she was born.

I run outside to ask Chas about the guys coming to dinner tonight. Of course, he gives me a hard time about it, but then says, "Sure, whatever for my dear sweet Kimberly."

I run back inside to see if my lunch is finished. "Nanny, Nanny! He said the guys can come! Is lunch ready? I have to go call Kylan!"

Nanny practically drops the cornbread with all my excitement. Thank goodness she didn't because she makes the most delicious cornbread I have ever tasted!

I fly down the hallway to my bedroom to grab my phone. When I pick it up, I notice two missed calls from Maria. Oh crap! I checked, and my ringer is still on vibrate. I better call her back.

As she answers the phone, I interrupt her before she can even say "Hello."

"Maria! I have the best news for you! Nanny and Chas are taking us to dinner tonight!" Maria doesn't speak. "Want to know what's even better? Kylan and Peyton are allowed to come too! Isn't that awesome? Nanny said we are starting my birthday celebrations tonight! I'm so excited!"

Maria still doesn't speak. "Maria, are you ok? I'm sorry I missed your call. I was talking to Nanny."

"Um," Maria hesitates. "Yeah, I guess I'm fine now. I'm done with my interview. Officer Jane was the one talking to me. I told her everything, Kimmy. I mean...everything. I didn't leave any details out. She knows everything from our day at the beach with Oscar to when we woke up at your house, and you had a hangover. I didn't hold anything back."

I sit and think about what Maria just said. Then I wonder: When is that officer coming to my house? Neither my mom nor my Nanny said anything to me about it. Really, I don't have much to say.

"Do you feel better now that you got that all off your chest?" I ask Maria, trying to make conversation.

"You know, I do," Maria replied with relief in her voice. "My mom and Alex were there with me while the officer asked me the questions. So, now they know everything as well. Please don't be mad at me. I told them all about you and Kylan and me and Peyton. I made my mom promise that she wouldn't tell your mom. Of course, my mom's English probably isn't good enough to tell your mom anyway." Maria giggles.

"Ok, that's cool. Now, get your butt over here so we can start deciding where we are going to dinner."

As soon as I hang up the phone, I hear our doorbell ring. Oh no, it's my turn. I grab my sketch pad and head for the living room.

Officer Jane was very nice. I gave her my notes. Nanny explained how sometimes my brain doesn't process things very fast. I also asked to talk to Officer Jane alone. Nanny went outside for a few minutes while I told Officer Jane about me drinking beer that night and not being able to remember what happened. I told her how I got sick the next morning, and I remember the room spinning. I explained to her how Maria filled me in on some of the stupid things I did.

I was so embarrassed about what I told Officer Jane. She reassured me that what I told her was confidential. Since nothing bad happened to me that night, she didn't even have to tell my mom. Now that's over with, I can breathe a sigh of relief.

Maria finally got back to my house just in time to eat lunch with us. Nanny kept the food warm until I was finished with the interview. I thoroughly enjoyed my sauerkraut, smoked sausage, and cornbread. Nanny is one of the best cooks I know!

Maria and I decided to go to the Rum Kitchen for dinner tonight. She reminded me that they have some of the best specials in town. Nanny reminded me about the almost bottomless mimosas. Nanny also reminded me that those are adult drinks, and we aren't allowed to have any. Maria and I looked at each other and laughed.

CHAPTER 22

I'm so nervous! This is kind of like a date. What should we wear?" Maria asks as she paces from my closet to her bed and then back to my closet.

"No worries, I have a ton of clothes to choose from. Let's dress a little more casual tonight though," I say as I grab a pair of white shorts from my drawer and hold them up. "What do you think?" I ask Maria.

"For me? Or for you?" Maria says.

I really wanted to wear these shorts, but if Maria wants to, I will let her. "It doesn't matter to me," I say back to her as I hold them up against my waist. "These would go perfectly with that pink strappy tank top you brought over here."

Maria goes over to the closet and sorts through my sundresses. "I'll let you wear the shorts and tank tonight. I think I'll go with a dress. Nothing fancy though. I think dresses are a little sexier than shorts and a tank top." Maria smiles. "The past few times I've seen Peyton, I've looked like crap. I want to look my best tonight. I want him to know how much I like him."

Maria definitely has a point. I looked terrible the last time I saw Kylan. That was at Ashley's wake, and my eyes were all swollen from crying so much. "Ok, let's dress to impress tonight, but not like we did the night of the party."

We both laughed, thinking about how ridiculous we looked when we left the house that night. I'm pretty sure we looked like we were going to a Halloween costume party. I can't believe Ashley let us leave looking like that.

When I called Kylan to tell him about all of us going out to dinner, he sounded hesitant. He said he was nervous about eating with my grandparents. I told him they were cool and drank like sailors. I promised him they wouldn't be listening or paying attention to us. We could practically sit on the other side of the restaurant, and we wouldn't even know they were there. I told Kylan that we would try to get there early and get us a table in the back corner, far, far away from Nanny and Chas.

As we pull into the parking lot, I spot what looks like Peyton's car already parked. "Hey, isn't that Peyton's car?" I ask Maria as I roll down the window of Nanny's Subaru. Nanny's car windows are tinted so dark that at night you have to roll down the windows to see anything. Chas says it's dangerous to have such a dark tint on her windows, but Nanny says she's just being a hip grandma.

Maria rolls down her window to get a better look. "Yeah, I think you're right. I thought you told them we were going to get a table?"

"I did. I told them to meet us at seven o'clock. It's only six forty-five. Maybe they went into the Goodwill to kill some time," I say as I try to figure out where they are.

Maria and I get out of the car and straighten our clothes. We both ended up going with sundresses tonight. We decided this was kind of a special occasion since it was the beginning of my birthday week celebrations, and special occasions always call for a cute dress.

"How's my hair look? Are my curls still bouncy?" Maria asks as she spins around the car. I grab one of her curls, and it springs back up to her head.

"Yep! Still bouncy!" I say back. We both giggle with excitement.

Nanny and Chas walk ahead of us as we take our time in the parking lot admiring each other's hair, makeup, and outfits.

As we walk toward the restaurant, we notice it looks dark inside. "Is the place even open?" I ask Nanny, knowing good and well that they are always open during dinner hours. Nanny turns around with a smirk on her face and nods yes.

Maria and I decide to walk in like we are models on a runway. I put one foot in front of the other and pranced into the restaurant. All of a sudden, the lights start flashing, and I hear, "SURPRISE!"

I look around the restaurant and see my mom, dad, Alex, Kylan, and Peyton. Sitting next to Kylan is my sweet Grandpa Eugene! I am in complete shock!

I look over at Maria, who has the biggest smile on her face. "Did you know about this?" I ask her, wondering how she kept a secret from me.

"Um...you could say that. I promised your Nanny that I wouldn't speak a word. She made me pinky promise her."

Then I remember Nanny and Maria walking back into the house together after Officer Jane left. They were laughing and carrying on about something, but I was so distraught after my interview that I didn't even bother to ask.

I point over to Kylan and Peyton. "How'd y'all know about this?"

Kylan laughs. "Let's just say a little birdie told me," he says as he stands up and walks toward me. Kylan takes me by the hand and pulls me in for a hug. As he leans in, he whispers in my ear, "You look beautiful Kimmy." Then he kisses me on the cheek.

My face instantly turns beet red. I put my hand on my forehead and look toward the floor, hoping nobody notices how flushed my face is right now. I walk over to where my mom, dad, Grandpa Eugene, and Alex are seated.

"You all got me good this time! I had no idea anything was going on," I say to them as I bend down to hug Grandpa Eugene.

"Well," Mom says. "This was Nanny's idea. She wanted to kick start your birthday celebration early. We were able to bust Grandpa Eugene out for a few hours tonight, so your dad and I took the evening off, and we knew Alex could use a break from babysitting," Mom says as she pats Alex on the shoulder. I do have the best family!

Dinner was absolutely fabulous. We all ended up sitting at the same table. Well, half of us sat in the booth while the rest sat at the table that was moved up next to the booth. We sat in the booth. Kylan was by the wall, and I sat between him and Grandpa Eugene. Maria, Peyton, and Alex sat across from us. Nanny, Chas, Mom, and Dad ate at the table.

Throughout the entire meal, Kylan held my hand and whispered something in my ear every once in a while. Then, just when I thought we were getting ready to leave, several servers came out of the kitchen, holding a huge birthday cake and singing the happy birthday song. They sat the cake in front of me with thirteen lit candles on it. I made a wish and blew out every candle in one breath.

Kylan kisses me on the cheek again and asks, "What did you wish for Kimmy?"

I turn and look at him with a huge smile, and one eyebrow raised. "If I tell you, then it won't come true. You'll find out soon enough," I say as I squeeze his hand.

I turn my head to talk to Grandpa Eugene and notice that his eyes are shut. I tap him on the shoulder, and he opens his eyes. "Grandpa, were you sleeping?" I say in my sweetest tone.

"Nah Honey, I was just resting my eyes. When you get as old as I am, your eyes get tired and just close sometimes." Grandpa pats me on the arm. "You know, I'm so proud of you and the beautiful young lady you're becoming." Then he whispers, "I even like your little boyfriend, Kylan, over there. We had a very nice conversation while we were waiting for you. I made sure to let him know how lucky he is to have you," he says as he winks at me.

I smile at Grandpa Eugene as I feel my face turning red again. "I'm so glad you got to come tonight. This was such a wonderful surprise. I have been missing you Grandpa." I lay my head on his shoulder, and he pats the top of it.

"I know Dear. I always miss you. When you start driving, you can come to see me whenever you want to. You know, I plan on buying you your first car. So, you better start looking now because you'll be sixteen before you know it Sweet Pea."

We ate almost all the cake except for a tiny slice of it. Mom wrapped it up for Grandpa Eugene to take with him. We always send food back home with him whenever he visits.

Mom, Dad, and Grandpa Eugene left first. Grandpa said it was way past his bedtime and that he would see me soon with my birthday present. As we were walking out of the Rum Kitchen, Kylan grabbed my hand and said he needed to tell me something, but he was not sure how. I just smile at him and keep walking. I'm still in awe that everyone was able to keep this surprise dinner a secret from me.

The guys walk us over to Nanny's car. Nanny and Chas get in, and we stand behind the car to talk, hoping we are out of sight. Maria and Peyton walk around the side of the car. I guess they needed some privacy or something. Kylan takes both of my hands in his and pulls me next to him.

"I just want to tell you one last time tonight how beautiful you look. You are a pretty amazing girl!" He leans in and kisses me gently on the lips. "You know, I really like you a lot. Do you think we could go down to the beach this week together? The weather is supposed to be nice all week," Kylan says as I lay my head on his chest.

I wrap my arms around his waist and listen to his heartbeat. "I'd love that. Let me see what I can do," I say as I look up at him. He kisses the top of my head and holds me until I see Maria and Peyton walking toward us out of the corner of my eye.

After one last kiss from Kylan, he opens the car door for me, and I slide in. Maria gets in on the other side and waves goodbye to Peyton. As we drive away, I roll down my window, hoping he can see me. I wave to him and blow a kiss. He must've not seen me because Peyton just kept driving.

Then I feel my phone vibrate in my purse. I go to grab it and see I have a text message from Kylan. I open the message and read three simple words, "I love you."

CHAPTER 23

The day after my epic surprise pre-birthday celebration, we attended Ashley's funeral. It was held at Our Lady of the Gulf. It's such a beautiful church. It is located right on the beach. When you walk inside the sanctuary, you are pretty much mesmerized by the Bible scenes on the stained-glass windows. My parents don't go to church, so I have had to learn about the Bible from Maria. She goes to Mass every Sunday and has attended since she was a baby. I don't consider myself to be religious, but I believe in God, and I try my hardest to pray. Although I'm not sure I'm doing it right, Maria says I am.

Ashley's funeral was the saddest thing I have ever gone to in my entire life. Her casket was up front, along with so many flowers sent from people all over the world. I had forgotten that the Hernandez family was in Mexico and Central America. They even have a cousin who lives in Spain. Instead of them coming to the funeral, I guess they sent flowers.

Maria told me ahead of time that Catholics typically have open-casket funerals, but Ashley's would be closed. Her parents did not want anyone to see how bad she looked when she died. They wanted everyone to remember Ashley like she was, beautiful and full of life.

My mom, dad, Nanny, Chas, and I sat near the front of the church, close to the Hernandez family. Nanny gave me a little packet of tissues to use for the service. I cried nearly through the whole thing, especially when the priest talked about how we are all on this earth for such a short period of time and how Ashley's short period was cut even shorter.

He shared several stories from the Bible and how we need to forgive people for their actions. I'm not ready to forgive the person who did this to Ashley. Maybe I need to start going to church with Maria so I can work on forgiveness.

The end of the service was very painful for us all. We had to walk up to the casket, hug the Hernandez family, and then say one last goodbye to Ashley. They had her senior picture on her casket, along with many other pictures on the sides. There were pictures of her from when she was a baby. There was even a picture of me, Maria, and Ashley with Oscar when he was a puppy.

When we got to the family, I couldn't speak. I gave side hugs to Mr. Hernandez and Alex. Mrs. Hernandez was sitting in a chair, so I hugged her around her shoulders. When I got to Maria, I hugged her so tight that I could feel every bone in her back. Maria is the closest thing I will ever have to a sister. I love her just like she's my mother's child. I still cannot believe what we are all having to go through.

When I turned around to walk down the aisle, I spotted Kylan, Peyton, and Peyton's parents. They were sitting toward the back of the church. Kylan and Peyton both had their heads bowed. About the time I walked by, Kylan raised his head and waved to me. I just looked at him and nodded.

We all waited in the parking lot for the family to come out of the church doors. Kylan and Peyton, as well as Peyton's parents, came out just before the Hernandez family. They didn't see me as they went and got in their car.

As the Hernandez family was coming down the church steps, I saw that right behind them was a bunch of men carrying Ashley's casket. I could not watch this. I looked down at the ground while they loaded her up in the hearse. We all got in our cars and followed each other to the cemetery.

It felt like we drove forever to get there. Maria had told me that her parents had a hard time finding a plot for Ashley. They eventually found something in Kiln out in the middle of nowhere. Cow pastures surrounded the cemetery. I also saw a group of old FEMA trailers from Hurricane Katrina off to the side. It looked like someone had made them into a little trailer park or something.

Our time at the cemetery was not very long. The priest said a brief prayer, we sang Amazing Grace, and then it was over. Maria and all her siblings were at the burial. The little kids were actually sitting quietly under the tent during the service.

When they started throwing dirt on the casket, I felt a tug on my arm. It slightly startled me. I turned around and saw Kylan standing there next to my dad. He leaned in and hugged me. His warm embrace made me realize that even though this terrible tragedy has occurred, we all must move on with our lives. That's what Ashley would have wanted.

Chapter 24

The last few days have felt almost normal. Mom and Dad have gone back to work full-time. Dad has been coming home every night around eight o'clock from the shipyard. Mom is still working a lot of hours, but she keeps saying it won't be forever. Nanny and Chas went home for a few days. They said they would be coming back for my birthday, which is tomorrow!

Even though it's been fairly normal around here, a lot has happened since Ashley's funeral. My mom let Kylan and Peyton come over for dinner the other night. Mom even let us light candles at the dinner table so we could pretend we were at a fancy restaurant. Peyton and Maria almost broke up. That's a whole other story. And, most importantly, we found out who they suspect killed Ashley...Jason! Can you believe it?

They arrested Jason for Ashley's murder because the police found his DNA on her and inside the car she was in. At least, that's what Ken told Kylan. I don't know if it's true, but I do know that the Hernandez family is content with this.

I just have a tough time believing that Jason would do something to hurt Ashley, let alone kill her. He absolutely adored her. I talked to my mom about this, and she told me that sometimes people act crazy when they love someone. She reminded me of an episode of Forensic Files where the wife thought the husband was cheating on her. The wife burned down the house with her husband inside. The police used forensic evidence to convict the wife.

So, I'm satisfied that if Jason did do this, he will get his day in court and go to jail for the rest of his life. Maybe he'll even get the electric chair or something. I heard they still use a firing squad in Mississippi too.

I'm anxious to hear the results of Ashley's autopsy. Maria said the results were in, but the medical examiner was waiting on a toxicology report to make a final decision on what happened. I'm not sure what that means, but I guess I will find out soon.

I am glad that someone is locked up, so Nanny and Chas don't have to stay here anymore. I just hate that it has to be Jason. I love my grandparents, but they are a little strict on me, and I'm ready for some freedom.

In the meantime, I do feel a sense of relief knowing that we all don't have to watch our backs and keep looking over our shoulders to see if someone is following us. I just don't see how, when you love someone, you could hurt them. Maria said that her parents have suspected Jason from the very beginning, which is such a shame. I just knew that he and Ashley would get married one day and have beautiful babies.

Now that we don't have to worry about a murderer on the loose, my mom told me that when I turn thirteen, she will let Maria and me go to the beach by ourselves as long as we stay together. I'm not sure why she is making me wait until my birthday. Does she think I'm going to mature that much overnight or something?

Anyway, I'm ready to enjoy the rest of the summer. Kylan is planning a cookout at his house for the Fourth of July. The holiday is on a Sunday this year, and my dad has already said he will take us over there and pick us up when it's over.

Kylan has only invited me, Maria, Peyton, his cousin Elijah, and Elijah's girlfriend Macy. I've never met Elijah or Macy, but Kylan says they are nice. Elijah just graduated from high school with Ken and Ashley, and Macy will be a senior. Ken won't be coming because he will be helping at the fire department. Many fires get started on the Fourth, and they need all the help they can get. Kylan said his parents would probably invite some of their friends over, too. He asked if my parents would want to come. I told him my mom would definitely be working and Dad would be at home resting.

Kylan has this awesome in-ground pool. He told me it has a slide and a diving board. There is also a hot tub to get in after the sun goes down when the air gets a little cool. I'm so excited just thinking about it.

My parents have pretty much taken in Maria as their own. It has even reached the point that Maria doesn't ask her parents for permission. She asks my parents. She does go to her house at least once a day to check in, but she doesn't stay long, and I always go with her. She said she gets this really strange feeling when she walks into her bedroom—kind of like Ashley is still in there.

We have almost emptied everything out of Maria's bedroom. My mom brought home a bunch of boxes from the bar at the casino the other day, and we loaded them up with Ashley's things. Mom let us put the boxes in the closet by the carport, where they will be safe until we can start going through them. It's really not that much stuff. Apparently, Maria's family doesn't buy their kids many things. Maria told me that all her clothes and shoes get passed down to her younger siblings. Most of the stuff we packed up was clothes and jewelry that Jason gave her.

Maria wanted to burn everything Jason gifted Ashley, but I talked her out of it. I told her we could donate what we didn't want, take the valuables to Bay City Pawn, and maybe make some money off of them. Well, my mom or dad will have to take us. I called, and you have to be eighteen to sell items to them.

Now, being that my birthday is tomorrow, and I will officially be a teenager, I've got some party planning to do. I know that Nanny and Chas are coming tomorrow night for dinner. We are planning a seafood feast! Dad is picking up a bunch of shrimp, soft shell crabs, scallops, and my favorite, Redfish! Dad can get a lot of fresh Redfish at the shipyard. I think it's the best-tasting fish you can buy. I like mine grilled with blackened seasoning sprinkled on it.

My mom has invited the Hernandez family down for my birthday dinner. Maria doesn't think they will come though. Neither one of her parents has gone back to work yet. I'm not sure if her mom will ever go back. The other day, she talked about becoming a stay-at-home mom so Maria's dad could focus more on work. Maria told me that he has applied for a huge promotion at the casino and my mom thinks he will get it. If he does, it will allow him to have a few days off during the week, and he will have his own quiet office away from the casino floor.

"Are you ready for tomorrow?" I ask Maria as I grab a plate to put my toast on. Mom is resting from a long night, so Maria and I decided to make peanut butter on toast for breakfast.

"What's tomorrow?" Maria says as she turns to look at me with a blank stare on her face. Really? Does she not remember what tomorrow is? She smacks my shoulder and says, "I'm just kidding Kimmy. Of course, I'm ready for tomorrow, but the real question is, are you?"

I think about what she just asked me as I slather some peanut butter on my toast. My mouth is watering just looking at it. "What do you mean by that? Will something happen when I turn thirteen that I don't know about? Will I get magic powers or something like that?"

I go over to the kitchen table and sit down. "Girl, your Kylan, he's been talking to Peyton about what he's getting you for your birthday. I'm just making sure you're prepared for what you're getting."

"What's he getting me?" I ask with a mouthful of toast.

"You really think Peyton would tell me that? He knows I can't keep a secret from you. I just know he's pretty much got the whole day planned out. I told Peyton that your mom said we can go to the beach tomorrow, so all I know is that it has something to do with the beach."

I'm so glad Nanny made Maria and me get new bathing suits. Now, I will have a spare when mine gets wet, and I won't have a soggy bottom all day.

"I'm kind of nervous about going to the beach tomorrow. I know that Kylan loves me, but I'm scared that

I might get embarrassed and say something stupid in front of him. Did Peyton mention anything else?" I say to Maria as she joins me at the table with her toast.

"Nah, he just said to make sure we had our sunscreen and not to bring Oscar because we won't be able to watch him." Maria smiled and took a huge bite of toast.

I wonder what Kylan has planned. I haven't talked to him about it. I know he's coming over for dinner tomorrow night, and I just figured we would hang out at the beach tomorrow, but he's not mentioned anything to me about what we might be doing.

I enjoyed our last day on the beach. That was the day after the party when Ashley, you know, was killed, but before anyone knew. We were all happy as little larks splashing in the water and daydreaming about our futures. None of us had a care in the world.

"So, I'm guessing that I really shouldn't even plan anything for tomorrow? Do I just wait and let Kylan tell me his plans? What if he really doesn't have a plan? What if Peyton was just telling you that? I'm a little worried that if I don't say something to Kylan, he might think I don't want to hang out with him tomorrow."

Maria smacks me on the shoulder again. "You really think that Kylan would be like that? He's already told you that he loves you. He treats you like a princess. Just wait.

Maybe you should ask him what time he wants to meet us at the beach tomorrow and see what he says."

Maria always has the best ideas and knows exactly what to say. "That's a good point. I'll call him later. In the meantime, what are we going to do today?" I say as I take my last bite.

Maria hesitates, then slams her fist on the table, "Oh crap! I forgot that I have a stupid dentist appointment at two o'clock today. My mom reminded me of that yesterday. She said Alex will be taking me." Maria rolls her eyes. "I wish Peyton could take me, but my mom doesn't trust him yet. She likes him and thinks he's a good guy, but she says he hasn't had his driver's license long enough to haul precious cargo."

Maria hops up and runs to the refrigerator. "Hey! You wanna know what goes good with peanut butter and toast?" I shrug my shoulders. "Dr. Pepper! Let's drink it for breakfast. Who's to stop us? Your mom is in the bed."

I raise my eyebrows up at her and wonder what mom would do to us if she knew we were drinking soda for breakfast. Then I remember that I'm going to be a teenager tomorrow. "What the heck! Pour me a glass, too!"

Maria and I enjoy our peanut butter on toast with our Dr. Peppers as Oscar sits at our feet under the table. Several minutes of silence goes by. Sometimes, peanut butter is kind of hard to swallow. I wash it down with my soda and hope my mom doesn't get up and see what we are doing. She'd be pissed!

"I've been trying to process this whole Jason thing. I still don't understand why he would do this. What do you think?" I cautiously ask Maria. She has not talked much about this since we found out that Jason was the suspect in custody.

Maria leans back in her chair and runs her hands through her hair. "Well, my mom doesn't want me talking about it to anyone, not even you, but I know you won't say anything." I can tell that she truly doesn't want to discuss details with me, but I'm curious to know if she has heard anything else.

"I haven't told you this because I was hoping you would just wake up one day and remember, but since you haven't yet, here goes," Maria says. She stands up and goes over to the sink to put her plate in. It seems like she is trying to avoid looking at me while she is talking. She turns on the water, washes off her plate, and then places it in the dish drainer. She doesn't speak as I am watching her every move.

"Do you remember seeing Jason at the party?" Maria asks me as she settles back into her chair at the table. I look up at the ceiling, trying to think really hard. I look around the kitchen, hoping a memory will come to me, but nothing does.

"Nope, I sure don't. I guess I was so wrapped up with Kylan that everything else was just blocked out from that night, and you know, the alcohol probably played a role as well." I give Maria a shameful look as she continues.

"So, Jason showed up at the party and was drunk. At least, that's what Ashley told Joni. I actually didn't speak to him. I just saw him from a distance. Ashley was on the dance floor with another guy when Jason grabbed her by the arm and jerked her away. I knew something was off about him, so I followed them. They couldn't see me, but I could clearly see them. He forcefully dragged her outside as I watched the whole thing unfold. Jason was yelling at Ashley, and she was yelling back. They kept going back and forth until Ashley slapped him across the face. She must have busted something in his nose because blood started pouring down his face. Ashley grabbed a napkin from her purse and tried to wipe the blood off his face, but she ended up getting blood all over her hand. I could tell that Jason was thoroughly enraged at this point, and Ashley was trying to apologize, although I really couldn't hear what they were saying. Whatever she was saying wasn't working."

I'm not sure that I want to hear any more of this story. My stomach was starting to churn, and I was getting a shooting pain in my head. I was still trying hard to remember something, but it was like a black hole had swallowed my memories.

"About that time, Jason spotted me through the window spying on them and pointed in my direction. I ducked down to the floor, and when I popped back up, they were gone. That was the last time I saw my sister alive."

Maria looked up, and I could see the tears welling up in her eyes. Then she put her head down on the table. I stood up, walked over to her, and patted her on the back. She grabbed my hand and raised up.

"Why didn't I run outside and stop them from leaving? It's all my fault," Maria says, uncontrollably sobbing. "I could have saved my sister that night but was too scared. I didn't want them to know I had been watching the entire time."

There are times in our lives when no words will ever help a situation. This was one of those times. My mom has always told me that if you can't think of anything to say, it is fine to just not say anything. My words often come out mixed up anyway, so I just knelt down beside Maria and hugged her back as tight as I could. Life is hard enough already. It's even harder when your brain works like mine.

CHAPTER 25

Today is the day! I thought as I opened up my eyes. It's my birthday! I'm officially a teenager! More freedom, more fun, and most importantly, more Kylan!

I look over at Maria, who is still sound asleep. I roll over to check the time on my phone: six forty-seven. Geez...why am I up so early? I tiptoe over to my window and ease back the curtains. There's not a cloud in the sky. As I quietly walk back to my bed, I can faintly smell the scent of bacon and biscuits coming from the kitchen. Mom must be cooking us breakfast before she goes to work.

I lay back down only to realize that I can't go back to sleep. I'm too excited! I need to get up and let some of my energy out, so that's exactly what I do.

I throw the covers off me and try not to be too loud, but I kind of wish Maria would wake up. So, I "accidentally" dropped my phone on the floor, hoping Maria would hear it. No luck. So, I get up and turn on my closet light. Yep, that did the trick.

"Hey, what are you doing? You think it's your birthday or something?" Maria says to me as she pulls the covers up over her eyes. "It's not even daylight outside yet. Why are you getting up?"

I turn toward her and tilt my head. "Well, actually, it is daylight, and I'm ready to start celebrating. And...I smell breakfast. I'll go see what's cooking."

Maria rolls back over and pretends to be asleep. I see a big lump next to her. I guess Oscar came in last night and got under her covers. He's such a turd.

I slip on my flip-flops and head down the hallway. As I get closer to the kitchen, I hear music playing. It sounds like yacht rock—you know, the kind of music that old people listen to. That's strange! My mom never listens to music while she is cooking. If anything, she will have the TV on in the living room and listen to the morning news.

I turn the corner and walk into the kitchen. "Nanny! What are you doing here?" I ask as I see my Nanny standing over the stove mixing up some gravy.

"Well, good morning to you too!" Nanny says as she lays down the spoon and comes over to hug me. "I just wanted to be the first one to wish you a happy birthday, Sweet Pea. So, Happy Birthday! You're officially a teenager!"

I smile at Nanny, knowing that I couldn't have asked for a better grandmother. "Thanks, Nanny," I say, feeling bad for being grumpy with her. "Where's Mom?"

"She went in early to the casino this morning so she could get off this evening for your birthday celebration," Nanny says as she goes back to stirring the gravy.

"Um, did she say anything about me and Maria going to the beach today? Mom promised we could go without an adult today as long as we stayed together."

Nanny paused for a moment and turned her head toward me so she could see my face. "Hmmm...let me think. Your mom asked if Chas could go pick up a few things from town. She mentioned that Maria's parents might be coming over, so you girls must straighten up the house. I don't quite remember anything about a beach trip."

Oh no! Mom didn't tell Nanny that we could go to the beach. Crap! What am I going to do now? I can't call Mom because she won't answer if she's working. My dad probably has no idea that she gave me permission. Panic sets in as my mind is racing. My birthday is officially ruined.

As I am sitting at the kitchen table, I am so wrapped up in my thoughts that I don't even notice Nanny put a plate of food in front of me until I feel the steam hit my face. "Really Nanny? Mom didn't say anything at all to you?"

Nanny giggles and then sits down beside me. "Of course she did Kimmy. Don't be such a worry wart!" I let out a huge sigh of relief. She told me that you and Maria would be going down to the public beach and that I wasn't invited." Nanny puts her hands on her hips. "So, what time are y'all leaving? I've got a lot of work to do around here today to get this place ready for a party."

"I'm not sure. Don't tell Mom, but we are hoping to meet Kylan and Peyton down there around noon so we can hang out all day. Also, we would be safer with the guys with us. Don't ya think?" I laugh and wink at Nanny like she doesn't know we're up to something.

"I think that would be a great plan. I've seen how that Kylan looks at you, and I know he would never let anyone hurt you. He's a good one, I tell ya! I just hope he can keep his hands where they belong," Nanny says as she gives me a stern look, then smiles.

I go get Maria up so we can all eat breakfast together. "Nanny made a huge spread!" I say to Maria as I see Oscar's little nose popping out of the covers.

Oscar loves the smell of bacon, but he's allergic to pork. We found that out the hard way. When Oscar was a baby, my dad fed him a few bites of leftover bacon one morning. Not even two minutes later, Oscar started getting hives all over his face and body. We rushed him to the emergency vet only to find out that he had a severe allergy to pork. Who would've thought? Anyways, that led to a bunch of allergy tests, and three days later, we found out that Oscar was pretty much allergic to everything—poor little guy.

Nanny, Maria, and I take our time eating the delicious breakfast. Nanny made eggs, bacon, biscuits, and gravy. She even brought some of her homemade blackberry jam, my favorite!

We all pitch in to clean up the kitchen. Maria volunteered to vacuum the living room while I took a shower. She said that I shouldn't have to do housework on my birthday. Maria is so great!

After my shower, I don't even bother putting on regular clothes. I go straight to my swimsuit! As Maria is getting cleaned up, I decide I should put on just a tiny bit of makeup. Maybe just a little mascara and eyeliner. I don't want to look like a ghost!

I text Kylan to make sure he and Peyton are still meeting us. Hoping he would reply immediately, I lie back in my bed with my wet hair and close my eyes. He doesn't respond. *Hmm...that's strange*, I think to myself.

So, I decide to get up, make my bed, and straighten up my desk in case Kylan is allowed to come into my bedroom tonight. I don't want to look like a slob.

"Swimsuits already?" Maria asks as she walks into the bedroom. She is wearing her robe, and her hair is wrapped up in a towel on top of her head.

"Duh. What else?" I say back as I smack my forehead with the palm of my hand. "I'm not wearing a moo moo to the beach today," I say, laughing at how Maria rolls her eyes at me.

"I texted Kylan just to make sure we were still on for today, and he hasn't texted me back. Do you think everything is ok? He hasn't even told me happy birthday yet." Which I think is very strange. Don't boyfriends know that they should text or call their girlfriends first thing on their birthday? Maybe I'm Kylan's first girlfriend, and he doesn't know that yet. I will be sure to let him know.

Maria grabs her swimsuit and turns away from me to put it on. She is very secretive about her body. She always turns in the opposite direction of me when she gets dressed or changes clothes. I wonder why and if she has something to hide.

"Peyton called while you were in the shower," Maria says as she wrings the water out of her hair onto the towel. "He was on his way to pick up Kylan. They had some errands to run before they met us. I told him we would see him around noon at the marina. Then we could walk over to the beach together."

I felt a huge relief when Maria told me that. I don't know why I worry so much about Kylan. I guess I'm always thinking about the worst-case scenario.

"That's good. Hurry up and get dressed so we can go. I want to get out of here as soon as possible. I don't even care if we are a few minutes early," I say as I fold up my beach towel and grab some sunscreen. I throw everything in my beach bag and sit down on the edge of my bed. I still feel butterflies in my stomach.

Just then, someone knocks on my bedroom door. "Hang on," I say. "Maria is getting dressed." Nobody responds. That's strange. Usually, the person on the other side will say "Ok" or "Come out when you're done," but nothing.

Maria sprays conditioner on her hair and proceeds to comb out the knots. I had no idea that her hair got tangled until she moved in over here. She has really thick hair that gets easily snagged up. And the shedding...OMG...I've never seen anyone's hair fall out as much as Maria's does. I don't know how she's not bald. I even had one of her hairs in *my* hair the other day. My mom had asked if I had dyed my hair. When I told her no, she pulled a big, long black hair off my head. We both had a pretty good laugh!

"Ok, I guess I'm ready. I don't need any makeup today. The ocean water will just wash it away," Maria says as she slings her long, wet, black hair off her shoulders.

Maria never needs any makeup. I'm actually a little jealous. She has such a beautiful complexion and tanned skin year-round, kind of like Kylan. I get pretty dark in the summer, but I have to work hard for my tan, which they get naturally. Mom says that I will have skin cancer when I grow up if I don't use enough sunscreen. I tell her that I want to look beautiful and tanned while I'm young and that I will worry about cancer when I get older.

Maria packs all her stuff and reminds me to bring an extra swimsuit. I'm so glad she mentioned that, or I would have forgotten and had to walk around with a soggy, wet bottom all day.

Maria walks toward the bedroom door and reaches for the handle when she stops and turns toward me. "Hey, why don't you go first? Whoever was out there was probably wanting to talk to you anyway."

I wrinkle my forehead at her and cross my eyebrows. "Come on, don't be weird. Just go," I say, a little bit annoyed.

As Maria walks out of my bedroom, I can hear voices in the hallway. I grab my bag and head to the door.

"HAPPY BIRTHDAY, BABE!" I squeal and nearly jump out of my skin as I am face to face with none other than my sweet, sweet boyfriend, Kylan.

"OMG! You just scared the bejesus out of me! How did you get into my house?" I say as I am still in awe at the sight of Kylan in my house.

He grabs a hold of me and plants a kiss smack dab on my lips. "Your Nanny let us in. When Peyton talked to Maria, we agreed it would be best to surprise you. I didn't want to ruin the surprise by calling you," he says as he holds on to my arms and leans out to get a good look at me. "Dang Kimmy, you're so beautiful!"

I can feel my face getting hotter by the second. "So that's why Maria wanted me to go first out my bedroom door. She knew you guys were coming here, didn't she?"

Kylan shrugs his shoulders like he is innocent. "Really? I don't believe a word you say," I tell him as I roll my eyes and grin.

"How does it feel to be a teenager now?" Kylan asks as we stand awkwardly in my hallway.

"About the same as it felt yesterday not being a teenager," I laugh. "But you know what? Now that I'm a teen, I get to go to the beach without a babysitter. Woohoo!!" I shout.

Kylan puts his hands on each side of my face. "You know something?" I look up at him. "I love you even more now that you're thirteen. Actually, I love you more and more every day." Then he leans in and slowly kisses my lips. He works his way to the side of my neck and then goes back to my lips. I get cold chills all over my body.

"Hey, we should probably go. We can do more when we get to the beach," I say to Kylan, as I'm afraid Nanny will see us.

When we walk into the living room, Peyton and Maria are sitting on the couch with Oscar between the two of them. Nanny is over in the recliner, and Chas is on the loveseat. All four of them look at us like we were committing a crime or something.

"What took y'all so long?" Maria asks as she jumps up off the couch.

Kylan and I look at each other, and at the exact same time, we say, "Nothing!" We all bust out laughing. They definitely knew what we were doing.

Chapter 26

As soon as we get out of my house, Kylan grabs my hand. Maria and Peyton are several steps ahead of us. They aren't holding hands or even walking close to each other. They are acting like they just met each other. It's bizarre. Oh, well.

"I can't wait until tonight," Kylan says as he puts his arm around my shoulder. "Actually, I'm really nervous. I'm so nervous that I'm excited! You know that feeling you get when you know something fun is getting ready to happen, but you're not quite sure what it is? That's how I feel."

I stop and turn toward Kylan. "Yes, I know exactly what you're talking about because I feel the exact same way right now. I know today is going to be awesome, but I have no idea what we are doing, so I'm a little nervous too."

I'm not sure if I should have told him that. I don't want him to think I'm nervous to be around him, but I want him to know that I understand how he feels. I really have no idea what we are doing today. I would be totally fine with just hanging out in the water and sunbathing on the beach. I need to work a little more on my tan, so my white shorts really pop against my tan legs.

"So, what are we doing today?" I nervously ask. Kylan's eyes dart off into the distance like he is trying to find an answer.

"Oh, it's a surprise Babe! I can't tell you, or it will ruin the surprise."

We continue to walk toward the beach. I see the cemetery starting to come into view. "Hey, can we not walk by Cedar Rest? It creeps me out. And it also makes me sad because it reminds me of Ashley."

Kylan jumps in front of me so I don't see the cemetery. "Close your eyes. I'll guide you down the street. You will have to trust me."

I close my eyes and squeeze them as tight as I can. It's hard to close your eyes in the daylight and not peek. I can feel my eyelids flickering up and down. Kylan hooks my arm in his like he is escorting me to a fancy restaurant. This is actually pretty romantic, but I bet I look stupid walking down the street in broad daylight with my eyes closed. I just really don't want to look at that cemetery.

"Ok, we are past Cedar Rest. The coast is clear," Kylan says as he once again takes my hand in his. I open my eyes and can barely see. The sun is so bright, and my eyes feel extremely sensitive all of a sudden.

I look around as my eyes adjust to the sun once again. "Where's Maria and Peyton?" I ask as I have a slightly uneasy feeling. "I thought they were just ahead of us?"

"Well, they were until we stopped at the cemetery. They cut down Second and walked right in front of the cemetery. We went around it and came out at the school. I didn't want you to walk blind any longer than you had to. I'm sure they will meet us on the other side. Peyton knows where we are going," Kylan reassures me.

I've never had any trust issues in my life. I have been very fortunate to have great parents who have made sure that I am always safe. Ever since all that happened with Ashley, I feel like I need to be constantly aware of my surroundings when I'm away from my parents. I am extra protective of Maria, too. I cannot imagine what I would do if something happened to her.

Kylan and I finally make it down to the marina. "Where are they? Did something happen? They should be here by now!" I feel my heart start to beat faster. My palms are sweaty, and my thoughts are becoming jumbled.

"It's ok Babe," Kylan says as he turns me toward him. My body is so tense that if I fell over right now, I would break into a thousand pieces. Kylan starts to rub up and down my arms, from my shoulders to my hands. For some reason, this is actually helping. I can feel my body start to relax as I take in a deep breath and then let it out.

I gather my composure and wrap my arms around his waist. "How did you know to do that?" I ask Kylan with a slight tremble in my voice.

"I don't really know. I've seen my dad do that to my mom when she gets upset. I could tell that something was wrong with you, and I thought it would help," Kylan says as he continues to rub my back while holding me tightly. I rest my head on his chest and feel an overwhelming sense of peace as I can hear his heart beating. It's like the rhythm of a ticking clock.

"Hey guys! We're over here! You can stop making out now!" That's Peyton's voice, I think to myself. I jerk my head up and see Peyton and Maria running up to us from the boat docks.

"What took y'all so long? Did you have to stop for a make-out session?" Maria says as she grabs my arm and hugs me.

I let out a huge sigh of relief and a giggle. "Um, no, and if we did, it would be none of your business," I joked back with her. "So, what's on our agenda for today?" I ask the gang while we are all back together for now.

"Well, my Kimmy, we have to make it down to the beach, and you will see," Kylan says as he kisses me on my forehead. "But first, I need to make a quick phone call to make sure everything is set up. I'll be right back."

Kylan takes a few steps down the sidewalk while Maria, Peyton, and I sit down on the steps. I can hear his voice, but I can't quite hear what he is saying.

Peyton and Maria are huddled up now like it's the middle of January in the Arctic. He's cute, but not like Kylan. To me, Kylan is the most attractive guy I have ever seen. He's way hotter than that R.L. guy we ran into a while back. R.L. was hot, but he's got nothing on Kylan.

As we are waiting on Kylan, I look out over the marina at all the fancy boats. I can see some of the names and laugh as I read them: *Gettin' Nauti*, *Unsinkable II*, *The Doctor's Office*, and *Bullship*. The funny thing about boat names is that most of them mean something to the owner. That's what my dad says. Someday, I would love to have one of those huge yachts. You know, the ones you can be way out in the ocean and not even feel the boat rocking. I have major seasickness, so if I ever get a boat, I will probably have to take something before I even step foot on it.

I look over at Peyton and Maria. They are full-on making out right here in front of everybody. *Eww, gross*! I look around, slightly embarrassed, to see if anyone is looking in our direction. "Y'all, come on! Can't you wait until we get out in the water?" I say as I tap on Maria's shoulder. As she pulls away from Peyton's mouth, a massive string of spit comes out of her mouth. I think I might vomit!

"Sorry Kimmy. I guess we got a little lost for a few." Maria's face is about as red as I've ever seen it. "I kind of forgot you were sitting right here next to me."

Kylan to the rescue! He bounces back over to us with an ear-to-ear smile. "Ok guys, let's go!" Kylan says as he lifts me up off the steps.

We walk ahead of Maria and Peyton down to the beach. I can see what looks like Ken and Alex in the distance. That's strange. I wonder why they are here. Next to them, there are a bunch of surfboards. Why would they bring surfboards to our beach? We don't have any waves to ride here.

"Surprise!" Kylan says. "Are you ready for our adventure?"

I look at him, puzzled, not knowing what to say. "I'm not sure. What are we doing? I don't think there are enough waves here in the bay to surf."

Ken starts laughing so hard as if I told a funny joke. I don't see anything funny about what I just said. For real, you can't surf on our bay. The waves are about one inch tall.

Kylan punches Ken in the arm as Alex gets paddles out of a huge duffle bag. "I'm not teaching you how to surf today. I'm teaching you how to paddle board today!"

Maria has her hand over her mouth like she's trying to hide her smile. "Really? You are teaching me to paddle board today? I've always wanted to do this, but I've never seen anyone out here on the bay doing it. A few years ago, we went to Panama City Beach on vacation, and they were paddle boarding all over the place. I've wanted to learn ever since."

"I know. That's what your mom told me when I asked her permission to take you out today. The only thing she said was to make sure we don't go past the buoys. She doesn't want us to get caught up in any boat propellers or get bit by a dolphin." Kylan laughs.

I cannot believe that he asked my mom's permission for today. He is such a gentleman! I would have never guessed that he had such an amazing day planned.

"Hey man, you good?" Ken said to Kylan. "I've got a ton of stuff to do. Just call me when you're done, and I'll come back to get them." Ken starts to walk off, then stops and turns back around. "Oh, by the way, have you heard the latest?" Ken hesitates, then takes a step toward us. "Jason's out on bond. So be on the lookout. He's supposed to be on house arrest with one of those ankle monitors, but you never know."

Geez...why did he have to tell us that? I could have totally gone through my day without that information. I knew I had a strange feeling when we were walking down here earlier. It's kind of like I am psychic or something. I roll my eyes at Kylan as he waves to Ken.

"Hey Babe, don't let it ruin your birthday. I have a full day of fun planned for us. Now, put your stuff in this dry bag, and I'll put it on my board. I sure don't want you to lose it."

I shake off the thought of a killer roaming around my town again and try to forget what Ken just said. It's going to be hard, but at that exact moment, Kylan pulled me into him. "I'm here to protect you. I'd never let anyone hurt you. Please trust me. Remember Kimmy, I love you." Kylan gently moves my hair out of my eyes and kisses my cheek. Then he moves over to my mouth and softly kisses my lips. There's just something about Kylan that takes all my worries away.

As we load up on the paddle boards, I realize that I am not a very steady person. On my first try, my board completely flipped over with me underneath. I think I might've scared Kylan. My second try was a little better. I made it up on the board, but as soon as I tried to stand up, I toppled over into the water. Thank goodness the ocean is only knee-deep right here. It takes me three tries to finally get my butt on my board. Kylan decided it would be best to get off his and hold mine still so I didn't get wobbly. That worked! Of course, everyone else was able to make it up on their first try.

After sitting on my board for a while, I decided it was time to try standing back up again. Nope! It didn't work. Back in the water, I went! "Maybe you just need to get your sea legs Kimmy," Kylan says as he starts paddling back to me. I just don't understand how everyone else is an expert, and I'm over here like a drunken sailor.

My parents have always suspected that I have mild cerebral palsy. At least, I think that's what it's called. When I was a baby, it took me forever to hold my head up and crawl. I didn't walk until I was almost 18 months old, and my body parts just don't coordinate together like everybody else's do. I used to fall down a lot when I was little. I would be covered in bruises. I'm sure people thought I was getting abused at home, but my parents would never do that to me. I guess you could say I've just learned to live like this. Mom has always told me that I would grow out of it.

"Don't worry, you'll get it!" Maria shouts from across the bay. She and Peyton have paddled out about as far as they should probably go. A few minutes ago, I watched a boat pass by them, fearing they would get run over.

"I've been doing this since I was a baby. My family always goes to a little beach town called Flagler Beach on the East Coast for vacation. It has massive waves you can actually surf on. Ken and I always wanted to learn to surf, but my dad said it was too dangerous," said Kylan.

I love to watch Kylan talk. Have you ever heard someone say they smile with their eyes? Well, Kylan does. His stories are so detailed and interesting that he always gets my full attention.

"So, when we were little, Dad bought us a couple of these paddle boards. He strapped life jackets on us and let us take off into the deep blue sea. Well, kind of. Dad always goes out with us, and Mom sits on the beach and watches in case she needs to call rescue. For the past few years, Dad has let us go out on our own. I guess you could say I'm a pretty experienced paddle boarder." Kylan winks at me and helps me back on my board.

I could sit here all day long and listen to Kylan talk. The sound of his voice calms my soul, and his facial expressions make me feel at home in a weird kind of way, like he is the person I'm supposed to spend the rest of my life with. Yeah, I know I'm a little young to be talking like that, but I'm in love. What can you expect?

After numerous attempts at trying to stand up on my board, I decided that squatting on my knees would be best for me right now. I can paddle all around the bay like this. The only problem is that my knees are getting sore, and I'm getting hungry for a snack. I have really worked up an appetite!

I hop off my board, on purpose this time, and drag it back to the beach. Kylan, Peyton, and Maria are out near the pelican poles. So, I decide to walk out to them. I get about halfway there and feel a strange sensation under my foot. I stop immediately and look down, but the water is so brown that I can't see past my calf. I ease up my foot just enough to take a step. *SWOOSH!*

"A STINGRAY!" I shout as loud as I can. "A STINGRAY WAS UNDER MY FOOT!"

Kylan jumps off his board and runs through the water to me as fast as he can. I stand as still as a statue until he gets there, afraid I am surrounded by stingrays. Typically, they travel in a large group called a fever. I learned that in science last year when we took a field trip to the aquarium.

"Are you ok?" he says when he is almost to me. "Don't move. I'm sure there are more. I'm going to scoot my feet through the sand so I don't step on a barb."

Kylan starts moving a little slower. I can tell he has done this before. "I'm ok," I say. "I don't think it got me. It just scared me a little."

"Ah...there's one right here," Kylan says as he points down to the water. "I can see it flapping."

As Kylan reaches me, he picks me up and makes me wrap my legs around his waist. "Are you sure you can tote me?" I ask, slightly concerned that he might drop me in the water on top of a stingray.

"OMG Kimmy, you're like 85 pounds soaking wet. I could carry two of you right now without any issues."

I wrap my arms around his neck and cross my ankles behind his back just to make sure. I lay my head on his shoulders and can still smell the scent of his cologne, or maybe it's his deodorant. Whatever it is, I like it!

When we get back to shore, I unlock my legs, and Kylan places me back on dry ground. "I could've carried you like that forever. Don't ever forget it either!"

"Thank you for saving me from the scary stingrays. My dad got stuck by one of their barbs when we were on vacation a few years ago. He refused to go to the doctor, and it got all infected and nasty. We ended up having to go home early. Dad finally went to the doctor and had to get a shot. I sure don't want that to happen to me or you for that fact."

Kylan grabbed my hand and gave me a gentle kiss. "I just love you so much! I hope this will be the happiest birthday you've ever had!"

We spread out my blanket and sit on the beach while Peyton and Maria paddle around the bay. We laugh as Peyton takes a plunge into the drink. Then, he pulls Maria down with him.

Kylan laid back and pulled me down with him. "Look!" he said, pointing to the sky. "It's a family of pelicans!" I squint my eyes and put my hand up to shade the sun. Sure enough, a family of pelicans were flying directly over us.

"Close your mouth!" I say as I quickly put my hand over Kylan's mouth. "We don't want any accidents to happen in there." I laugh.

Kylan rolls over and props himself up on his elbow. He stares at me for a few minutes. Neither one of us speak a word.

"What are you thinking about right now Kimmy?" Kylan says as he starts to play with my hair.

"Oh, nothing really." I roll over so I face Kylan. "You know how I love to close my eyes and dream about the future. Well, that's what I was doing. I was imagining that we were on one of those big fancy boats down in the marina." I close my eyes. "We were all alone with no parents or friends around. We were lying on the bed in the cabin and kissing heavily. Then we started to take each other's clothes off."

I open my eyes up to look at Kylan. His eyebrows are raised, and his mouth is wide open. "Then what happened?" he asks.

I look up at the sky like I am trying to remember. "Nothing. That's when you asked me what I was thinking, so my thoughts were interrupted."

"Oh, dang it!" Kylan snaps his fingers. "It was starting to get really good."

I naughtily smile. "How about you finish what I was thinking, and we will see if we're on the same page." I twirl my hair around my finger and thumb.

"Oh, I know we're on the same page. In fact, we are even on the same word in the same sentence," Kylan says as he leans in for a kiss.

Then he whispers in my ear, "If we were alone on this beach right now, I'd be taking off your swimsuit and sliding my body on top of yours." Kylan's hand starts to move up from my waist to my chest and back down my stomach.

"Hey! What's going on here!" I open my eyes only to see Ken standing over us. "Enough of that hanky panky, you two! We gotta get these paddle boards up before the storm gets here."

I roll over on my stomach, thoroughly embarrassed that Ken saw us messing around.

"Y'all should really get a room." I hear Alex mutter from a distance as he is dragging our boards up the beach.

"I've been expecting your call for a while now. I just got one of those emergency reports over the radio that a strong storm is headed this way and to take shelter immediately," Ken says as he starts gathering up our stuff. "Hey, get those two fools off the water. We don't want anyone to get struck by lightning."

I look over at Kylan, confused. "But it's not even cloudy out here." I look up at the sky, out to the ocean where Peyton and Maria are, and then I look toward town. "Oh, I see. Yeah, that's looking pretty bad."

I run over to the water's edge and holler at Maria and Peyton. I point to the sky so they get the message. As I walk back to Kylan, a huge lightning bolt strikes, followed by a clap of thunder loud enough to wake the dead. Yep, Ken was right for once. It's getting ready to storm.

CHAPTER 27

I gaze out the window of Cuz's as sheets of rain fall from the sky. Suddenly, I feel like a lost little girl. The last time I sat here was the last day we spent on the beach with Ashley. I am overcome with emotions, but I don't want to let them out today. It's my birthday, and my best friend is across the table from me, and my amazing boyfriend is by my side. How could my life be any better?

But something still is not right. I look over the menu and feel Kylan's hand on my thigh. I bite my bottom lip as I turn my head toward him. I fight back the tears with all my might, but I still have a tiny little one trickle down my cheek.

As Kylan leans in my direction, I see a look on his face that I have never seen before. It is like Kylan and I are connected, and he can read my mind. For a moment, I thought he was going to cry. I see tears well up in his eyes. He looks down at his lap, then over at me. He raises his hand to my face, gently wipes the tears, and mouths the words *I love you*.

Maria and Peyton never even notice anything going on between us. They are too busy laughing about how Peyton fell off his paddle board when the lightning struck earlier, and Maria almost peed on herself at the same time. They are definitely two peas in a pod.

I'm trying to eat a little healthier like Maria, so I chose water today instead of my normal fruity drink. I can't decide what to order, though. I really don't want a salad, so I think I'll just get some bisque and toast. That's pretty healthy, right?

When I checked my phone, Nanny had called three times, and Mom had texted, too. I'm sure they were worried about the storm. I texted both of them, letting them know that we are safe and sound inside Cuz's right now. I haven't received a response from either, though.

"So, what are our plans now that it is monsooning outside?" I ask as the waitress sets a hot bowl of bisque in front of me.

"Well, I don't really have anything planned. I didn't anticipate this rain. I guess we could just hang out in here for a while until it stops," Kylan says as he takes a huge bite of his shrimp po boy.

And that's just what we did. We hung out at Cuz's for a couple of hours until it stopped raining. It was still cloudy and muggy outside, so we decided to head back to my house to get ready for my birthday dinner. Kylan and

Peyton walked Maria and me home. Then, they went over to Peyton's to take showers and get cleaned up. Maria and I freshened up as well while we were waiting for them to get back.

"I got you something for your birthday Kimmy." Maria hands me a small paper bag. "It's not much, but I wanted you to have this."

I hold the bag for a moment, deciding whether to open it. "Don't you think I should save this for the party and open it then?"

Maria looks down at the floor and then back up at me. "It's something very special, and I want you to wear it tonight. Please open it now while we are in a private place."

Ok, that's strange. I'm nervous now. What on earth could be in this brown paper bag that's so special? The bag is small, like one you would put your lunch in, and it's not heavy at all.

I sit down on my bed, and Maria sits right beside me. She's so close to me that our shoulders touch. The bag is folded down several times. I unroll it so I can look inside. I see a tiny little box. I look over at Maria.

"Keep going," Maria says. "You have to open the box."

I nod my head back to her. I reach inside the bag and get out the box. All of a sudden, I get a strange feeling in my stomach—almost like when you know something is about to happen, but you don't know what.

I hold the box in my lap and gently remove the lid. The tiny little box is filled with cotton. I remove the top layer and reveal a beautiful, shiny silver bracelet.

Maria holds out her arm. "It's just like mine, see." She rolls her arm around so I can see hers. Then, she takes a deep breath and lets it out.

"It was Ashley's bracelet. My mom and dad gave it to her when she turned thirteen. Then, when I turned thirteen, they gave me one that matched hers. I asked my mom if I could give it to you for your thirteenth birthday, and she said she wouldn't have it any other way. We might not have the same parents, but you are my sister always and forever."

I put the box to my heart, knowing this is a very special gift. I turn and hug Maria, and we both start crying.

"Thank you, Maria. You have no idea how much this means to me. You are the best sister that I could ever ask for. Now, every time I look down at my wrist, I will think about you and remember Ashley too." I grab some tissues off my nightstand and pat the tears off my face.

"She was such an amazing person. I still can't believe that she's gone. It almost feels like she's just on a trip or something. Do you remember last summer when she went to Florida for a few weeks? It feels just like that. Like tomorrow, we will wake up, and she will be standing in the doorway waiting for us to get ready so she can take us down to the beach," Maria says as she sniffles into a tissue.

"I didn't want to upset either of us with this gift. So, let me help you put it on so we can fix our faces and go celebrate you," Maria says as she snaps the bracelet on my right wrist.

"Now, look at us," I say as we hold our arms together and take a picture with my phone. "Sisters for life!"

I walk over to my mirror and check my makeup. My eyeliner is slightly smeared, and my face has blotchy red spots. I wave my hands back and forth to dry my cheeks.

"Here, use this." Maria hands me a cosmetic bag. "Ashley would have wanted you to have this. You know, I don't use much makeup, and I don't want it to go bad."

I look down at the bag and then up at Maria. "I can't use Ashley's makeup. It just wouldn't be right."

Maria grabbed the bag and pushed it toward me. "Yes, you can. Please use it. Jason gave her all these very expensive products. Please, I don't want them to go to waste."

I put the bag down on my dresser and start looking through it. I pull out a tube of concealer. "Ok, I definitely need this today," I giggle as I begin making dots on my face to cover up all the red spots from crying.

Knock, Knock, Knock

"Girls, there are guests here waiting for you. Come on out when you're ready." The door slightly opens, and Mom pokes her head in. "Are y'all decent in here?"

Maria and I laugh. "We are now," I holler back. "Who's here?" I ask Mom as she goes to close the door.

"Just a few people. Hurry up girls, they want to see y'all."

Mom closes the door back. I look over at Maria and say, "You ready for this?"

Maria grabs her sweater off my bed and wraps it around her shoulders like she's cold. "Oh, come on, Maria. It's like 100 degrees outside. You don't need a sweater."

Maria continues to push her arms through the sleeves. "You know me, I'm always cold no matter what the temperature is outside. Plus, I don't want Peyton to see that my shoulders got sunburnt today. It's kind of embarrassing when a Latino gets too much sun. Our skin isn't supposed to burn. At least that's what society thinks."

As we walk out of our bedroom, I can hear voices in the kitchen. It sounds like a lot of people and maybe even some kids. Who would bring little kids to our house? The only people I know who have small children are Maria's family.

As we round the corner to the kitchen, I see Nanny standing by the table, getting it set up for the party. "Hey! They're out of hibernation," Nanny says as she comes over to give us each a hug. "Happy Birthday, Sweet Pea. I love you!" Nanny whispers in my ear as she squeezes me tight.

"Look Nanny, at what Maria gave me." I hold up my arm so she can see my new bracelet.

"Oh Dear, that's beautiful!" Nanny says as she looks over at Maria. "You did a good job picking that out for Kimmy. It fits her perfectly."

Maria smiles and says, "It was Ashley's." I can see the tears welling up in her eyes as she looks away. "I have one just like it." Maria raises her arm up to show Nanny. Then, we put our wrists together.

"See Nanny, we are real sisters now." Nanny embraces us both in a big bear hug. As we are leaning out of the hug, I see a glimpse of a small child from the corner of my eyes.

"Maria, is that your little brother?" I point down to the little guy, who is probably no more than two years old. He doesn't speak much, but he sure can run fast.

One day back in the spring, when the weather was just starting to get warmer, we took him over to the park next to my house. Ashley went with us to make sure we were safe. We all enjoyed playing on the monkey bars and pushing her little brother on the swings. We were ready to leave, and that little booger started running laps around the playground when we told him it was time to go home. I was chasing him in one direction. Then, Maria would try to catch him in another. You should have seen us! I'm sure it was hilarious for anyone watching. Finally, Ashley came in from behind and scooped that fellow up, and gave him a smack on his butt. Then, of course, he started crying.

"Mom! Dad! You made it!" Maria shouts across the kitchen as she sees them walking up the steps of the back porch while talking to my parents. She hurries over to them and gives them both a hug. She looks down at her mom's belly, rubs it, and gently kisses it.

"Only a few more days, Mom, and he'll be here. Are you excited?" Maria asks as she puts her ear to her mom's stomach. Mrs. Hernandez just smiles back at Maria and then looks over at me.

"Oh, come here, my sweet girl Kimmy," Mrs. Hernandez says in a thick Spanish accent. "Feliz Cumpleaños!" She holds her arms out, signaling to me that she wants a hug.

I walk over to Mrs. Hernandez. As I raise my arms, she grabs my wrist with her hand and pulls it up close to her face. She carefully examines the bracelet that Maria just gave me. For just a moment, I thought that we were going to be in trouble. Maybe Maria didn't ask permission to give it to me.

"Nina, come here!" My mom runs over to Mrs. Hernandez like she is going into labor or something. "See." Mrs. Hernandez swiftly moves my arm over to my mom so she can see the bracelet. "It's perfect! I knew it would fit her perfectly!"

Mrs. Hernandez then drags me over to Mr. Hernandez. I'm still not sure that I am supposed to have this bracelet. I am starting to get a sick feeling in my stomach.

When Mr. Hernandez turns around from talking to my dad, Mrs. Hernandez pushes my wrist in his face. He looks at me, then at his wife, and back at me.

"Kimmy," he says as he takes a deep breath. "When a girl in our culture turns thirteen, it means they are two years away from their quinceañera, which is her fifteenth birthday. A quinceañera is the celebration of a girl transforming into a young woman. As you know, Kimmy, our family celebrates everything in a big way: births, deaths," he puts his hand over his heart and pauses, "and most importantly, birthdays."

Mr. Hernandez motions for my mom and dad to come over to us. "We know that the past few weeks have been especially hard for not only our family but for yours as well. Lucia and I consider you and your parents part of our family Kimmy. You all have been there with us through thick and thin. That's why I didn't hesitate to say yes when Maria asked to stay here while we were getting everything sorted out at home."

I look over at my mom, who has tears streaming down her face. My dad is patting her on the back.

"With that being said, we want you to have this bracelet in honor of our beautiful daughter, Ashley. The bracelet that Maria is wearing was given to Lucia when she turned fifteen. The bracelet you have, Kimmy, was the gift Lucia's sister received on her fifteenth birthday."

I look down at the bracelet and realize how important this is to the Hernandez family. "All we ask is that you take good care of it and hand it down to your daughter or granddaughter one day." Mr. Hernandez grabs a hold of my shoulder and gives me a gentle squeeze.

I look up at Maria and her mom. Both of their faces are red and soaked with tears. I open my arms and wrap them around Mrs. Hernandez. As she is holding me, I can feel my whole body relax all the way down to my toes. Mr. Hernandez comes over as I open up my arms and let him into our hug. My mom and dad follow up from behind and hold me tight.

For the first time since we learned about Ashley's passing, I finally feel a sense of peace rush over me. I have such a wonderful group of people surrounding me who will always be by my side no matter what. I know that there is nothing we can do to bring her back. What I do know is that I will never have to look very far for someone who loves me.

The rest of my birthday party was quite amazing! The seafood feast was better than any restaurant could have fixed. We had all my favorites, including Nanny's homemade crawfish casserole. It was delicious!

I received some great gifts as well. Nanny and Chas got me a bunch of new clothes and shoes. Mom and Dad gave me a subscription to a makeup bag that comes once a month and has the latest and greatest products for girls my age. My favorite gift was definitely my bracelet from Maria, but what Kylan got me for my birthday was the most romantic.

When I opened his present, I wasn't sure what to expect. I knew no one could top Maria's gift, but I was excited nonetheless, just knowing the thought he put into it. And that he did! Kylan gave me a gorgeous necklace with two hearts intertwined. He told me no matter where we are or how far apart we might be, our hearts will always be connected. He said this necklace should serve as a symbol of love and hope for our future, and I melted.

CHAPTER 28

The day after my birthday was July 4th, which meant that Maria and I would be going over to Kylan's house for his Fourth of July party today. I was beyond excited and extremely nervous to meet his parents. Luckily, they both loved me! They especially liked it when I told them I was the one Kylan was square dancing with when he broke his ankle. I think I embarrassed him by telling the story, but it was funny.

Kylan has a huge house! I don't know exactly what his parents do for a living, but they sure are rich! His pool reminded me of one that you would see in a magazine. It had a diving board, a slide, and even a little waterfall flowing into the pool. After dark, we spent most of our time in his hot tub connected to the pool. Even though the days are in the nineties here in BSL, the nights still tend to get a little cool.

You could say that our Fourth of July ended with a bang. As my dad was on his way to pick us up from the party, he had a wreck and totaled his truck. Dad was fine, but the truck was completely destroyed. Maria and I ended up staying much longer at Kylan's than originally planned. We had to wait until my mom got off work from the casino to pick us up. I didn't complain. It just meant we would get to hang out with the guys even longer. I'm really sad about Dad's truck, though. He just bought it less than a year ago. It's midnight black with tinted windows and blacked-out everything, even the wheels. It's also a diesel, which, for some reason, I just love. Hopefully, Dad can get him another one just like it.

Since it was so late, Kylan's parents were asleep. This gave Kylan and me some much-needed alone time to chill and enjoy each other's company in the hot tub. We kissed and held each other for what seemed like hours. We watched the neighbor's fireworks and gazed at the stars when the fireworks ended.

I'm not sure where Maria and Peyton were during this time. They slipped inside to change and never came back. Kylan said that Peyton pretty much has his own room there, so I'm guessing that's where they went. I didn't want to be nosy, and plus I had my own business to worry about.

It was way after midnight when my mom finally picked us up. Suki, Kylan's dog, was barking like an intruder was getting ready to rob us, and that's how we knew Mom was there. I'm really glad Suki alerted us because I sure didn't want to get caught doing something my mom wouldn't approve of if you know what I mean.

When we got home, I realized that I had left my wet bathing suit at Kylan's house. I texted him to let him know. He said he would deliver it to me tomorrow after his mom washed all the chlorine out of it. *Sigh*. I'm glad I have an excuse to see him tomorrow. The thought of going a single day without seeing Kylan makes me want to cry.

You could say the rest of the summer was quite excellent! So much happened! After my birthday party, we tried our best not to talk about what Jason did to Ashley. Nanny said it was time to heal and ask God to forgive Jason for his actions.

Speaking of Nanny, she and Chas decided to sell their sailboat and buy a huge cabin cruiser. It's big enough for ten people to sleep on. I was so afraid to go out on it the first time after they bought it. But guess what? I didn't get seasick on it. It's a miracle! Nanny said that the sailboat rocked back and forth much more than the cruiser. That's probably what was making me so sick. We are planning an overnight trip on it this fall once the weather cools down.

Mrs. Hernandez had her baby a week after my birthday. Maria and I were down at the beach with the guys when Alex came to get us. He said that their mom had gone into labor and needed Maria to help with the delivery. We quickly packed up, and Alex took us both to their house.

The midwife told me I could stay in the room if I wanted, and I did until things got really gross. I could see the baby's head starting to come out, and I thought I was going to throw up. I don't think I want to have kids, at least not anytime soon.

Do you remember me saying that Maria's new sibling would be a boy? Well, guess what? I was sitting in her living room talking to Kylan on the phone when Maria came running down the hallway screaming, "It's a girl! It's a girl!" They ended up naming her Ashlynn Ruth Hernandez. Ashlynn was in memory of Ashley, and Ruth was in honor of me since that's my middle name. Mrs. Hernandez said she wanted to do something special for me since I am such a huge part of their family.

I'm pretty sure that Kylan and I have been together every single day since his Fourth of July party. My mom has been so cool about him coming over to our house when she's there. Her only rule is that we keep the bedroom door open. We've been meeting at the park and the beach when she's not home. Mom has also let me go over to his house to swim and hang out. His parents already treat me like family. I love it!

Maria and Peyton are still hot and heavy. I think they've been sneaking around a little more than Kylan and me. Maria has been telling my mom that she needs to go home for a while, but I think Peyton is picking her up down the road and taking her for a ride. She told me they have done pretty much everything together except for "it," if you know what I mean. They just can't keep their hands off each other.

Kylan and I have messed around quite a bit this summer, but he is very respectful of my body. We've talked a lot about saving ourselves for marriage and how we would like to try to do that. I just get so tingly when he touches me, and it always feels so good. Our teenage hormones are flaring, and I'm not sure if we can last that long, but we will sure try.

Last week, we said farewell to Ken as he set off for college in Tennessee. Kylan's parents drove him to a town called Murfreesboro. I think it's close to Nashville. He said we could come to visit sometime, and he would take us to see Music City USA. Even though Kylan and I didn't really hang out with Ken much, I'm really going to miss him while he's gone. He said he'll come home at Christmas, but it won't be the same around here without him. Maybe I can talk my parents into letting me go up to Tennessee with Kylan's family at Thanksgiving.

After Ashley's funeral, Ken and Alex became pretty close. I thought it was strange that they were all of a sudden besties. I think Ken's personality was starting to rub off on Alex because he was being nice and pleasant to hang out with. Later, I found out that Ken was helping Alex get a job at the fire station. Alex actually ended up taking over Ken's job at the station, and he's getting a good paycheck now. Alex is still doing some landscaping jobs on the side.

Now that we are back in school, I don't get to see Kylan as much, which absolutely tears me apart. He often reminds me that absence makes the heart grow fonder. When I miss him, I remember to look at my heart necklace, and I feel instant comfort.

Did I tell you that Kylan is in the marching band at the high school? Yeah, he plays the snare drum. He's played at two football games so far. I've been to both of them. Kylan's mom picked Maria and me up for the games, took us out to eat, and drove us home when they were over. Kylan typically has to stay after school on ball game nights, but he rides with us when his mom takes us home. Peyton has been meeting us there since he can drive himself. He and Maria snuggle up together beside me in the bleachers. Watching them makes me a little jealous because I can't sit with Kylan.

I'm considering joining the band next year when I go to high school. I've always wanted to play saxophone. Nanny said she would buy me one if I wanted to learn. If I were in the band, Kylan and I would be together all the time, especially on Friday nights and all day Saturdays when they have band competitions out of town. They have a band at my middle school, but I think the band teacher is creepy, so I probably won't be joining this year.

We are now about four weeks into the new school year. Maria and I are not in the same homeroom but have lunch together daily. Our classes are entirely different, too. She has all honors classes, and I have all inclusion classes. That's ok with me, though, because I always have two teachers in my classrooms to help me. I'm hoping we can take some of the same classes when we go to high school. I would love to take cosmetology and learn how to do hair. I know that Maria plans to take that class and get her certification. She will be great with that!

Maria and I ride the bus to and from school every day. I hate the bus. The kids at school call it the "Cheese Wagon." It's so embarrassing! There's this really annoying boy who rides the bus. His name is Jon. I'm pretty sure he likes Maria, but he says mean things to her to get her attention. The other day, he was calling her a wet back. I had no idea what that meant until I asked Maria. It's not good. Actually, it's awful. One of these days, I'm probably going to punch him in the throat! I'm hoping that Kylan will have his driver's license next year, and he can pick me up for school and take me home in the afternoons.

I'm actually counting down the days until this school year is over. I like middle school, but I'm ready to be with Kylan. Not that I am worried that he will cheat on me, I just want to be able to see him whenever I want. We can hold hands down the hallway, eat lunch together, and I can give Kylan a goodbye kiss as he walks me to class. I only have 158 more middle school days left until all my dreams will become my reality.

<h1 style="text-align:center">CHAPTER 29</h1>

Something terrible has happened. Well, maybe I'm exaggerating. I should've just said something happened: Kylan got into trouble at school the other day. I know, I can hardly believe it, too. He didn't do anything, though; at least, that's what he says.

Kylan had gone to the bathroom to send me a text. That's how we check in with each other during the school day. Kylan will ask to go to the bathroom, and while he's there, he will text me. See, we aren't allowed to have cell phones at school. You are supposed to keep them in your backpack or at home. If a teacher sees the phone or even hears it ringing, they will take it up and turn it into the office. No warning or anything! Then, your parents must come to school to get your phone from the principal. Yeah, they're really strict!

Anyway, Kylan had gone to the bathroom to text me, and according to his story, some other boys were in there too. Kylan started smelling cigarette smoke, so he quickly flushed the toilet and went to wash his hands.

About that time, a teacher came into the bathroom and stopped Kylan before he could leave. The teacher made the other boys come out of the stalls. All the boys were searched. Cigarettes and lighters were found on all of them except for Kylan. The teacher accused Kylan of passing it under the stall because one of them had two packs of cigarettes. Long story short, Kylan got in trouble even though he didn't do anything wrong. So now, he's got a week of ISS-In School Suspension.

I believe Kylan. He doesn't smoke or do stuff like that. The only time that I know of him having alcohol was at Joni's party that night when I got stupid drunk. Other than that, Kylan's a really good person.

So, this week, I won't be getting any texts from Kylan during the school day. When I talked to him last night, he told me that yesterday, he was in a portable classroom out in the middle of the courtyard of his school. That's where the ISS classroom is. He said this nice old man, Coach John, is the ISS teacher. He's one of the football coaches, but he teaches ISS too. Kylan said that Coach John kept falling asleep during class yesterday. The kids in ISS giggled when he snored and woke himself up. The other boys, the ones who were actually smoking, were in there with him too. Since he's a freshman, he was afraid to say anything to them. They're all seniors.

I see Maria from across the cafeteria and wave. She finally sees me and starts making her way in my direction. "Hey, Sis! How's your day going?" Maria says as she plops her lunch tray down across from me.

"Oh, you know. Just thinking about Kylan and what we're going to do this weekend. You?"

I look over at Maria as she has her phone under the table. She is looking down, and her fingers are going a mile a minute. She raises her head up and looks at me. "Huh? Sorry, I didn't hear you."

As I take a big bite of my hamburger, I nod to Maria. "I was just asking about your day," I say with a mouth full of half-chewed hamburger.

"Sorry, I was just texting with Peyton. This is his lunch too, remember," Maria says sharply as she chomps down on her chips.

I briefly think back to last year, when life seemed much less complicated. There were no boys to worry about, no bullies on the bus, and no moody Marias to deal with. I love Maria, but gosh, she sure can get grumpy!

"So, what are your plans for the weekend?" I ask Maria hoping she can focus on our conversation for a minute.

"I'd like to go to a movie this weekend with Peyton, but I doubt my mom or your mom will let me. We want some alone time if you know what I mean." Maria flicks her hair over her shoulder and gets out her makeup compact to check her teeth. "You know, we've been talking a lot about taking our relationship to the next level. I think it just might happen this weekend! EEK!"

Is she being serious? "I thought we made a promise to each other to save ourselves for marriage. Are you really going to give yourself to Peyton? He's not even given you a ring or anything, has he?" I ask Maria as I inch closer to her face. "What if something happens and you accidentally get pregnant? We're only in eighth grade. How would you support a baby right now?"

Maria rolls her eyes and pushes me out of her face. "Come on Kimmy, you're being a little extreme. I just want to have a little fun. Peyton and I are so sexually attracted to each other that we are ready to make the leap. We've talked about it a lot and know the risks. He's got protection ready for when it happens. Please don't try to talk me out of it because all it can do is hurt our friendship."

Oh my gosh! Who am I talking to right now? This is not the Maria that I know. Why is she acting like this? I'm afraid if I ask her, she might bite my head off. I decide to change the subject and talk about something else. Plus, I'm starting to feel slightly uncomfortable talking about this right here in front of everybody. This is a conversation that needs to be had in private.

After a long, awkward silence, the bell rings for us to return to class. "I'll see ya at the bus Kimmy. Have a great rest of the day!" Maria says as she waves bye.

Wow! How could she be so angry with me one minute and then the next act like nothing's wrong between us? I think her hormones might be out of whack. Geez...I had no idea being a teenager would be this hard.

I'm walking back to math class, and I feel my pocket vibrate. I can't check my phone because I'm not supposed to have it out at school. I'm not sure who would be texting me right now. Mom is at work. Kylan is in ISS. Dad doesn't know how to send a text, and Nanny knows not to text me while I'm at school. Who else would it be? I need a plan. I know! I'll ask to go to the bathroom in a few minutes. I'll tell Mrs. Lisa that it's an emergency. She'll let me go.

My plan works! As I make my way down the hallway to the bathroom, my phone starts vibrating again. I'm pretty sure someone is calling me now. I am to the point of a full-on sprint. Something is definitely wrong. I can feel it. I barely get inside the girl's bathroom, only for my phone to stop vibrating. I jerk it out of my pocket and almost drop it in the toilet. One missed call. Six new text messages.

I sit down on the seat with my pants still on. My hands are so sweaty I can't even open my screen. Finally, it recognizes that my finger is swiping—a missed call from Kylan. I can't call him back. What if someone walked into the bathroom and heard me talking? I'd for sure be busted with my phone and probably never get it back, because there's no way my mom or dad could come up here and get it.

I take a deep breath. Why would Kylan be calling me? Does he want to break up? Is he hurt? My mind is racing, and my heart is pounding. *Come on, Kimmy, get it together!* I tell myself.

I end up taking five deep breaths and open my text messages.

Kimmy. Can you talk? (10:10 am)

Hey! Are you still at lunch? (11:05 am)

I need to talk to you ASAP! (11:17 am)

Go to the bathroom and send me a text. (11:19 am)

I just called you. I don't want to tell you through text message. (11:35 am)

This can't wait. Please let me know when you can talk. (11:36 am)

What is going on with him? He needs to talk to me in person? He is definitely breaking up with me. Well, I might as well call Nanny to come pick me up because I sure can't spend the rest of my day here. I think I might throw up right now.

I take a deep breath and formulate my thoughts. I study his name on my phone. If I touch on his name, it will call him. If I talk in the bathroom, I risk the chance of getting in big trouble. Is it worth the risk? I settle on sending a text.

Hey! I'm in the bathroom at school. (11:43 am)

I need to talk to you. I can't text this. I just don't feel right about it. (11:44 am)

Are you breaking up with me? If so, you can just do that through text messages. (11:44 am)

KIMMY! HELL NO! WHY WOULD YOU ASK ME SOMETHING LIKE THAT? I LOVE YOU! (11:45 am)

I let out the huge breath of air that I was holding in. If he's not breaking up with me, what is so important that he can't text?

> *Ok, sorry that I thought that. What's up?* (11:46 am)

I'm in ISS and bored out of my mind. Coach John fell asleep, so I pulled my phone out to look through the pictures. I came across some pictures of us at Joni's party. Some of the pictures have Ashley in them. I don't think Jason killed Ashley! She didn't leave the party with him. She left with someone else. Jason was still at the party after she left. I have pictures to prove it. (11:46 am)

> *What? Are you serious?* (11:47 am)

Yes (11:47 am)

> *Don't tell anybody, especially Peyton or Maria. Can you come over after school?* (11:48 am)

I have band practice after school, but I'll have Peyton swing me by there on our way home. Try not to worry so much about me. I love you. (11:48 am)

> *I love you too.* (11:49 am)

I cannot believe it! I knew from the beginning that Jason was innocent. He was so in love with Ashley that I knew he couldn't hurt her. I can't tell Maria this until I see the pictures. Her family is sure that Jason did all that terrible stuff to Ashley.

"Kimmy, are you in here?" Oh no, I've been gone from class for way too long.

"Yes, I'm in here. Who are you?" I ask as my voice trembles.

"It's Ellie. Mrs. Lisa sent me to check on you. She said you've been gone for a while, and you might need help or something."

I sit very still for a moment. I look down and realize I still have my pants pulled up as I'm sitting on the toilet seat. Can Ellie see that from where she is standing? "I'm ok. My stomach is just a little upset. Tell Mrs. Lisa I'll be back in a few."

Ellie hesitates with her response as I can hear water running in the sink. "Ok, I'll let her know." She turns the water off and gets some paper towels. I can hear her footsteps leaving the bathroom. Whew, that was a close call! Now, I guess I should try to use the bathroom, so I don't need to go later.

Chapter 30

The last three hours of school have crept by. I had a social studies test and science quiz, and I worked on my English paper in study hall. I haven't seen Maria since I texted with Kylan. I'm sure she will want to talk about Peyton while we are on the bus. Maybe I can suggest that we plan something for the weekend to distract my thoughts about what Kylan told me.

Kylan has band practice every Tuesday and Thursday after school until around four-thirty. Peyton stays to wait on him after school. I'm not sure what he does during that time, but whatever. Sometimes, the guys will bring McDonald's or Burger King to eat dinner with us. Other times, they call ahead and see if my mom put anything in the crock pot before she left for work. When she knows she has to work a double or thinks she might have a late night at the casino, she will put on a roast, so Maria and I can have something healthy for dinner. Other times, Mom knows that the guys will take care of us or we can fix something on our own. We always have an endless supply of noodles and TV dinners, just in case.

Maria makes it to the bus before I do. I can see her sitting toward the back as I bounce up the steps. I'm really anxious to see the pictures on Kylan's phone. I'm just not sure how we can get away from Peyton and Maria so he can show me. Maybe I'll text Kylan to tell Peyton I need to talk to him privately when they get to the house. I'll tell Maria the same.

"So, I've been thinking about what we talked about at lunch. By the way, I'm so sorry I was such a jerk. It's that time of the month, and my emotions are running high right now," Maria says, looking up at me as I slide in next to her.

"Oh, that's ok. I understand. I'm sure I can get that way sometimes too. Just don't do it again!" I laugh and smack her on the shoulder. "So, what have you been thinking about?"

Maria turns her head to look at me then turns back to look at the back of the seat in front of us. "I've been thinking that we both need to keep our pact of waiting until marriage to be with a guy. That's what marriage is for. You're right when you said we were too young. I don't want to take any chances. We've got our whole lives ahead of us, and I don't want to ruin it by doing something stupid like having sex. There are plenty of other things we can do with our boyfriends that don't involve high risks like getting pregnant."

Whew! I'm so glad she just said that. Maria has been heavy on my mind when I've not been thinking about what Kylan has to show me this afternoon. I don't want her to let her hormones get in the way and make poor decisions. If Peyton truly loves her, he will wait until marriage, and Kylan will, too.

I listen as she continues talking about how she and Peyton have already been planning their wedding. I tilt my head to the side and look at her like Oscar looks at me when I ask him if he wants to go outside. "Really, Maria? Do you think you will marry Peyton?" I say, tilting my head in the other direction.

She shakes her head up and down really fast. "Yep! I'm quite certain. I know we've not been dating for very long, but it's one of those things with us. When you know, you know! That's why I'm totally fine with waiting until marriage. I know he will be the one I marry."

Ok. I sit in awe as I stare back at Maria. I don't know how to top that, so I don't. I try to gather my thoughts and say something clever, but nothing comes to mind.

"So, what's on your agenda for the weekend?" I always go back to that question when I don't know what else to say.

Maria stares down at her phone while she texts. I'm guessing she is texting Peyton since I am sitting right beside her. I know it's not me. "Um, probably nothing," Maria says, not even looking up from her phone. "If the weather is nice, I would like to have a picnic with Peyton, but that's a stretch."

"Why would that be such a stretch?" I ask. "Picnics are pretty cheap, and the beach is the perfect place to eat lunch. Except for the seagulls. They're a pain in the butt if you drop any crumbs."

We were all at the beach a few years ago with Maria's family. Her little sister was eating some cheese puffs and ran over to try and feed one of the seagulls. At the same time, she ended up dumping the entire bag of cheese puffs on the ground. Before we knew it, she was swarmed with a thousand birds trying to get a cheese puff. Poor baby was so scared that she screamed her head off for hours after that. It freaked me out too. I'd never seen anything that scary in my life. I was afraid her little sister was going to get her eyeballs pecked out!

"My mom wants me to come over and babysit the little ones while she catches up on some sleep. She is considering returning to work soon and wants to see how the kids do without her. I don't know. I guess I could ask if Peyton could come over and help me. She really likes him."

As the bus takes off from the school, James, my friend from class, starts walking toward me down the aisle. "Hey Kimmy!" he says as he sits down in the seat in front of us. "I heard that you were dating Kylan. Is that true?"

"Yeah, why?" I ask as I look over at Maria. She shrugs her shoulders.

"I was just wondering. I saw you all at the beach the other day. I wanted to come hang out, but I feared Kylan would get mad. I've heard he's very possessive over you."

"You should've said hi. Kylan is definitely not possessive. Who told you that?" I snarl up my nose at him.

"My big brother, Kevin, is a senior at the high school. He's in the percussion section with Kylan. He said that you're all Kylan ever talks about. I just figured that he wouldn't want me talking to you," James says as he puts his head down. Then, he pops his head back up. "Can I tell you something Kimmy?"

I feel my forehead wrinkle as I zone in on James. "I guess."

"I'm really sorry about Maria's sister." James leans forward to see if Maria is paying attention. "Kevin used to have a huge crush on her. He said she was the most beautiful girl he had ever seen, and she was nice too. Kevin said she always spoke to him whenever they saw each other. He knew she was out of his league though."

An overwhelming feeling of sadness moves through my body. I can feel my heart actually skip a beat. "Thank you, James. I appreciate it." I lower my head and feel a tear fall on my bare leg. I am still grieving the loss of Ashley. We all are. Nanny said that when you lose a loved one, it gets easier as the days go by, but the pain never goes away.

I nudge Maria to get her attention. She was entirely in her own world. I don't think she heard anything James said.

"Did you know that Peyton and Kylan are coming over after school today?" Maria looks at me with a huge smile on her face.

I try to act like nothing is wrong. "Yeah, Kylan texted me earlier that he wanted to see me this afternoon. You know, he's been going stir crazy since he's been in ISS these past couple of days."

"I'm glad they are coming over. I need to talk to Peyton about a few things. Hopefully, we can take a walk down the street if the sun is still up. Mom said I'm not allowed to be out after dark right now. She's still afraid Jason might try to find us and do something bad."

I'm dying to tell Maria what Kylan said earlier, but I can't until I see the pictures. I can't indicate that I know anything, either. Gosh, this is so hard. Maria is my best friend, and I tell her everything.

"I don't think Jason would do anything to hurt us. I'm still not convinced that he hurt Ashley. He just never seemed like the kind of person who would do that."

Maria scoffs at me. "OMG Kimmy!" she yells in my face. "He killed my sister! Why can't you get that through your thick skull?" Maria thumps my head with the palm of her hand.

Emotions start to take over again. I look over at her. "Why did you hit me on the head? I was just telling you how I felt. We don't have to agree on everything." Tears start streaming down my face.

I look up just in time to see my house coming into view. I jump up out of the seat and make my way to the front. I don't care if Maria is behind me or not.

I run up the steps to my front porch without even looking back. I open the front door with as much force as I have in my entire body. The screen door slams behind me as I stomp down the hallway to my bedroom. I shut the door with my hand flying over my shoulder and start sobbing uncontrollably on my bed.

I must have forgotten to lock my door because I felt a hand on my shoulder. By the way it felt, I knew it was Maria's. I didn't look up and just continued to cry. I hope she feels bad for how she has treated me today.

"Please don't cry," Maria says as she pats my back. "We've cried enough over the past few months."

I don't respond to her. I don't even move to acknowledge that I heard her.

"I'm still hurting, too. That is why I get so angry when people talk about Ashley or what Jason did to her." I can tell that Maria is starting to cry. I raise my head up off my bed and wipe the tears from my eyes.

"I've been keeping a secret Kimmy. I promised my parents I wouldn't tell anyone, not even you, but I think you need to know this." Maria gently sits down beside me on the bed. "When my parents got the autopsy report back, I had to read it to them. Even though my dad is fluent in English, he still has difficulty reading it." Maria hesitates as I push myself up. "It was awful Kimmy. So bad that I had to stop several times to take a break while reading it."

Maria puts her hand over her mouth and shakes her head. "I can't believe I am telling you this. I never in a million years thought I could tell anyone this."

Maria takes a deep breath, looks up at the ceiling, and back at me. "Ashley was pregnant. There, I said it. I know I told you she wasn't, but my parents didn't want the word to get out to anyone before Jason went on trial. He would for sure get the death penalty, and my parents don't believe in that. They want him to rot in prison for the rest of his life."

I don't know what to say. All my thoughts just instantly left my mind. Maria and I sit there in silence until she says, "She was about four months pregnant, according to the pathologist's report."

Maria stands up and walks across the room. She paces for a few minutes until she finally sits down in my desk chair. I am still at a loss for words.

"You know, I told you that I saw Ashley and Jason fussing that night at the party, and she hit him?" I nod my head yes. "I think that's when she told him she was pregnant. When I saw her hit him in the face, I suspect he told her that she needed to get rid of it. I also think Jason knew that having a baby would ruin his life. That is why he killed her."

My phone vibrates, but I can't check it right now. I am still in too much shock to speak. Maria continues, "There was always something about Jason I couldn't put my thumb on. He was constantly buying Ashley gifts and doing nice things for her, but there was a different side to him that we never saw. Ashley told me several times that Jason would talk down to her and treat her like a baby because she was so much younger than him."

Maybe Maria is right. Maybe Jason really did kill her. Even if he didn't, there is no way that I could ever convince Maria to think otherwise.

"I'm so sorry Maria. I had no idea. Well, I kind of had an idea. Do you remember the last day we spent with Ashley at the beach? She had to sit down on the sidewalk because she was tired as we walked over to Cuz's. And all that food she ate for lunch? It was like she was starving or something."

My mom pokes her head in our bedroom. Maria and I about jump out of our skin. "Hey girls! I'm here for a few but heading back to work. I'm picking up a shift for Mel. Dad will be home later. Do y'all need anything?"

Neither one of us speaks. At the same time, we nod our heads no, then look at each other. "Everything ok?" Mom asks.

"Yeah, we're fine. We've just been thinking about Ashley today," Maria says.

"I understand," Mom says. "Any chance the boys might be coming over this afternoon?" She raises her eyebrows as she looks at us very seriously.

"Well...they were planning on it," I say with hesitation.

"That's fine. Just don't leave the house and lock the door when they leave. Dad will try to be home before dark."

Mom closes the door back, and I look over at Maria. "Can you believe Mom trusts us to be home alone with the guys?"

"I feel so much better now that I have told you about Ashley. I feel like a huge weight has been lifted off my chest. Please promise me you won't tell anyone, not Kylan, not Nanny, and especially not your mom. Ok?"

"Ok, I promise."

"Can we also promise not to keep secrets from each other? I couldn't stand knowing something and not being able to tell you."

I didn't respond to Maria, so she poked me in the arm. "Ok Kimmy?"

"Yeah, sure. Let's get ourselves ready for the guys. My face is a hot mess, and my hair looks like a rat's nest," I say as we giggle all the way to the bathroom.

CHAPTER 31

A couple of hours pass as we chill at the house, waiting for the guys. We decide to fix some chocolate chip cookies. You know that premade dough that you keep in the refrigerator? It tastes almost as good as homemade. I end up eating three cookies, and Maria eats two.

"Let's make sure to leave some for the guys. Do you know if they're bringing anything over for dinner?" Maria asks. "I'd love a good greasy cheeseburger! All these salads are getting old."

"I'll text Kylan and ask. In the meantime, I'm going to finish my math homework."

"Ok, remember our promise. Please don't say anything to him about what I told you about Ashley." I give Maria a thumbs-up and head back to my bedroom.

I need some time to process what Maria told me. Until I have everything squared away in my head, there's no way I could even formulate the words to tell someone else.

I work for a solid forty-five minutes on my math homework until I hear a knock on my front door. It must be the guys. I close my book and shove it in my backpack. Then, I take a quick look at myself in my mirror and take off running down the hallway.

When I get to the living room, I see Kylan standing there with a single rose in his hand and a bag of fast food. I jump up in his arms, nearly knocking him over.

"Great to see you too, Babe!" Kylan says as he lays a big kiss on my lips. I hop down and take the rose and bag from his hands.

"Where's Maria and Peyton?" I ask as I look around the room.

"They went outside. Maria said she needed to talk to him about something. Do you know what that is all about?"

"No. She mentioned something about needing to talk to him, but I didn't ask what. I just figured that would give us enough time to look at those pictures on your phone. Come on, let's go back here to my bedroom. I'm dying to see what you have." I motion Kylan back to my room.

"Are you sure it's ok for me to be in your bedroom?" Kylan asks.

"Um, yeah, my mom isn't here. I think my dad will be home later."

"That's what I mean. Would your mom be ok with me being in your room without them here?"

I study Kylan's face for a minute. He's absolutely gorgeous and very serious. "They will never know if you don't tell them."

He grabs me by the arm and swings me into him. He brushes my cheek with his hand and gently kisses my lips. "I just love you so much! Please don't ever change Kimmy."

We get back to my bedroom and sit side by side on my bed. Yeah, my mom would probably not want us sitting here on my bed, but who cares! We're not doing anything we shouldn't be doing yet.

Kylan flips open his phone and proceeds to scroll through his pictures. I see a lot of pictures of Suki and some of his mom's flowers. Then, he gets to the party pictures. Most of them are pretty dark. I do remember the lights being out, and some colored lights were flashing.

"Look, here's the first one." Kylan places his phone in my hands. I look closely. It's a picture of Ashley standing by a dark-colored car. The background is pretty light. I can see every detail of the car, including the brown leather seats inside.

"Ok, notice this car." Kylan switches to the next picture. "Now, what do you see here?"

I carefully examine what he is showing me. I squint my eyes and pull his phone closer to my face. "It's Ashley inside that same car."

"Correct. From what Ken told me, I'm about ninety-nine percent sure this is the car they found her in that was wrecked. Now look at this." Kylan switches to another picture and hands me back his phone.

I lean back on my bed as I study the picture. I give Kylan back his phone. "Did you see the same thing that I saw?" Kylan asks as I raise up.

"I saw Ashley sitting in the passenger side of a black car with brown leather seats waving goodbye and someone else in the driver's side, but who was it? It's not Jason. That person has a tattoo, and Jason doesn't have any."

Kylan scrolls to the next picture on his phone. It was taken after the picture of Ashley in the car. There is a big crowd of people on the dance floor. "Look, there's Jason with his hands in the air. See? No tattoos." Kylan points to the far right of the picture. "Jason was still at the party when Ashley left. He wasn't driving that car when it wrecked."

I close my eyes and shake my head. I slowly lean all the way back on my bed and lay there for a minute. Then, I raise up so fast I give myself an instant headache.

"Kylan, give me your phone back. I think I know who is in the driver's seat," I say as the realization hits me like a ton of bricks. I grab his phone and bring it as close to my eyes as possible while still seeing the picture.

"What? What do you mean?"

I put my finger over my lips to hush Kylan. "I know exactly who it is. Oh my God, Kylan! Jason didn't kill Ashley."

"Hey, lovebirds! What are you guys doing?" Maria says as she bounces into the bedroom with Peyton on her heels. Kylan and I look at her like a deer in headlights. "Did we interrupt something?" she asks.

She didn't hear us—thank God she didn't hear! I can feel my hands starting to shake and my palms getting sweaty. "No...no, not at all," I manage to get out. "Come on in."

I look over at Kylan. I'm pretty sure he is thinking the same thing that I am. Maria and Peyton have the absolute worst timing of anyone on this earth! We all sit on my bed in awkward silence. No one speaks.

"So...whatcha doing?" Maria asks with a smile as she bounces up and down on my bed. She must've thought we were fooling around or something, but we definitely weren't doing that.

"Oh, nothing. We were just talking," I say with no expression whatsoever on my face. I'm sure she thinks we are up to something. "Y'all want to go eat? By the way, what's for dinner?" I look over at Kylan and wink.

"You know, the usual. A couple of greasy ole cheeseburgers for the princesses and chicken sandwiches for the peasants. There's plenty of fries for all!"

Maria and Peyton jump up off the bed and head toward the kitchen. Kylan puts his arm around my shoulder and leans so close to my face that I can feel his breath on my lips. "Tell me what you saw in the picture," he whispers.

I swallow hard and ball both of my hands into fists. I can feel my fingernails cutting deep into my skin. I press them harder until I can no longer stand it. I look Kylan straight in the eyes and say, "R.L."

Kylan wraps both arms around my shoulders and embraces me. "Kimmy, take a deep breath. It's ok." He can tell that I am almost about to go into a full-on panic attack. He starts rubbing my shoulders and stroking my hair. "Breathe, Babe, breathe."

I start having flashbacks from that day at the beach. We were sitting at Cuz's. R.L. and his friends walked up to our table, and I vividly remember staring at the tattoo on his arm after he kissed my hand. I thought it was such a strange-looking tattoo. Why would anyone want a scorpion on their body? I can understand the cross, but a scorpion? Then, I started remembering the party and running into R.L. at the drink table and how I spilled beer all over him when my cup went flying up in the air. It's all coming back to me now.

I feel my breathing start to regulate and my heart rate slow down. I lean over and put my head on Kylan's shoulder. "What are we going to do? I don't even know his real name. All I know is that his initials are R.L."

Kylan grabs my hand and wraps his fingers around mine. "I think we need to call Ken. He still has his connections at the fire station. He can at least lead us in the right direction."

"Until then?"

"Babe, you're just going to have to trust me on this one. All you need to do is relax and remember as much about the party as possible. We are kids, but we have some evidence on my phone that could free an innocent man and convict a guilty one."

CHAPTER 32

I've heard people talk about the days being long but the years being short when they reference raising children. I asked my mom what that meant. She said that the long days refer to sleepless nights parents have when they bring their babies home and all the pain and heartache that comes along with raising a child. Then, when you blink, your child is grown. That is what the short years part means. I can't relate to raising a child since I'm only a child myself, but I do know that the past twenty-four hours have been the longest twenty-four hours of my life. The past day has felt like a year. I keep blinking my eyes, hoping that time will pass quicker, but it doesn't.

I have avoided Maria like the plague. I told her I had a huge test I needed to study for and couldn't hang out. She offered to help me study, but I told her no.

When Kylan got home from my house yesterday, he called Ken immediately and told him everything. Ken was going to call a few of the guys at the fire station to see if they could figure out who this R.L. guy was. I've been texting

Kylan nonstop, hoping he has heard something from Ken. Nothing yet.

Kylan and I decided to tell Maria and Peyton about our findings after we hear back from Ken. We want to make sure that we are taking the proper steps before we spill the beans. I already know that Maria is going to freak out. That's why I'm very hesitant to tell her. She's also going to be pissed that I've been keeping a secret from her, but she'll have to get over it.

As I look at my phone, trying to pick a good song to listen to to pass the time, I get a text from Kylan. He wants to know if I can talk. Of course, I can talk!

I tiptoe to my bedroom door and very quietly turn the button on the knob to lock it. At least no one can bust in while I'm on the phone. Then I tiptoe over to my closet, climb inside, and shut the door. I get comfortable on the floor between a few of my old stuffed animals. I open my phone and proceed to call Kylan.

"Kimmy, is that you?" Kylan asks as he answers my call.

"Yes, it's me," I say back in barely a whisper.

"I just got off the phone with Ken. He gave me a lot of information. Are you ready for this?" he asks as if I would say no.

I take a deep breath. "Go for it," I say.

"Ok, the black car that Ashley was in came back as stolen. It was registered to a man in New Orleans who reported it gone over six months ago. The police already knew that, but Ken just found that out today before he called me. Jason's DNA was found all over Ashley, but we already knew that. I told Ken about how Maria had seen her sister hit Jason in the face, bloody his nose, and then try to clean him up. That would explain his DNA being all over her."

Kylan stops talking for a minute. "And?" I say.

"And this R.L. guy, his real name is Rhett Lucas Walker. Kimmy, you're not going to believe this. Rhett's father is U.S. Senator Raymond Walker. I'm sure you studied about him last year in seventh grade Mississippi government class. You know that boat they were on? The big yacht that was named something about children's inheritance. It's the senator's boat. He keeps it down at the Pass Christian marina. They all live up in Jackson full time but have a house in Long Beach that sits right on the ocean."

"Did Ken find out anything else?" I ask quietly, hoping no one can hear me in the closet.

"Oh, yes, he did. R.L. has been in and out of drug rehab centers all over Mississippi and Louisiana. I'm sure that's why he doesn't want anyone to know his real name, so he goes by his initials. By the way, R.L. is twenty-three years old. He's been arrested around ten times or so for different things, but he always gets off because of his dad. Ken said this is very risky for us to take on, but we will be protected since we are minors. Our parents, on the other hand, will not be."

"So, what do we do now?" I ask, still whispering.

"Ken said he can call his friend at the sheriff's department and let Officer Jane know that we remembered some more things about the party. He said she will contact our parents to get consent to talk to us again. Then, we will show her the pictures and tell her everything we now know," Kylan says confidently. I love how reassuring he always is to me about everything.

"That sounds pretty simple," I say, hopeful that we can get Jason off the hook sooner rather than later.

"But there's a catch," Kylan says as I can sense worry in his voice. I knew it couldn't be that easy.

"Senator Walker is a very powerful man who will do anything to protect his name, even if that means hurting others. Ken said we must have our ducks in a row when we talk to the officer. If not, everything could backfire on us."

I sit in dark silence in my closet. I take the phone away from my ear to listen to see if anyone is out there. I crack open my door to make sure. I'm still safe.

"How are we going to tell Maria and Peyton? I should tell Maria, and you tell Peyton. I don't think they need to be together when we tell them, just in case Maria has a meltdown on me again. That was pretty bad yesterday. She is bound and determined that Jason did all that stuff to Ashley. Can I tell you something? You have to promise not to tell Peyton?" I peek out my closet door again just to check.

"Yeah, Babe, I promise. What's up?"

"When Maria and I had that full-on blowout yesterday, she confessed to me that Ashley was around four months pregnant when she was murdered. Her family thinks that Jason killed her because he didn't want to support her and the baby."

I can hear Kylan take a couple of deep breaths on his end. He must be taking after me. "This does not help our case out, but all we can do is tell the truth and share what information we have. That's what we promised the officers, so that is what we will do. That's all we can do at this point."

I sit and think for a moment and listen again to see if I hear anyone. Nope. "Ok, tell Ken to go ahead and call his friend to get everything set up with Officer Jane. In the meantime, let's just keep all this on the down low."

Kylan agreed, and we said our goodbyes. I'm sure he'll call me back later and tell me what Ken has found out.

I ease my closet door open so nobody hears me. I raise up on all fours and crawl out from underneath my clothes. As I start to stand up, I hear a noise. I ever so carefully shut my closet door and see Maria standing behind it.

"What the hell are you doing?" I say in a panic. "Were you listening to me? How'd you get in here? I locked the door!"

"No, the real question should be, what the hell were YOU doing in that closet whispering on the phone? WTF Kimmy!" I can tell that Maria is furious with me. Her face is beet red, and her teeth are clenched together. "And what are you keeping on the down low? What secret are you keeping from me?" she says as she lunges at me.

As I stare at Maria, trying to think of something to say, I hear the lyrics of an old song that Nanny likes to listen to pop into my head. They sing about getting busted down in New Orleans. Well, that's me right now. Then I hear my mom's voice say: *Honesty is always the best policy. The truth will set you free Kimmy.*

Maria puts one hand on her hip and then the other. I'm pretty sure if looks could kill, I'd be dead right now. My mouth goes completely dry, and my brain goes blank. For a moment, I think I even stopped breathing. Then I choke on my own spit and start violently coughing. When I catch my breath, I look over at Maria. Her expression hasn't changed. She now looks more like a lion getting ready to attack someone rather than my best friend. I guess now is a better time than ever to tell her.

"I was talking to Kylan." I drop my head down and look at my floor.

"Well, I figured that much! I'm no idiot!"

I look around the room, hoping to find something that will spur a thought or even distract me. Nothing. I look up at my ceiling fan and back down at the floor.

"Can you please stop staring at me like that? You're making me nervous, and I am forgetting my thoughts," I say as Maria doesn't move a muscle. "Ok, at least come sit down on the bed with me."

I walk over to my bed and sit on the edge. I pat the bed beside me, hoping Maria will take a seat. She's still standing by the closet door with her arms folded, looking like she's about to pounce.

"Ok, well anyway, I have something very important to tell you. I am not keeping a secret from you. I just needed to gather more information before I shared it. I wanted to make sure I had all the details." That was good. I sounded very genuine and caring, which I am.

Maria finally relaxed her shoulders and walked over to my bed. "Really Kimmy? What is so serious that you needed to get more details about?" she asked as she eased down beside me.

I told Maria everything, from Kylan discovering those pictures while he was in ISS to the calls with Ken. I told her who R.L. really was, how much trouble he had been in, and who his dad was. I even told her about telling Kylan that Ashley was pregnant when she died. It felt really good to get all that out. Now, I'm sitting here waiting for her response. She hasn't spoken a word since I finished.

We've been sitting in complete silence for at least five minutes. I've had several text messages come over my phone, but I'm afraid to move. I don't know how Maria is going to react. She showed absolutely no expression on her face when I told her everything. No tears, no frowns, no nothing. Just a solid blank stare. I'm actually quite scared. I'm worried that she is going to do something drastic, like start flogging me like a chicken. I'm not sure if my body can handle something like that right now.

Just when I think Maria hates me forever, she turns toward me and wraps me in the warmest hug I've ever felt. I instantly relax all the muscles in my body. For the first time in several months, I no longer have the urge to cry, and neither does Maria.

She slowly pulls away from me and looks me directly in the eyes. "Let's go get that asshole that murdered our sister!" And just like that, I knew everything would be all right.

CHAPTER 33

We've all been keeping a pretty low profile the past few days. We haven't heard anything from Officer Jane or anyone else. Kylan completed his last day of ISS yesterday, so I am looking forward to things getting back to normal with him.

Kylan has a marching band competition today, so his mom is coming to pick me up so I can watch. I've never been to one of those, so I'm not sure what to expect. Kylan said it's like back-to-back halftime shows all day long. Then, they pick a winner at the end. It sounds pretty cool!

Maria decided to spend the day with her family. Her mom called last night and asked if we would be interested in coming over to hang out. She told her that I already had plans. I think Peyton is planning on going over to Maria's today to hang out with her family as well.

Ever since I came clean to Maria, things have been great! We have been able to talk about Ashley without crying. Maria convinced me that we both needed to write down notes of what we plan on telling the officer, so we don't forget anything this time. I suspect that Kylan and I will be talking to her together, but just in case, I have a cheat sheet to take with me. I made one for Kylan, too.

I'm not sure what to wear to the band competition today. Kylan gave me one of his high school spirit shirts to wear, but it's a little big on me. I think I'll just put a hoodie over it. Even though we live down south by the ocean, it still gets cool here in the fall when the sun goes down. If we stay until the end, I will need something a little heavier.

I hear a car door slam outside. It must be Kylan's mom. I jump up and check my makeup in the mirror to be sure it's perfect. As I run down the hall, I hear someone using a key to open my front door. Who could that be? Mom is at work, and Dad went to New Orleans to help Chas with something.

When the door opens, I see Nanny's big purse. "Hey Nanny?" I say, puzzled. "I didn't know you were coming today."

Nanny comes in and sets her purse down, along with a huge box. "Your mom didn't tell you I was coming?"

"No."

Nanny looks around, expecting someone to jump out from behind the curtains. Then she picks the box back up and carries it into the kitchen.

"What's in the box Nanny?" I say as I follow her to the kitchen.

"Oh, nothing, Honey. It's just your mom's blender that Chas fixed." She takes the blender out of the box and sets it on the counter. "Your mom really didn't tell you I was coming today?"

I stand in the kitchen and stare at the blender. I look around the room, trying to rack my brain. I don't remember my mom saying anything about Nanny coming today.

"Um, no. I'm supposed to go with Kylan's mom to his band competition today. I'm expecting her to be here any minute."

Nanny plugs in the blender and turns it on to make sure it works. "Perfect!" she says when it starts up.

"Honey, come sit down at the table for a minute. I think your mom forgot to talk to you about something very important." Nanny pats me on the shoulder and ushers me to the table.

"Do you remember when that police officer came over here back in the summer to talk to you about what happened to Ashley?" I nod my head yes, and a thousand thoughts flood my mind. "Well, that same officer is stopping by today to ask you a few more questions."

I sling my head back so hard it almost falls off my shoulders. Then, I slowly raise it up, being careful not to give myself whiplash. This can't be happening. I don't have the pictures. They're all on Kylan's phone. What am I going to tell her? That my boyfriend has some evidence for her?

"She can't. I mean, I can't. No, that's not what I mean." My words are all jumbled, and I can't think of what I want to say. "Nanny, I have plans. And, plus, I don't have the evidence. Kylan does." As soon as I say that, I put my hand over my mouth and regret my last words.

"What do you mean, Dear? What evidence are you talking about?" Nanny says as she inches closer to my face.

"Nanny, can you keep a secret? I mean, a real deep, dark secret?" I ask her this, knowing she can do it, but I still need confirmation. I can tell my Nanny anything. She would never tell my mom unless I was in danger. I have told her so many secrets in my life that if she were ever to get mad at me and tell my secrets, I could probably go to jail or something.

"Of course. What's on your mind?"

I take a deep breath and open my mouth, but nothing comes out. So, I take another deep breath and try to decide whether I should tell her everything or just the important facts.

I hold up one finger to Nanny, indicating she needs to give me a minute to collect my thoughts. But then I realize that Kylan's mom will be here soon, and I need to get this out as quickly as possible. I don't want to be explaining things to Nanny in front of his mom.

So, I open my mouth again, and words come gushing out like an open dam. I tell her everything. I tell her how Ashley took us to Joni's party. I tell her about me drinking alcohol and acting stupid. I explain how I don't really remember much from the party. I even tell her how I woke up in my bed with Kylan on the floor—every single detail.

I run to my room to get my notes for Officer Jane and read them off to Nanny. I share with Nanny how Kylan was bored in ISS last week. That's how he found those pictures. If he hadn't been wrongly accused of smoking in the bathroom, he might have never seen them.

Nanny got up from the table and grabbed a clean washcloth from the kitchen drawer. She ran it under the tap and wrung it out. Then she folded it in half and placed it on her forehead.

"Darling, I'm not really sure what to say to all this. You've just thrown me for a loop. So, you're telling me that Jason is innocent? And some guy whose dad is a U.S. Senator is the one who killed Ashley?" Nanny patted the washcloth against her head, then wiped her eyes as she eased back down in her chair.

I shake my head, yes. "Nanny, are you crying?" I ask.

"Honey, you just overwhelmed me with information. I'm going to need a minute to process everything."

Nanny gets up and takes a glass from the cabinet. She opens the refrigerator and gets Mom's bottle of wine out. Mom keeps it there for emergencies, so she says. Nanny fills her glass to the top and takes a sip.

"Kimmy, I would say you've got a pretty big case on your hands. Why have you been keeping this from your parents?"

I feel my face starting to flush. "I was too embarrassed to tell them, and I thought they would ground me for life if they found out." I put my head down on the table.

I feel Nanny's hand rubbing my back. "It's going to be just fine," she says as she takes another sip of wine. "Everything you told me, you must tell the officer when she gets here. Do Maria's parents know all this?"

I try to remember what Maria said she told her parents. "I think so, but not the picture part. We just found that out this week, like I said. Why didn't my mom tell me that the officer was coming today? She knew I was going to the band competition?"

"Your mom probably didn't want you to worry. You know, she's pretty good at keeping secrets, too," Nanny says as she winks at me. I think that wine is starting to take effect on her.

When Officer Jane arrived, I was ready and willing to share everything with her this time. I held nothing back, and Nanny sat right beside me the whole time and even held my hand when I started having a hard time with my words.

Surprisingly, Officer Jane already had the pictures from Kylan's phone. They were printed off and enlarged. You could see so many details that we didn't even notice when we looked at them on his phone.

I was able to identify everyone in the pictures. I told Officer Jane how R.L. had approached us at Cuz's while we were waiting for our food. I explained how we all thought he was God's gift to women. That's before I ran into Kylan at the party. I also told her about how he kissed all our hands and tried to win us over. I made sure to tell her that he was especially nice to Ashley. I told her about my hair getting snagged under the table and how he called me "Little One," and I thought that was so odd.

When I finally finished telling her everything I knew, she had me look at the pictures one more time to see if I could put a time frame on them. I was stumped. Then, all of a sudden, I remember Ashley saying that we had to be home by midnight the night of the party. I remember looking at my phone as we were leaving, and I was disappointed that we left before midnight. I made sure to let her know that according to Kylan's pictures, Jason was still at the party long after Ashley had left.

I asked Officer Jane what would happen now. She couldn't tell me much, but she did say that they would be bringing in a new suspect for questioning. I asked if that suspect was R.L., but she couldn't give me that information.

As soon as the officer left, I called Maria to give her a heads-up. While I was talking to her, a police car pulled up in her driveway. It was now Maria's turn.

I still had so many questions, though. The only thing I knew to do was to call Kylan. He told me he'd be busy all day at the competition, but since his mom texted that she was running late, what else am I supposed to do?

I called Kylan, but he didn't answer, so I sent him an extremely long text. He immediately texted me back. I told him about how the officer showed up and had all the pictures from his phone already printed off. Come to find out, Kylan had sent the pictures to Ken, who in turn sent the pictures to his friend at the police station. I gave Kylan a heads-up that Officer Jane would probably be coming to see him soon and to be ready to spill his guts about everything.

Kylan's mom finally made it to my house. She apologized like a thousand times. When she went to get in her car this morning, she had a flat tire. She had to wait for Kylan's dad to get home to fix it for her. Typically, Ken or Kylan could have done it, but since Ken is in Tennessee and Kylan was already at the competition, she had to wait. I told her it was no big deal and that I had some business that needed to be taken care of anyway.

We had so much fun at the band competition! Kylan is a fantastic drummer. His percussion section ended up winning first place out of all the bands there. I was so excited when I finally got to see him that I kissed him right there in front of his mom and everybody. When I realized what I had done, I was so embarrassed that I couldn't speak.

That evening, we all met back up at my house. Nanny was still there and had a big pot of her homemade gumbo going on the stove. I could seriously smell it before we even opened the front door. I invited Kylan's mom to have dinner with us, but she said she needed to get back home. Nanny made up two to-go plates for Kylan's parents and sent his mom on her way.

We spent the rest of the evening talking to Nanny about everything that had happened in our lives over the past few months. I always knew Nanny was a cool grandma, but I never realized how cool she was until tonight.

Before we knew it, we had talked the entire night away, and it was after eleven o'clock. Nanny said it was too late for the guys to drive home and suggested that they sleep on the couches in the living room and go home in the morning. She made both of them call their parents and talk to her to make sure it was fine with them, and it was.

So, instead of going to bed, we all stayed up and watched a movie. Nanny turned in before the movie had finished. Kylan, Peyton, Maria, and I fell asleep on the couches. Kylan and I were snuggled so tightly that I felt like a wrapped burrito. Although slightly uncomfortable, I wouldn't have moved for a million dollars.

We would have slept that way all night long if it hadn't been for Nanny coming in to wake us up. She said Maria and I better go get in our beds before my mom got home. She probably wouldn't approve of our sleeping arrangements.

I was ok with that. I sure don't want to test my boundaries with my mom right now. When she finds out about everything, I'm sure I'll be treading on thin ice. Maybe Nanny can help smooth things over for me.

When I finally laid my head down on my pillow, I rolled over and looked at my clock—2:46 a.m. I couldn't go back to sleep. I was so giddy that Kylan was sleeping in my living room and would be there when I woke up. I wanted to get up and sneak back to see him, but I talked myself out of it.

I just lay in my bed with my eyes closed, thinking about how everything has played out. Ashley would still be alive if we hadn't gone to Joni's party. But on the flip side, if we hadn't gone to the party, we would have never met Kylan and Peyton. That's a terrible way to think about it, but I'm trying my best to stay positive for myself as well as for my best friend and sister, Maria.

CHAPTER 34

The last few months have been extremely busy. So much has happened! First off, Maria's dad got that huge promotion at the casino. He moved up to an office and has access to all the security cameras whenever he wants, even at home. His favorite restaurant is over in Pass Christian. So, we loaded up in several vehicles, traveled across the bridge, and surprised him with a celebratory dinner. He had no idea why we were all driving to The Pass. When we pulled into the parking lot, he finally figured it out.

Speaking of promotions, my mom also got promoted to head cocktail waitress. The casino must've been feeling generous here lately. Mom said her hourly wage will stay the same, but she will get a monthly bonus check. Her check will be a percentage of all the waitress and bartender tips taken in throughout that month. She said it should be quite a bit. I can't wait to see how much it is! The only bad thing is that she might have to pick up more shifts. I already feel like she works all the time.

Kylan and I are doing great! Since marching band season is starting to wrap up, I'm looking forward to a little more downtime with him. I've been trying not to smother him, but I really miss him when he's doing his band stuff. I guess it might be something with Maria and Peyton being able to see each other all the time.

Mom has been a little more lenient about the guys coming over. Ever since Nanny let them spend the night on the couches, Mom has been chill about them staying on the weekends. Almost every Saturday night since then, Kylan and Peyton have crashed at my house. We always end up falling asleep watching a movie, and Nanny has to wake us up before Mom gets home. When I get up in the mornings, Oscar is always snuggled up next to Kylan. I think he is Oscar's new favorite person.

Nanny has been coming up every weekend since Mom's promotion. Mom says the boys can stay as long as Nanny is there, but they have to go home if Nanny isn't there. That's why I said they've stayed almost every weekend. Last weekend, Nanny had something to do with the retired teachers club in New Orleans and couldn't come. Maria and I were both devastated that we had to spend Saturday night without the guys by our sides, but we survived by calling and texting them all night.

You know how my dad wrecked his truck on the Fourth of July? Well, it was determined that it was the other person's fault, and their insurance company had to buy my dad a brand-new truck! He ordered a black diesel, just like his old one, but with many more features. It should be here any day now. It feels like we are waiting for a baby to get here. I'm so excited to see it!

Ken called Kylan when I was with him the other day. He said he would be coming home for Christmas next week. He has the whole week off from work and wants to bring his new girlfriend to meet the family. I'm beyond excited to meet her. He says she is really nice and very pretty. He sent Kylan a picture of her, and Ken was not lying when he said she was pretty. She has long blonde hair and a beautiful fair complexion. You could say she looks like a Barbie doll. Barbie and Ken, Haha! I'm hoping I can go over to Kylan's Christmas night and have dinner with them.... My fingers are crossed!

Alex is still working at the fire station. He actually has a girlfriend now too! Do you remember Ashley's friend Joni? Well, they started hanging out during the summer, and I guess sparks started flying. They didn't tell anyone they were dating until about a month ago. The Hernandezes were over the moon excited. They've always loved Joni and her family.

Ever since Maria caught me in the closet talking to Kylan and I told her everything, we haven't fussed a single time. Actually, we have become so much closer. I didn't even think that was possible! We promised each other never to keep a secret unless we were gathering more information. We both agreed that would be the only reason.

As for Maria and Peyton, well, you know, not much has changed. She told me they talked about waiting until marriage, and he understood. Not only did he understand, she said he wanted to do the same. I'm not sure if they are in love or lust right now, but I'm glad they could mutually agree on that subject. They are still all over each other when they're together.

A lot has transpired with the investigation into Ashley's murder. Kylan and I had to go to the police station to record our story. Our parents went with us. Even my dad went. He said this was very serious, and the whole family needed to be there.

They took us back together to a room with no windows and a solid metal door that locked behind us. It was very creepy and freaked me out a little. I'm glad I had Kylan by my side because I'm not sure I could have done it without him. Since we were minors, they kept our identity confidential. We had to speak into a microphone and tell everything. I feel like I've told this story so many times that I relive it in my dreams every night. I can't wait until all this is finally over.

Officer Jane told us that our story and the pictures were very helpful in catching the lead suspect. She couldn't tell us who that was since we were kids, but we knew she was referring to R.L.

Come to find out, R.L. was wanted in Louisiana on similar charges. Not only was his DNA all over Ashley, but his DNA had also been found at the scene of another crime that was very similar to what happened to Ashley. They traced everything back to that black car that had been stolen. To everyone's surprise, R.L. had stolen the car, changed the license plate, and was using it to lure young girls into it so he could take advantage of them. After the story broke and R.L.'s picture was on the news, over twenty girls came forward and accused him of sexual assault. Who would've thought such a handsome and wealthy guy would do such nasty things to young girls?

That hand of mine that he kissed, I wanted to burn it off when I found all this out. Kylan talked me out of it, and I'm glad because it is the hand I write with. I would've had to learn to write with my other hand. As if my handwriting doesn't look like chicken scratch already, it really would have then.

It didn't take long after R.L. was arrested for Jason to get released. They were able to clear him from Ashley's murder by using our testimony. By Maria saying that she saw his blood all over her ter, it proved that is how Jason's

DNA got all over her hands and arms. Those were the only places his DNA was found.

I'm not sure what's in store for R.L. He hasn't gone on trial yet, but they are keeping him locked up until he does. My parents talked to another officer at the police department. He reassured them that R.L. would probably never get to see the light of day for the rest of his life, kind of like my mom's uncle. They said this is something his daddy won't be able to get him out of this time. Just in case, my parents consulted with a lawyer on what to do if he is released before his trial. The lawyer pretty much said the same thing the officer said, but my parents have taken out an order of protection just to be on the safe side.

Getting back to Jason. Maria's parents did not welcome him home with open arms like we thought they would. Mr. Hernandez was very hesitant about even letting him come to their house. He said that Jason should've been protecting his daughter. Ashley would still be alive if he had been doing his job as her boyfriend.

Maria was at her house when Jason first got cleared of the charges, and he called her dad. He yelled at Jason and cussed him out in English and then in Spanish. A few days later, Jason stopped by Maria's house and sat down with Mrs. Hernandez. Maria had to translate the conversation because Alex was working at the fire station and Mrs. Hernandez's English is still not very fluent. Maria was very careful to make sure she accurately translated all words back and forth. She said it was so intense that she barely remembers any of the conversation.

Jason pretty much told Mrs. Hernandez everything that had happened. He even said that he had no idea Ashley was pregnant. She was keeping everything a secret from him. He said if he would have known, he would have done the right thing and married her as soon as he found out. Jason emphasized the fact he was devastated that the Hernandez family thought he murdered their daughter. Maria said that Jason pretty much cried the entire time he was talking to her mom.

I guess after that, Mrs. Hernandez convinced Mr. Hernandez that Jason was a good man. They are doing their best to mend their relationship with Jason. He comes over to their house at least three times a week now for dinner. I always knew deep down inside that Jason was innocent, but I didn't know how to prove it until Kylan showed me those pictures.

There are so many things that would be different if Kylan hadn't looked back over those pictures. Poor Jason would still be in jail waiting for his trial, and R.L. would be out and free to hurt more girls. It's crazy to think about.

My mom has always said that whenever something bad happens, there is always a silver lining, just like when a rainbow appears after a storm. I guess the silver lining for what happened to Ashley is that R.L. will never be able to inflict pain on anyone ever again, and his victims will finally get their day in court.

CHAPTER 35

So, it's the last week of school! I can't believe it! And it's my last week of eighth grade! I'll be in high school next year and get to see Kylan every day. Woohoo! I'm beyond excited!

Last week, the high school had an eighth-grade day. Maria and I got to pick our classes for next year. At the high school, they are on a block schedule which means that you only take four classes each semester. I will have regular standard classes next year. No more special education classes for me! My teachers said I tested out of everything in middle school, and I'm good to go. I will still have an Individualized Education Program, or IEP for short, just in case I need a little extra help, but no more reading or math intervention for me!

Maria and I have the same guidance counselor at the high school. I guess it's because F and H are close in the alphabet. We got to sit by each other during the class planning process. I decided to take English, algebra, geography, and band for my first semester. Maria is taking pretty much the same classes, but hers are honors classes except for geography. We're pretty sure that we will have geography class together since there is only one teacher who teaches freshman geography. And, of course, we will have band together! Maria also convinced Peyton to sign up for the band next year too. He doesn't know how to play an instrument, but the band director said he can learn.

Do you wanna know the best thing about being in the band next year, other than getting more time with Kylan? Band camp! We will spend an entire week in July this summer at a state park just south of Hattiesburg, learning all about band stuff. Kylan said he had so much fun last year. They even got up one morning to practice fundamentals, and there was an alligator on the football field. The band director had to use one of the flag poles to chase it away. I can't wait!

For some reason, I'm a little sad about leaving middle school. I have really liked my teachers and the smallness of the school. Everybody knows each other, and I don't have to worry about homework because we never have any. One thing I haven't liked is riding the stupid bus every day. I hope that when Kylan gets his driver's license in August, my mom will let me start riding to school with him. Maria is already planning on riding with Peyton when school starts back if her parents are ok with it. I'm pretty sure they will be because they absolutely love him.

I guess you'd like an update on Ashley's murder case. Well, not much has happened. R.L. is still in jail awaiting his trial. It has been scheduled for October. My parents still have the order of protection against him, but even more girls came forward, and he's looking at life in prison without the possibility of parole. There's even a slight chance that he might get the death penalty. My mom said that probably won't happen because of who his dad is though.

Speaking of Senator Walker, he is up for re-election in August. Surprisingly, he's already announced that he won't be running for office again. He said he will be retiring when his term is over. That's probably for the best since his son is in so much trouble right now. I guess he could come out of retirement later and run again, but he probably wouldn't get elected. Who wants to elect the father of a murderer to represent our state? Not me, that's who!

This afternoon after school, we all decided to take a walk on the beach before we met Nanny and Chas at Cuz's for a celebratory dinner. I'm not sure what we're celebrating. Possibly the last week of school or maybe mine and Maria's eighth grade graduation. Nanny said she had a surprise for us but wouldn't give me the slightest hint of what it might be. Whatever it is, I'm sure it will be good!

As I am sitting on the beach with my boyfriend to my right and my best friend to my left, I try to remember what life was like this time last year before my world was turned upside down. I was getting ready to wear a bikini for the first time and was so excited about becoming a teenager. If I had only known how last summer would turn out, I probably would have just crawled under a rock and hidden until it had all passed, but then I would have never run into Kylan.

"So, what's your plans for the summer Kimmy?" Kylan asks as he wraps his arm around my waist. I look to the ocean and think about all the fun we had out here last year. I look over at him, then lay my head on his shoulder and stare out into the distance. The ocean is such a marvelous creation. It's hard for me to comprehend its vastness.

I grab his hand and pull it tightly around my body. "Oh, you know, just spend some time with you and work on my tan. Hopefully, this summer will be a lot less eventful than last."

I glance back out to the ocean as I can feel Kylan's heart beating against his chest. Out of the corner of my eye, I can see a fluttering. I raise up just in time to see a family of pelicans flying overhead. Not a day goes by that I don't think about Ashley, but whenever I see the pelicans, I have peace knowing that she is up there flying high with them.

Acknowledgements

A very special thank you to my mother, Patsy, for being my editor-in-chief. Without your help, this book would have been a mess.

Thank you to my mother-in-law, Jane, for being one of the first ones to read my book and the wonderful feedback you gave me. It was much appreciated.

Thank you to my very patient and loving husband, Ken, for the listening, proofreading, and brainstorming you have done over the past year to help me reach my goal. I am especially thankful for all the trips to BSL you have taken me on just to get some "inspiration." I would have never attempted this endeavor without you.

Without the love and support from my family, *The Pelicans Fly High* would have never been written. Thank you all!

For more information on books, events, and
news from Christie Peavyhouse, follow her on
social media @christiepeavyhouse

www.ingramcontent.com/pod-product-compliance
Lightning Source LLC
Chambersburg PA
CBHW022019310726
48972CB00006B/1728